Something Decidedly

Oddd

Lesley A

Published by New Generation Publishing in 2022

First Edition

ISBN
       Paperback   978-1-80369-262-3
       Ebook   978-1-80369-263-0

www.newgeneration-publishing.com

 New Generation Publishing

Wednesday 10 July

There he was again. The third time that morning. And he had the audacity to smile directly at me. He strolled over, picked up the frozen peas I'd dropped and placed them carefully in my trolley. He didn't speak. He simply smiled courteously and with a brief nod, turned, clasped his hands loosely behind his back and sauntered towards the cereals. I was astounded. He wasn't even trying to be discreet. No more keeping a safe distance, pretending he had some other purpose beyond following me, which he clearly was doing. I aborted my shopping list, swallowed and then marched as resolutely as my shaking knees would allow, towards the checkout.

I bundled the shopping hurriedly into the boot, left the trolley where it was – I never do that normally – threw myself into the car, started up the engine, released the handbrake, stalled, turned off the engine and sank back into the seat. I felt as if I'd been punched. My lungs didn't seem to want to make the effort to breathe. I tried to steady my racing heart, but it ignored me and carried on racing, blood pounding in my temples. I stared blankly ahead trying to make sense of what had just happened. My thoughts echoing my galloping heart as I pieced together my previous encounters with this odd little old man.

I'd first been aware of him two weeks before when I was at the garden centre choosing bedding plants with Toby, my next door neighbour. I was increasingly conscious that someone was watching me, a kind of sixth sense that made me feel uneasy. I turned and glimpsed him briefly as he disappeared behind a display of ceramic planters. There was something about him, something I recognised, something about his features that I couldn't quite pin down. Toby was oblivious. He was busy making a crucial decision about whether to opt for Gazania Firecracker or Gazania Sunrise, or possibly a medley of both and, in his own inimitable way, he'd blotted out the rest of the world.

I tried to let it pass, shrug off the incident, forget about it. But then, the following morning, when I arrived at Costa to meet Alice and Jess, there he was at the table right next to them drinking coffee and reading the free newspaper. The only seat left for me was facing him. I sat with some trepidation, poised to escape if he approached me, consoling myself that he was alone whilst I had the protection of my friends. To my relief, he didn't look up when we left and he didn't follow.

Later that day, when I went to pick up Ben from school, I saw him standing with the rest of the parental straggle that had arrived to collect the prepubescent onslaught about to erupt into the playground. He hadn't seemed to be with anyone. I hadn't been aware of having seen him there before, but no one else seemed surprised by his presence. I convinced myself that that was why I thought I recognised him at the garden centre.

Only, suddenly, he was there every day. Every morning and every afternoon, without exception. I told myself it was just that I'd never noticed him before and it was only now I was making a thing about checking if he was there, that I kept spotting him. The fact that I never saw him speak to anyone and never saw him with a child was an irritation I chose to ignore. I mentioned him to Alice, but Alice couldn't recall seeing him, not even in Costa. She said she'd look out for him the next day, only she was in a hurry and she forgot.

After that he seemed to keep popping up wherever I went. Coming out of the dentist's as I was going in. Going into the deli as I was coming out. Sitting on a nearby bench when I took Ben to Hegley Lawns to fly his new kite. Ahead of me in the queue at the bank. A fellow guest at my cousin Robert's wedding for heaven's sake. Rattling a collection tin for Oxfam in the market square. I even recognised him in the crowd on a local TV news report about an art exhibition. There'd been a brief close-up of him and it seemed for all the world that he was smiling at me personally through the screen. I rewound and paused it to check.

Maybe I should have been alarmed by all this sudden attention, but for some reason it never occurred to me and I have to admit I was intrigued. I'd lain awake in the small hours going over the encounters, persuading myself they were coincidences, suppressing the niggle that he might be stalking me. After all, he didn't look like a stalker. He was a little old man; old enough to be my grandfather. I'm five foot four. He was at least a couple of inches shorter and although sprightly, probably well into his eighties. And besides, he looked quite dapper in his suit and tie, smart, well-dressed; someone who takes pride in his appearance. He didn't seem in the least threatening or intimidating. If anything he had a serenity, no a tranquillity, rather a peacefulness or a stillness about him. I couldn't quite put my finger on a more exact definition that fitted with the sensation. Yes, I was unsettled by his unpredictable sorties into my life, but I also felt his calmness extend to me. I felt less frayed at the edges, as if his gentleness spilled over onto me. The thought of him as an aggressor made me smile, it just didn't fit with the qualities I'd witnessed.

Anyway, I mused, how could he know exactly where to find me?

Everything had been fine while he'd kept his distance and hadn't attempted to make contact with me. I even looked forward to discovering where he'd turn up next, but when he deliberately smiled and then picked up my packet of peas, I panicked. At arm's length the meetings – if they could be called that – were an entertaining diversion. Actually acknowledging me was a different matter altogether.

A woman with two noisy toddlers walked past and brought me sharply back to the present. Goodness knows how long I'd been sitting in the car lost in my thoughts. I heard Mother's voice in my head telling me to pull myself together and felt foolish for making such a fuss so, dismissing the battle with my nerves, I gingerly restarted the car and made my way to the exit.

He was standing at the exit. He waved. He waved! And he was smiling.

My hand raised itself and waved back.

I drove home on autopilot.

I sensed the change in the feel of the house the moment I stepped into the hallway. The air was markedly wrong. The whole house seemed to throb with a new vibration. Tangible. I could even taste the difference. I'm being ridiculous, I thought, quashing my suspicions – I've had a lot of practice at doing that – as I made my way into the kitchen.

For the second time that day, I dropped my shopping.

He was sitting at the table. Smiling.

The shopping tumbled from the carrier bags. I watched mesmerised as a tin of beans rolled across the floor.

'Hello Ruby,' he said. His voice was surprisingly melodious.

He knows my name. I looked around at all that was familiar in the kitchen. It was just as I'd left it. The wall clock said nine fifty-eight and continued to tick away the seconds with the same reassuring swagger that it always has. I would have spoken, but could think of nothing to say. In fact I had no thoughts of any kind. I just 'was'.

'Do come and sit down.' He gestured to the chair next to the window as if it was his home and I was the visitor. 'We have a lot to talk about.'

My legs carried me to the chair and I sat. I heard a distant voice say, 'I ought to put the frozen stuff in the freezer.' It sounded remarkably like my own voice.

He leaned forward slightly with his arms resting on the table, clearly waiting for me to tell him something of great importance. I was vaguely aware that this would be a good time to challenge him as to how he'd got into my kitchen and what exactly he was doing there.

The thought evaporated.

I had the distinct impression I was sitting opposite an old friend. *Is this prearranged? Has it somehow slipped my mind?* He was looking directly into my eyes. *How rude.* He knew me well, I could see that from his manner. Only someone who knows you really closely is quite so… familiar.

Oh my days, he's going to murder me! What should I do? Call the police? Scream?

My limbs were heavy, they didn't want to move. My voice seemed to have deserted me. Any urge I had to call for help or to insist that he leave limped into a dark corner to hide. *He's drugged me. That's what it is. I've been drugged…* I felt like an observer watching the scene unfold. Both aware of the anxieties running amok in my mind, whilst also disconnecting from them. He had such an affable, open face. He looked good natured and kind. Actually, it felt comforting sitting at the table with him. It reminded me of when I'd sat at the same table with Paul.

'Take your time. I'm not in any hurry.'

The fug in my head wasn't so much clearing as shifting position, trying to get more comfortable, settling in for the duration.

'How did you get in? Why are you here?' I blurted, trying to sound self-assured and poised but instead sounding tentative and uncertain.

He smiled.

It was unsettling.

'Will you please stop smiling?'

'I'm afraid I can't.'

'Excuse me?'

'I'm here at your invitation. You summoned me. Remember?'

'I did?'

'Uh huh.'

'When did I do that?'

'When you were in the speedboat.' My heart somersaulted.

'Ah, now you remember'.

'How can you possibly know about the speedboat? I haven't told anyone about the speedboat.'

I'd been having a recurrent nightmare ever since my husband, Paul, was killed. Sometimes I'd go months without it happening and then it would revisit several nights in a row. The previous month had been the tenth anniversary of his death and the regularity and intensity of the dream had become so extreme I'd been afraid of going to bed. And then, a couple of weeks later, it stopped, as abruptly as it had started.

The nightmare hardly varied; it always began and ended the same way. I was in a speedboat, racing out of control on the open sea with no land in sight. There was no one at the helm. The thrust of the boat and the swell of the waves made it impossible for me to reach for the wheel. It was frightening, terrifying, yet, at the same time, a tiny bit exhilarating. When I mulled it over in the comfort and safety of the day, I connected it to Paul's death. That's how it felt when he was snatched so suddenly; speeding into a dangerous unknown and being helpless to prevent it.

The intruder gently interrupted my thoughts. 'What was it you said, when you were in the speedboat?' he prompted. There was tenderness in his voice. 'What did you ask for?'

My eyes filled with tears. Gradually it came flooding back; what I'd prayed for, that last time I'd had the nightmare. And with it the realisation that that last time had been in the early hours of the morning I went to the garden centre with Toby, the day I first saw the old man. The significance of the timing was hanging within reach. The whole idea was madness. The prayer I'd invoked felt stupid now, not something I would ever say or think when I was awake and I was embarrassed to repeat it. I felt myself blushing and hoped he wouldn't notice.

He reached out and took my hand. 'Sometimes prayers are answered.'

When he touched me it was as if I was floating, wafting on a sweet sensation of wellbeing, like being wrapped in a soft warm blanket.

'I was desperate. Petrified. It didn't feel as if I was dreaming. I thought I was really there. As if it was really happening.' I hesitated, still not sure I wanted to admit to what I'd prayed for, but with the words thundering in my head demanding to be repeated.

'Go on.'

'So I prayed,' I began cautiously and then the words flowed easily as I relived the moment I'd spoken them. 'I prayed with every fibre of my being. I said, "Dear God if there are such things as Guardian Angels, then I need mine to come to my rescue right now." I don't know where the words came from; I was dreaming.'

'You summoned me.' And he smiled.

I smiled too. 'I don't believe a word of it. This is some kind of practical joke, yes?'

He stood up to leave. 'I think that's probably enough for today, you've the shopping to put away and the washing machine to empty and you need to press on with finishing the German manual. I'll see you tomorrow and we can chat again. Would you like me to prepare your coffee before I go?'

He was already filling the kettle. He switched it on, took my usual mug from the rack of four, a teaspoon from the drawer, the coffee jar from the cupboard and milk from the fridge. I stared in disbelief. 'There. All ready for you to pour. I'll let myself out.'

And like the Cheshire cat's grin, his smile left after he did.

I didn't move.

The house gradually returned to its usual ordinariness. It was like being in a jumbo jet coming in to land. There was a rolling sensation in my stomach and my ears popped as the pressure reverted to normal. I, on the other hand, was feeling anything but normal. I couldn't cope with feelings like that. I decided it must have been another of my day dreams. If he had really let himself into my kitchen, I would have called the police and had him arrested. In real life I certainly wouldn't have accepted his presence so passively. I would have taken command of the situation, been pro-active, been assertive and insisted he left. I questioned whether he actually existed at all or I'd just been imagining him.

The kettle boiled and switched itself off. The coffee cup was sitting on the worktop waiting for me.

I rose to my feet a little unsteadily and began picking up the shopping bags. Time to resume my safe orderly routine. It always had steadying effect when life leapt into the unpredictable; kept away the demons. I opened the freezer door. The cold crispness was calming. I stared at the contents. Everything was stored neatly and methodically as always, but somehow it didn't give me the customary frisson of satisfaction from testament of my organisation and efficiency. I shoved the peas – the bloody peas – and the other frozen foods I'd bought, indiscriminately into the freezer ignoring their designated shelves promising myself I'd rearrange it all properly later. I sought refuge in emptying the washing machine trusting that such a mundane task would be sure to help me put the whole absurd incident to one side.

Guardian Angel indeed. Huh, did he really think I was so naïve? I'll sort it all out with him tomorrow and get to the bottom of it. He'll probably tell me he's one of Santa's elves or something.

I redirected my energy to my habitual stop-thinking-and-just-get-on-with-it mentality and busied myself with damp socks and tee shirts, ignored the raucous itch in my brain – I was used to doing that, after all – and reminded myself I had work that had to be done.

I sat with my coffee in front of the computer. Finishing translating the manuscript, "Compliance with European Safety Regulations in the Use of Fork Lift Trucks, Hoists and Power Tools in Industrial Settings" from German into English was beyond me right then, deadline or no deadline.

As I sipped the coffee my thoughts wandered to Paul. I reached for his photo from the wall above my desk. He'd been dead for more than twice as long as I'd known him. We'd been married for barely a year when the accident happened yet I still felt his presence sometimes and held on to the feeling of the joy in his laughter. It grew more difficult over the years to recall his face in detail – until I caught his smile in Ben's and the memory of him came bouncing back as if it was only yesterday.

If he'd died when he'd been called out on a shout I might have better come to terms with it, but to die riding his bicycle, just because some idiot decided to turn left suddenly without checking his mirror or signalling, was a despicable way for a firefighter to lose his life. A shameful, worthless waste of a man who'd devoted his life to rescuing other people from danger. Ben wasn't even born. The wallpaper for the nursery was chosen and waiting next to the unopened pots of paint, but Paul never got to hang it.

My world exploded, but I coped. I'd coped because I had to. Ben was due to make his arrival only eight weeks later, what other choice did I have? It wasn't the horror of the accident I thought about so much anymore or the loss of our hopes and dreams for our lives together, it was the perforated memories of our first meetings; the day he proposed, our wedding day, our honeymoon in Jamaica, buying the house and moving in, the confirmation of my pregnancy. Reassuring, rose-tinted landmarks that couldn't be diminished by his death. The pain of it was no longer a constant presence that engulfed me, but a dull ache that hovered and claimed my daylight attention less and less frequently. I'd even ventured into relationships with other men, skirted the fringes of romance a couple of times and, although I'd not yet met anyone I wanted to make a commitment with, I was open and optimistic about the possibility of it happening one day.

Meanwhile, I filled my time with projects and plans and procedures and undertakings and endeavours and responsibilities and, most of all, lists. I filled Ben's time too, with Cubs and clubs and societies and piano lessons, which he tolerated, and swimming lessons, which he loved. Our lives were ruled by timetables and appointments and pressing engagements. It was predictable and safe. There were no hidden surprises to jump out and grab us.

I steadied myself by checking the neat colour coded wall planner written on the specially constructed whiteboard in the hallway. It was a Wednesday. Wednesdays were karate for Ben at five, then choir for me at seven. Toby always popped round and stayed with Ben until I got back home. I felt mollified by the security of returning to the regular routine. I scribbled don't forget – 20 mins piano on a Post-It note and strategically placed it at Ben height on the fridge door. This was a method I used frequently to remind him of his calendar of obligations. Except of course, because they'd become part of his normal environment, Ben generally didn't even notice them. I ran a finger along the sticky edge of the note to make sure it would stay in place, anyway.

At eleven fifteen precisely, I was compelled by an abrupt yet insistent urge to continue with the half-completed translation. I replaced Paul's photo on its hook, then, all else forgotten, the battalion of words marshalled themselves, stood to attention and quick marched from Germany to England all present and correct. I had found the moment, was in the zone, in the groove. At ten minutes to three, a day ahead of my deadline, I pressed 'Send' and shut down the computer. I even had time for a beetroot, alfalfa and radish sandwich before I had to leave to pick up Ben.

In the evening, on impulse, I decided to break with our usual routine. We didn't rush our meal so Ben could get to karate for five o'clock. Ben didn't go to karate. I phoned Toby to tell him I wouldn't need him to baby-sit after all and Adrian to say sorry, I couldn't make choir practice. Instead, we played on the Xbox all evening, Ben's choice, dodging under, around and over obstacles, rafting rapids, bursting bubbles and laughing so much it hurt.

After Ben went to bed I phoned Mother about nothing in particular, just to catch up and check all was well.

I generally felt apprehensive about going to bed, but that night I felt strangely calm after my encounter with the little old man in my kitchen. In fact, bizarrely, I'd been more troubled by the incident in the supermarket. I'd been tempted to say something to Mother, but decided against it. We don't have the kind of relationship where we discuss anything that really matters.

I climbed under the duvet with trepidation as always. It had been my nightly ritual ever since Paul's death to mull over the details of my day in the hope I could settle my mind ready for sleep. It was in my dreams, however, that the disquieting fears had a habit of rising to the surface and I was out of control. After all that had happened that day I was feeling even more anxious than usual. I wanted it to be true, wanted to discount the common sense that said Guardian Angels don't make impromptu appearances with offers of help.

And aren't angels supposed to have wings and a harp?

But what if…? Wouldn't it be wonderful if…?

And with that thought, unaware of the turmoil about to explode in the next two weeks, I slipped into a dreamless sleep.

Thursday 11 July

I woke the following morning at seven amazed that I'd slept so well after the previous day's happenings and tried to act as if nothing out of the ordinary was afoot. Ben seemed not to notice. He paid his usual visit to Toby's garden to inspect the progress of the runner beans he'd planted and then chatted happily about the Xbox games we'd played.

I arrived home from the school run full of anticipation, expecting the old man to be in the kitchen again. Driving home, I'd rehearsed how I would react. I visualised opening the door, stopping to take out the key as I casually called out, 'Hello?' before closing the door, throwing the latch for safety and walking into the kitchen dropping the key back into its designated pocket in my handbag. Usually there was no one to say 'Hello?' to, but 'Hello?' would be easy to sneak into the routine and it would give me the upper hand. He wouldn't be expecting that, would he?

However, as it turned out, my plan failed to match the reality. I knew immediately he wasn't there because the air remained undisturbed and there was a distinct lack of fug in my head. I was surprised by how disappointed and irritated I felt. I'd set aside the whole morning to finish the German commission, but since it had translated itself already, I had no programme scheduled. It should have taken me a good fifteen hours to complete. I'd expected to stay up most of the night to get it done; something I do every now and again to meet impending deadlines without interfering with my regular regime.

There were four long hours stretching ahead of me before I was due to leave for my yoga class. Four unscheduled hours. I didn't do 'time to relax', 'time to chill', 'time to spend unwinding'. I preferred to stay wound, thank you very much. I once joined a book club to fill a perceived gap on Tuesday afternoons, but found that actually sitting and reading a book was impossible. It gave my mind time to wander and, God forbid, think about where my life was taking me. I switched to Zumba classes instead. There's no window for contemplation with Zumba.

The agitation and anxiety that descended whenever there was a gap in my timetable or a hiccup in my itinerary was a familiar foe. I was teetering on the edge of an abyss fighting a compulsion to jump. My mind was in overdrive, searching for explanations: He had definitely said he would see me again today, so why isn't he here? What on earth am I supposed to do now? Sit and wait for him? Twiddle my thumbs until he condescends to arrive? Why wasn't he at the school yesterday afternoon or this morning? I knew I was working myself into a panic-driven frazzle, but I couldn't stop it. It was his fault.

I vowed to get a silent replacement for the wretched wall clock with its infuriating nerve-jangling ticking, reminding me that I had time on my hands and nothing to do with it.

I checked my emails. Dominique was offering me an unusual commission from a company called Allerbestes Tierenfutter to translate the wording on 15 kg bags of "Fleischige Güte Hundekuchen" from German to English, to Italian and to French. Twelve hundred and twenty eight words paying €900, significantly more than my usual rate. Perfect. I would make a start straightaway. I scrolled down to read the details only to find my deliverance from an empty morning was short-lived as the work would not be available for another week.

The doorbell rang.

'Huh,' I muttered, 'now he bothers to follow convention.' Nevertheless, I felt self-conscious opening the door.

It was Toby. He was holding his trademark briarwood pipe to his lips, empty, of course.

'Toby!' I tried to disguise the irritation in my voice. He was the last person I wanted to see.

'You all right?' he asked; always a man of few words. It made conversation difficult.

'Oh. Yes. Um yes, yes,' was the best I could manage.

We stood in silence for a moment, each waiting for the other to speak.

'Um, would you like to come in for a coffee?' It was the first thing that came into my head; he hasn't come to my front door for years.

'Only it's not like you to miss your choir.'

'Oh, choir.' I'd assumed he'd asked about my wellbeing because he'd noticed my confusion. 'Yes. No. It's fine. I'm fine. It's Ben, no not, he's not, he's fine too. We just decided to spend the evening at home together, that was all.'

'That's good then.' He took a long puff on the redundant pipe, leaned back on his heels slightly and half scratched his head, as if surveying the sky for inspiration.

'Tea? Coffee? Come in, come in.'

'Well actually...' Another puff. I waited. 'I saw your myrtle's getting leggy.'

'Myrtle?'

'Been neglected too long. Thought I'd cut her back, see if we can save her.' He pointed to his bag of garden tools leaning against the wall.

'Oh, in the garden. Of course, it's Thursday, you're here to do the garden. So why didn't you let yourself into the back?'

'She's got bind weed and cleaver clinging to her. Clear that away, give her some space.'

I opened the door a little wider and gestured for him to come in. He waited for me to go first. I made my way through the kitchen into the conservatory, unbolted the French doors and we stepped out onto the decking. It was a glorious morning. I hadn't noticed when I'd dropped Ben off at school. The sun was shining, the sky was cloudless and I heard the distinctive song of a chiffchaff. It was going to be a beautiful day. In another life it would have been a day for being out enjoying the summer, not a day for shutting myself indoors and working.

'Lovely day,' said Toby. Not the guarded, being-polite, dreary Toby I'd grown used to, but Toby totally at ease, Toby in his element. Ben told me he'd be outdoors from dawn to dusk if he could. Already he was scanning my garden with an obvious impatience to start work. His eagerness took me by surprise, made me feel flat and uninteresting by comparison. I found myself looking at him as if seeing him for the first time. He's tall and wiry with raggedy eyebrows and a rugged outdoor complexion. He's recently turned seventy, but still has a full head of curly grey hair and would easily pass as someone ten years younger.

'Well, I'll let you get on then,' he said. It was my turn to be lost for words. 'I know how busy you always are.'

'Show me the myrtle,' I said. I don't have the slightest interest in gardens and Toby isn't the most dynamic company, but in that moment it seemed the perfect way to fill the empty hours. 'If that's alright?'

He made his way over to the tall fence that separates my house from the Marlows, my elderly neighbours on the left. (After living next door to them for eleven years I still didn't know their first names.) Brandishing the stem of his pipe he pointed at two spindly bushes, then bent down and scooped a garland of green leaves and trailing stems that grew around the roots. He held them up for me to see.

'Bind weed. Grows everywhere in the gardens round here. Ruddy nuisance.' I thought it was rather attractive, but decided not to say so. 'I've brought some hooks to screw to the fencing. I'll string up some nylon and train the honeysuckle to grow across.'

He indicated the area behind the myrtle and stooped to inspect the plant like a sympathetic doctor examining a sickly patient.

'The aphids have made the leaves misshapen. Look.' He invited me to see for myself. 'Think she'll survive with some organic blood, fish and bone. Might give her dry seaweed for a few months to give her some strength.'

'Seaweed?' I'd never heard him so loquacious. He was amazing. Why had I thought him dull? He was animated, knowledgeable and his enthusiasm was infectious.

' 'S'magic stuff. Slow release, nourishes the soil, though she's in good compost already. See this?' He waved his pipe in the direction of a spiral of leaves wrapped around the frame that had once supported Ben's swing and was now a vehicle for all things floral. 'Zephrin Druin. Has the most amazing scent, exquisite and no thorns. All but finished flowering now. There'll be more come back-end because I keep him deadheaded and twisting him round the post like this encourages his blooms. Did you see the glorious pink roses earlier this year?'

No, I hadn't noticed them this year or any year come to that, but I promised myself I would look out for them when they next flowered.

There was no stopping him now. He guided me across the perfectly manicured lawn, puffing on his pipe as if to catch the last vestiges of tobacco that might be lurking there, casting his expert eye over his protégés as we crossed, unmistakeably making mental notes of what needed attention and in what order.

'Your bay's gone mad this year. Grown up and wide. Should have thinned him, but couldn't disturb him while the pigeons were nesting in him. I'll leave him while October when the sap'll have stopped rising and I'll prune him then.'

I gazed up at the tree and gave homage from somewhere deep inside me to its presence and its majesty. I breathed in its sturdy solidity and watched the leaves seemingly reach out to capture and drink in the sunlight that spilled on to them. Toby patted the trunk as if saying, 'Bye for now' and turned his attention to a wild poppy, gently stroking the tall unfurling leaves.

He took me from plant to plant, shrub to shrub, tutting where the slugs had wreaked devastation. 'I cuts 'em in half and feeds 'em to the chucks.' His eyes were merry with delight at his gutsy payback. He glowed with pride when I marvelled at the displays of colour and the heady mix of fragrances he'd created. He encouraged me to feel the velvety petals of the red and the white pinks, held up the magnificent crimson roses for me to smell.

'They're called Paul's Scarlet,' he said as if it was the funniest joke he'd ever heard.

I was spellbound, in awe that my garden was a wonderland of abundance I'd never bothered to notice. Toby had been in charge of my garden for several years, ever since his own partner, by co-incidence also called Paul, died. It had suited me to let him get on with it; it meant I was relieved of the tedium of taking care of it myself. He wouldn't let me pay him, of course, so I salved my conscience by giving him the occasional lift (he doesn't drive) and inviting him for Christmas dinner. Having given neither him nor the garden much attention before, I was now overflowing with gratitude that he'd created and maintained it with such loving care. I felt more than a pricking of remorse that I'd never before truly appreciated its beauty or his hard work.

He reverted to his usual monosyllables once the tour was over. 'Er, if you like…? We could, er…? I could…?' He cleared his throat. 'Would you like to come over and see me seedlings?'

I wanted to say, "That sounds like an offer I can't refuse", but thought Toby wouldn't get the humour; our awkward friendship didn't stretch to making witticisms. I settled on a simple, 'I'd like that. Thank you.'

We made our way through the gate he'd put in from my garden to his – the route he normally uses to my garden. I'd glanced indifferently at his garden from Ben's bedroom window once or twice and thought it looked "nice", so I was totally unprepared for the paradise awaiting me. He'd bought extra land so it's more than double the length of my own. He took me through his Zen garden, with its squat Buddha and its elegant Japanese maples and ornamental grasses and a waterfall that fed into a huge pool teeming with fish.

'The red and white ones are koi, so are the black and white ones, see 'em there? The mottled ones, they're shubunkin, and the blue and gold? They're orfe. They always swim around in a shoal together like that. Couple of ghost carp in there too, can't see 'em right now. Smaller ones are goldfish, but they'll grow bigger eventually too. Got more'n a hundred and fifty fish in there now should think.'

'It's enormous. When did you build all this?'

'Oh years ago, before Paul got ill. Six thousand gallons of water in there. Have to keep the mesh over it cos of the herons. The fish are dinner for 'em.'

It was another world. No wonder Ben loved spending time with Toby in his garden. I decided it would be good to chat with him about it later.

'The lights are solar powered,' Toby said. 'Looks wonderful when they come on at night.'

We walked past the hen house with its spacious enclosed run on the way to the potting shed. I could taste his excitement and expectation as he beckoned me into his ramshackle, but obviously much-loved, shed with an extension to its extension.

I was greeted by a rich earthy smell and row upon row of small pots with seedlings and young plants on three tiers of shelving alongside the glass wall. There was hardly room for anything more. The wooden wall opposite had gardening tools of every shape and description fastened to it. I had to watch where I stepped because of the bags of various kinds of compost that were spread along the floor. He selected pots at random to show me what was growing, hardly able to contain his elation at having someone take an interest.

It was almost time for me to leave for yoga, but I was easily persuaded into the polytunnels to see the carrots, the red onions, the squash, the beans, the cabbages and the courgettes.

'You must just see the fruit tunnel,' he insisted. 'Do you want any plum tomatoes? Got loads extra even though I lost a few because Marmaduke decided to make a bed out of the seed tray on the kitchen window sill.'

Marmaduke is a huge ball of ginger fur and claws that passes for a cat. He intimidates all who cross his path, though for some reason, according to Ben, for Toby and actually for Ben too when he spends weekend or school holiday afternoons with Toby, Marmaduke is gentle, placid and agreeable.

'I really have to go. It's my yoga class at two.' I surprised myself, and him, by kissing him on the cheek. 'I've had such an enjoyable morning. Thank you so much.'

I struggled home carrying a wealth of fresh produce, a bowl of new-laid eggs and a warm mellow sensation of wellbeing pulsing through my veins.

Jess and Alice had bullied me into agreeing to the yoga class a few weeks earlier when we met for coffee.

'We want to persuade you to join our yoga class on Thursday afternoons. Our teacher, Acharya, is very special, you'll really like– ' declared Jess stabbing the table with her forefinger to hammer home her point.

'Yoga?' I was dumbfounded; that was the last thing I was expecting.

'He's amazing. The real deal,' added Alice.

'I absolutely don't have time for yoga,' I protested.

'It's only for an hour a week,' Alice insisted. 'You have to make time. You're good at that!' I wasn't sure whether to take that as a compliment or a dig.

'We've tried to say to you before: you're lighting the candle at both ends. You need to ease up, Ruby,' Jess insisted.

Alice nodded in agreement. 'We've been concerned about you for some time. You know that.'

I said nothing. I didn't want this conversation, though I knew they were right. Earlier that morning I'd noticed the dark circles under my eyes when I looked in the mirror. I was in the final stages of translating a huge dossier for a French Fashion house that was amalgamating with a company in Manchester. Two more days and it would be finished and I'd be able to catch up on sleep.

I made my reluctance clear, but Jess didn't give up. 'You're not listening again,' she said. She was always accusing me of that. It wasn't that I didn't listen, it's just that there were so many other things on my mind and sometimes she went on and on. Not that I wasn't grateful; she's a counsellor and often went into professional mode to help me when I had a problem.

'You'll not be disappointed when you see how much it can help you to be less... less frenetic.'

She studied me for a reaction. I could feel my face flush with embarrassment and was even more resolved to ignore their advice.

However, the following Tuesday I was invited to join the Friends of the Hegley Lawns Pavilion Working Party, an activity that would extend – I knew from past experience – way beyond the margins of one afternoon a week. Yoga was preferable to having to take on yet another well-intentioned commitment that would mean more unpaid hours and less time for Ben so I was able to turn the offer down with a clear conscience. 'I'm afraid I'm not free on Thursday afternoons,' sufficed as a regrettable, but reasonable, excuse. The downside was that I was then honour-bound to give the classes a go.

'I didn't know it was going to be so painful. Is it meant to hurt so much, all that stretching?' I asked after the first class. I watched as Alice and Jess looked at one another with resignation.

'It isn't about the stretching,' Jess told me. 'It's a meditation. Listen to what Acharya says. You just allow your body to move as far as it wants to go.' It was obvious that Jess was more than a little smitten by him even though she's in a long term relationship and has three teenage daughters.

'And it's only your first time,' Alice added. 'You'll soon get the hang of it and then you'll love it.'

The second, third and fourth times were no better though. In spite of Acharya's gentle reminders to breathe into the postures, I found myself forgetting to breathe at all. The classes were a battle of how far I could push myself into a stretch and hold it without screaming out loud.

'I don't think I'm cut out for this,' I moaned, hoping they'd release me from my promise, 'I'm just not flexible. I never have been really. And I have Zumba to keep me fit.'

'Persevere with it and you'll feel the benefit. It's a good way to relax the body. It's about body and mind balance and harmony,' Jess explained. 'The problem is you're trying too hard. Let go of over thinking.'

Simpler said than done. I'd been doing it for too many years. Sometimes I wished there was a pause button I could press to stop my brain from making everything seem so complicated.

This was to be my fifth class and after such a lovely morning I was feeling much more upbeat about it. Jess noticed immediately I walked into the changing room.

'Ruby, you look amazing. You're positively radiant. Have you had some good news?'

'I've been in the garden with my neighbour. I never realised gardening could be such fun. I've had the most glorious morning.'

'It shows. I'm really pleased for you.'

We were an unlikely pair as we walked arm in arm to the yoga class. Jess, a good six inches taller, strode out purposefully while gesticulating in animated conversation, her riotous red ringlets bouncing down her back. I admit I bathed in Jess's confidence and charisma, her compelling personality. Nevertheless, I also felt a little intimidated by her comments sometimes and often thought of myself as inept and awkward by comparison. Although we're both approaching our big four 0, I felt as if Jess was my big sister, keeping me in check.

Hegley is rightly proud of The Lakeside Centre; it's won an award for its design. It's an impressive circular building, with a rooftop garden, restaurant and bar. The swimming pools, gyms, sports halls and squash courts are enclosed in the centre, while the perimeter has a reception area with a hairdresser, spa, shops, cafes and studios and suites hosting a multiplicity of activities. Yoga is one of those. It is a long, carpeted, comparatively narrow room dominated by floor to ceiling windows on the curved outer wall that looks out onto a small patch of lawn leading to a hedge that screens off the car park. In the distance the tops of trees wave from the wood beyond, where the boating lake lives.

There were just seven of us in the class, one man and three other women as well as Alice, Jess and myself. We arranged our mats facing the window and Acharya began leading us in his soft Renfrewshire brogue through the postures, reminding us that the smooth movement from one posture into the next is as important as the posture itself.

'Remember to keep the breath flowing. The movement has its own purpose; you're not heading towards a destination and arriving, there's no difference in importance between the two.

The movement and the held posture are equal parts of a whole.'

He says that at the beginning of every class. It had never made sense to me before, but suddenly I began to appreciate what he meant. I forgot about the others in the class and tuned into myself.

'Smooth movement generates a calm mind. A calm mind will produce smooth movement,' he continued. 'Keep your focus. Breathe.'

Downward dog was usually my least favourite. I couldn't shift my weight without being jerky and uncoordinated and the stretch in my thighs and calves was no more than an exercise in mind control as the agony of it made me clench my teeth. This time, however, I closed my eyes as I bent my knees, shifted my weight effortlessly to my left while stepping back with my right foot.

'Your gaze should be on your big toe,' Acharya reminded the room at large.

I opened my eyes and did as I was bidden. I didn't beat myself up for getting it wrong. I just gazed at my big toe while I focused on breathing in and breathing out. I smoothly adjusted my weight again and then stepped back with my left leg as we were invited to hold the downward dog for three full breaths.

Acharya placed his hands gently on my back, easing my weight away from my hands to my legs. Previously when he'd touched me I flinched and bridled. This time I melted with no resistance and, although I felt a greater stretch, it wasn't pulling or hurting. On the contrary, it felt liberating, actually it felt amazing. I pushed my weight a little further back to test how that felt without noticing the rest of the class had moved on to the next posture.

I felt Acharya's touch again, lightly on my shoulder, as he whispered, 'Upward dog'. I began the descent and followed through into the upward counterpose with the positive energy still flowing unhindered through my mind and body. The movements felt like second nature now. This was what my body was meant to do. I raised my head slowly, remembering to keep my gaze straight ahead when, at the faintest feeling level, I became aware of the fug creeping up on me again, but this time distantly, barely within grasp.

As I raised my head my eye line went from the carpet to the windowsill to the grass outside and to a pair of brown suede loafers standing on the grass. The loafers contained a pair of feet that were attached to a pair of legs. There was a man standing on the lawn outside. It was the old man. I knew it without looking. The fug gathered momentum. Moving into the upward dog posture, I followed up the legs until I could see all of him. He was smiling, of course, and making a thumbs-up gesture. 'Yes,' he mouthed, approvingly.

In a flash the steady rhythm of the yoga, my concentration and my connection to myself left me. I was instantly electric with anger. It started from the base of my spine and shot through my body. My head was pulsing with rage. My fingers tingling with fury. I realised the class had stopped and everyone was watching me, but in the intensity of the moment I didn't care.

'What's the matter, Ruby?' Alice's concern would have been consoling at any other time.

I spat out, 'Don't touch me. Leave me alone,' as I shrugged off her embrace.

Acharya, as usual, was unfazed.

'No worries. No worries. This sometimes happens with spiritual work. It's nothing bad, nothing to worry about. I'll explain next time. I think we'll finish early without the sitting meditation today if that's okay with everyone?' I half-registered him glancing around to measure their approval and confirm that they understood. He stepped forward with his palms outstretched to the group and ushered them towards the door. 'Could you just give me some space alone with Ruby?'

The group nodded. This was no time to argue, not while I was gesticulating wildly and yelling incoherently at the window. I didn't care, didn't feel even a flicker of my usual awkwardness. They rolled up their mats in hushed silence and made a quick exit.

Alice hesitated a moment as she went through the door. 'Tell her I'll pick Ben up from school and drop him off later,' she said to Acharya as if I was unable to hear. 'Perhaps she could ring me?'

'Good idea. I'll do that. Thank you.'

I crumpled to my knees; still buzzing with the shock of seeing the old man so unexpectedly, I began sobbing uncontrollably.

Acharya sat cross-legged sideways on to me; close enough to be supportive whilst far enough away not to be intrusive. He didn't speak. His face was impassive. When the sobbing subsided, I felt drained, exhausted. I wanted to lie down and sleep, revert to childhood and have my grandmother comfort me. I was trembling slightly. My mind was full of thoughts, yet I had no thoughts. Any thoughts were trivial and though dimly aware of them, I paid them no attention. I felt detached. I allowed them to rant unrecognised and undisturbed, like muzak played in a shopping mall that blends into the background unnoticed.

'Sorry,' I said eventually, laughing without conviction to cover my embarrassment. The room suddenly felt huge with only the two of us in it; the space around us making me feel uncomfortable.

Acharya spoke very quietly, barely audibly. 'What's happened is really good. I know it probably doesn't feel that way right now. You connected at a very deep level to your soul and now you're releasing some of the shit you've been holding on to. There's a lot of pain suppressed in there, um? Pain you've suppressed for a very long time? You don't have to answer, it's okay. Try not to go over and over what happened just now. Put it behind you and be grateful that the healing has started.'

I met his gaze and held it. I didn't experience my familiar spontaneous reaction to look away. Eye contact was difficult for me, sometimes even with Mother, though never with Ben of course. I saw kindness and stillness in Acharya's eyes. I simply listened attentively to what he said.

'Thank you, but it wasn't any of that. It was the man outside staring at me through the window. He was supposed to have had an appointment with me this morning and he didn't show up. He was supposed to be helping me, but he let me down and then he turned up here. I didn't realise I was so angry with him, that's all.'

'You saw a man outside?'

'Yes, the guy who was watching me.'

'Didn't notice him, I'm afraid.'

He handed me my water bottle. 'Here, take some wee sips, take plenty. Are you going to be okay to drive home? I think you should have a shower first. No, I'm serious, really. Visualise the water carrying all that negativity away. Watch it drain away. When you step out of the shower, consciously leave it all behind you.'

'I don't have a towel.'

'You're making excuses. Go to one of the shops and buy one. Do it.'

And I did, but not without railing bitterly to myself about the inflated cost of the shower gel and bemoaning the fact that Acharya had bullied me into buying a towel I don't need as I stormed towards the changing room.

Nonetheless, the shower did have a soothing, calming effect and I allowed myself to imagine the cascading warm, soapy water carrying away the anger I'd felt and the tiredness that followed. It was easier than I thought it would be. I had never had time for all that visualisation nonsense before.

I wandered from the leisure centre towards the car park relaxed and in no particular hurry; enjoying the afternoon sunshine and feeling comfortable and contented. There was a lightness to my step. It made me realise how often I strode out with an urgency and purpose, as if the universe depended on me arriving at where I was heading in the shortest possible time. I was aware of how oblivious I generally am of the tension and strain I carry around in my body and how freeing it felt to let go of it. There was a bench by the bowling green so I sat for a while to think things over and watched the irrigation jets sending sprays of water across it.

'That's what Acharya must be talking about,' I reflected, 'when he says "movement has its own purpose". How does he put it? "You're not heading towards a destination and arriving, there's no difference in importance between the two." I think I'm starting to get it. Wow! He's not just talking about yoga; it's about all of life. I've never thought of it like that before.'

As such revelations often do, in a fraction of a second I was bombarded by a hundred examples of how I limited the opportunities available to me. How I restricted my life, and Ben's, to edited highlights of what it could be. Hurriedly preparing and eating meals with as little fuss and in as little time as possible so I could get on with something "more important". Taking Ben to school by car to save a mere fifteen minutes even when the weather was glorious and I didn't have a tight deadline, instead of enjoying walking together through Hegley Lawns. I couldn't remember when I'd last treated myself to half an hour soaking in a warm bath. Always a quick shower; in, out, move on. Oh and so, so much more, never allowing time to savour the moment and appreciate the everyday minutia for the sheer pleasure of doing it.

I resolved to be different. I resolved to walk with Ben to school in future. He would love it, be in his element; he loves

The Lawns. I set off for the car and remembered to breathe. The euphoria of the morning had returned.

This time when I saw the old man sitting in my car, I opened the passenger door and said patiently, 'Get out, please. You're not invited. You don't have my permission to be in here. And don't start that fug business again either.'

'Hello Ruby,' he said, grinning like a mischievous child who'd just stolen chocolate from the fridge. I waited expectantly, but he just kept on grinning. Finally I sighed, an exaggerated pantomime sigh, raised my eyebrows, shut the door and went around to driver's side and climbed in.

'So?' he said.

'So? So?' I snapped, all calm deserting me. 'What's with the "so"? Is that all you can say? "So"? No explanation? No apology? Stop that exasperating smiling, it's not funny. You turn up in my life, making all these claims, all these... promises, making me think you were there to help me. You say you'll turn up this morning and no sign of you. I'm just left waiting with no timetable because my work did itself! What was that all about? How did you do that? Why did you do that if you weren't going to turn up for our meeting? It would've made sense if it was to give you some time to help me, but oh no, no, just let me think I'm going to get some support and then wham bam leave me dangling. Let me stew. Let me get myself agitated and anxious and uptight? Huh? Is that it? Is that it? The joke's on me? Had a good laugh did you? I bet you did.

'Well, it may surprise you to know Mr Smarty-pants I had a wonderful morning. The best morning I've had for... And no thanks to you either. As a matter of fact. By the way. Incidentally.'

He nodded, but said nothing.

'And I was really getting into the yoga until you came and spoiled it, embarrassing me. How dare you? How am I ever going to show my face again? Well, all I can say is, consider yourself officially unsummoned. I'll not be messed about by someone who makes false promises he doesn't keep. Oh, for goodness' sake, false promises. Do you see what you've done to me? Do you see the effect you're having on me? I can't think straight with all this weird fug stuff in my head. Leave me alone.'

I paused for breath, at last, but only for a moment. 'Well, sort of. I don't mean for good. I just mean we have to come to a proper arrangement, make appointments, decide what's to be done and when and then stick to said arrangement. You're going to have to fit in around my other commitments. You must realise that's how it has to be? Let's be clear about this, that's understood, a given. There's no reason why we can't have an amicable working arrangement while we sort out these nightmare nightmares once and for all. Then we can shake hands and move on. Our contract brought to a satisfactory conclusion. Both parties satisfied.

'There, I can't be accused of not bending over backwards to be reasonable. I'm still angry, but I forgive you for messing me about today. We got off to a bad start but least said, soonest mended, as Mother would say. When shall we begin? I have to take Ben to school in the morning and then I have a hairdresser's appointment at nine thirty. I can be available from quarter to twelve until two, two thirty at a squeeze. How does that fit with you? Where would you like to meet? You're very welcome to come to the house and share some lunch if that's convenient?

'And why are you wearing a suit and tie on such a hot day? Wouldn't you be more comfortable in shirt sleeves?'

He nodded again. 'You can drop me here if you like,' he said, 'it's a nice afternoon for a walk.'

I didn't remember putting the key in the ignition. I didn't remember starting the engine. I didn't remember driving, but we were parked in the lay-by across from the south entrance to The Lawns, just around the corner from my house.

He released his seat belt and opened the car door.

'Hang on. I want answers. I demand an explanation.'

'Indeed you do,' he replied agreeably, getting out of the car and closing the door.

I watched him cross over the road and disappear through the gate into Hegley Lawns.

A real angel wouldn't ignore my questions. So, he was a fake after all.

Well, that's that then. What a let-down. Count me out. I'm managing perfectly well on my own thank you very much. End of. Joke's on you.

My phone rang. It was Alice. 'How are you?'

'Much better, thanks, but I'm going to be too embarrassed to face everyone again,' I replied attempting to sound as if my head wasn't gyrating.

'No, for goodness' sake, don't be. We all thought you were awesome, you completely let go. It was fantastic. You were magnificent.'

'That's what Ben calls Marmaduke.'

'Sorry?'

'Ben. "Marmaduke the Magnificent". It's his name for him.'

'Who's Marmaduke?'

'Toby's cat.'

'Oh… Who's Toby?'

'My next door neighbour. Ben's Ungrampa.'

''Fraid you've lost me on that one. I'm not sure where we're going with this.'

'Never mind.' I waited, but Alice didn't respond. 'Are you still there?'

'Yes… Ruby, should I be a bit concerned about you?'

'Me? Why?'

'You sound sort of, well, I can't explain it… different.'

'Good different or bad different?

'Weird different.'

Another stunned silence. This time mutual.

'Thanks for picking Ben up. Is he okay?'

'He's here now. He wants to ask you something. I'll hand you over.' I distinctly heard Alice whisper, 'Don't think your mummy's feeling too well, she might sound a bit strange.'

'Hi, Mummy. Sorry you're a bit under the weather.' I've grown accustomed to his use of expressions more suited to someone three times his age. Sometimes it feels like he's the adult and I'm the child. Too many hours spent with Toby probably. 'Can I stay over at Jake's tonight? Please? Please? His daddy's bought him a new game for his PlayStation. It's brilliant. Owen's here too and we're just having the best time. Oh please say yes, Mummy, please.'

'But Ben, Jacqui'll be here at six for your piano lesson.'

'No, don't you remember? She went into hospital yesterday to have an operation on her bunions.'

'I thought that was next week?'

'Noooooooo. It's on the calendar.'

A phrase I use to him so often. I could tell from his voice that his muddy brown eyes were dancing with laughter because for once I was the one to have forgotten a reshuffling of the normal pattern. I had to smile in spite of myself. 'Well, yes if that's alright with Alice?'

'She suggested it. Will you feed Mildred and Delilah for me? Bye, Mummy. See you tomorrow. Love you dots and spots.'

'Love you oodles and spoodles.' But he had already gone.

'Hello? Me again.' Alice said. 'I was just speaking to Pete and we wondered if you would like to come over too. Spend the evening here with us? Pete's just getting the barbie going. Jenny and Stuart and their kids are here already. We've got a fridge groaning with stuff. There's plenty to go round.'

'Oh that's so nice of you but no, I can't, I mean I'd love to but... it's my Italian conversation ladies on Thursdays, half seven till nine. You know how it is, I can't let them down. They do so enjoy it. I'm going to show them around the garden and get them practising talking about flowers and trees and grass and birds and oh, you know?' And all the while I was thinking: Stop now. Stop now. You're overdoing it. Too much detail. She'll know you're just making excuses.

'That's a shame. Enjoy the evening anyway. And Ruby, you can ring me any time, you know that. If there's anything, if you just want to chat. Yes?'

'Thanks but hadn't I better pop round with Ben's night things and a change of underwear for tomorrow?'

'No, don't worry. I'm sure we can find a spare toothbrush and pj bottoms somewhere and I'll swill his underwear out. No problem. See you after school tomorrow. Don't forget, phone me if you get fed up.'

'Yes, thanks. I'm fine. Bye.'

The truth is I do normally have an Italian conversation group with three feisty female friends in their late sixties and they do come on Thursdays from seven thirty until nine. However, at that very moment they were practising their Italian somewhere in the Italian Lakes, where they'd been for the past four days. I don't know why I do that; what it is that makes me lie with such frequency, even to my friends. I behave as if lying is the preferred option and being honest is the exception. I'd no other plans for the evening. I could have changed my mind even then, I hadn't committed myself, but I felt awkward about seeing Alice after the episode at yoga despite her reassurance. And, if I'm honest, I couldn't face pretending I felt fine, not with Alice and Jenny and their perfect marriages and their perfect families and their perfect lives.

I locked away the stupid lie, and the uncomfortable feeling lying always gave me, in the prohibited-access area of my brain, trusting it wouldn't seep out into my gut like it normally did.

I carried a jug of water into the garden to give to Mildred and Delilah. They'd already deserted their run and settled into the hutch, probably deciding on an early night because their adored Ben wasn't there. Does he shut the door to the hutch at night or is it safe to leave it open? I should probably make sure it's secured before I go to bed. I threw in some radish tops, chopped peppers and fresh hay as itemised on Ben's Thursday feeding list.

'Evening,' Toby was finishing tying up the honeysuckle. I hadn't realised he was there. 'Almost done. Looks much better now.'

I thought, Remarkable that talking about gardening seems to cure him of his shyness. I said, 'It's great, Toby. Thank you so much. It's transformed that whole area. Um, Toby? Have you eaten yet? It's just that Ben's staying at a friend's tonight. I wondered if you'd like to have some supper with me?' The random invitation surprised us both. 'It'll only be something quick, but…?'

He looked dumbfounded.

'Oh excellent,' I said, taking his uncertainty to be bashful assent. 'I'll go and have a rummage in the freezer and see what I can find.'

'I've made fresh salad and I have goats' cheese and crusty bread,' said Toby. 'Got some cream and some strawberries. Was going to sit out in the garden and eat. There's enough for two.'

We sat on the bench in his Zen garden and ate in silence. It was an easy silence.

'Thank you,' I said when we'd finished. I'd not felt so relaxed for as long I could remember. 'I'm not surprised you love gardening so much with all these amazing colours and smells. I'd not taken much notice before I must confess.' I searched his face for a disapproving reaction. There was none. 'Now I can see it must be wonderful to create something so beautiful.'

'Yes, well it is, but that's not it though. Not what excites me.' He hesitated, checking I was really interested. I smiled encouragingly, smothering the flash of recognition that mostly I wasn't. His eyes lit up with the exquisite secret he was about to share. 'It's the thrill of creating something from a seed. That's all it starts with, a tiny seed that grows into an abundance of life-giving energy.'

'I hadn't thought of it like that.'

'Just look at a tomato.' He held one up from the bowl left over from our meal. 'Might contain as many as, oh, I'm guessing, maybe fifty seeds. Each one of those seeds could grow into a plant producing, say, twenty tomatoes each, each with fifty more seeds. Think of the potential. You could eventually feed the whole world with this one tomato.' He gave me the tomato.

'That's a really beautiful way of looking at it, thank you. I'll remember that always.'

We lapsed into a contented silence again.

'Solar lights are starting to come on. Wait till it gets a bit darker and you'll see how grand it makes everywhere.'

I knew nothing of Toby's life. I'd met his Paul of course, but Toby and his Paul had kept themselves very much to themselves and rarely spoke above a 'good morning', a rhetorical 'how are you?' or an occasional 'would you mind taking a parcel in for us?' and those first years after my Paul's death were in any case a blur.

'Do you have any family, Toby?'

'A cousin in South Africa. Haven't been in touch for years. Not sure if she's even still alive. 'Spose she is.'

'Your parents passed away then?'

'Me ma died years and years ago and then me pa same year as my Paul.'

'I'm so sorry.'

'Don't be. The money from me pa's house paid for most of this. Gave me a tidy sum after it was sold. It was only a terrace in Huddersfield but it sold for more'n a hundred times what they'd paid for it in 1958. Could never have afforded the extra land and all the stuff to set up the garden without it. Quite ironic, really.'

'Ironic? Why?'

'He didn't know, me pa, never told him. Ma made me promise when she was dying that I wouldn't. He'd have disowned me. Never told 'em at work neither. Caused big arguments between Paul and me. That's what I regret most. Those last months when he was dying. We spent most of the time arguing. He was very bitter; didn't like being a secret. He thought that if I truly cared for him I'd have the courage to come out like he had. Couldn't make him understand. I knew me pa. Knew what his reaction would be. Perhaps if me ma had still been alive, might've been different... We never sorted it. Paul went to his grave still angry with me. Ah well, can't put it right now. Too late.' He rubbed his weathered hands up and down his brown corduroyed thighs in a business-like manner as if rubbing the regret away. 'Not sure I'd be any different if I got another chance anyway.'

'You're talking about being gay?'

'About being homosexual, yes.'

'But surely...?'

'Getting on for forty-nine years since Paul and I met. We were both students on the same biological chemistry course at the University of Bristol. Wasn't as easy in those days. You've no idea. There was no such thing as Gay Pride then. And it didn't travel this far from the big cities for another thirty years or more. We were queers, homos, benders, Nancy boys, fairies, faggots and worse. Wasn't uncommon for gay men to get a beating for doing nothing more'n being alive. You learned to keep your mouth shut. Careful who you told.'

'I'm so sorry, Toby. I hadn't realised people could be so horrid. Thank goodness it's not like that now.'

He didn't argue.

The lights finally revealed their full splendour; beams of muted pinks and greens and blues set into the gravel among the grasses and around the edges of the pool. The garden was transformed into a stage set for a whimsical ballet. I could almost hear ethereal music. I hadn't allowed my imagination to wander so fancifully since I was a child reading stories about fairies.

I fell into thinking about my own background. I've talked about it endlessly to Jess, trying to make sense of it all. My father left Mother for her so-called closest friend when I was four. He kept in contact with me at first, but when my stepbrother and then two stepsisters came along he had less and less time for me. I suspect Mother didn't make contact easy for him.

'Cuppa tea?' said Toby.

'Thank you. Would you like me to make it?'

'Sit tight, no problem' said Toby already out of his seat and making his way inside.

My dad was a travel writer and his work took him all over the world. He was often out of the country for weeks at a time and his promised holidays to far-flung places never materialised, again probably Mother's doing. A few years later he moved his new family to Rhode Island. I haven't seen him or my stepbrother and sisters since my wedding and even then they didn't stay for the reception because they "didn't want to spoil the occasion" for Mother. They didn't come to Paul's funeral, but they sent flowers and a card.

'Milk, no sugar,' Toby said handing me a mug of tea. 'Mind it'll be hot.'

I sipped the tea and felt at ease looking back on my relationship with Mother with none of my usual mixed feelings and ruminations. Toby seemed content not to talk.

There's an awkwardness between us, Mother and I. Jess is forever urging me to seek counselling about it, but it is as it is, she won't change now. The divorce took its toll on her, but she was a fighter and determined that neither her own life nor mine would be compromised. She had something to prove. Her doggedness and strength of mind were rewarded in her teaching career. She was promoted to Head of Modern Foreign Languages at a sprawling comprehensive on the outskirts of London. Four years later she moved to a school here in Somerset where she gained further promotion to Deputy Head and then, three years later, to Head.

She's widely recognised and respected for her innovative teaching of languages and was regularly in demand as a consultant and as a lecturer. Her several books on the subject are on reading lists for language teaching courses across the country and are still considered to be an authoritative reference for theory and practice. Nowadays, she works as an Ofsted inspector.

Yes, I acknowledge her career was and still is a great success, but it sits uncomfortably with me. Her record stands for itself, so why does she waste so much effort to make sure all and sundry are continually reminded?

'Penny for them,' said Toby, cutting into my thoughts.

'Oh sorry.'

'You were miles away.

'Yes, sorry.'

'No matter. I was happy watching the midges dancing over the pool.'

'I was just thinking about Mother and how hard she works.'

'So do you.'

'She's a hard act for me to follow.'

'Why do you need to follow?'

'Hah. Good question, because… it's what she expects me to do I suppose.'

'And do you expect Ben to be like you?'

'Gosh no. Definitely not.'

'It's coming up to ten,' said Toby getting up from the bench, 'Starting to get a bit chilly. I'm off to me bed. Come a long way today you and me, haven't we?'

It might just have been a trick of the light in the gathering darkness but I thought I saw tears welling in his eyes.

Friday 12 July

I'd expected to sleep well in spite of Ben's empty bed. It turned out to be providential he wasn't there, however. I spent most of the night throwing up. Five a.m. had come and gone before I was able to settle back in bed and, finally, fall into a deep sleep.

I became half-aware of sounds in the normally quiet cul-de-sac outside. Something about them prodded my memory. I groaned as my synapses fired and made the connection. It was Friday. On Friday mornings the rubbish is collected. I'd forgotten to put the wheelie bin out to be emptied.

I groaned again and groped for the clock on the bedside table. Holding it in front of me I opened one eye and squinted. Eight thirty. Ben would just about be leaving for school and I hadn't phoned to say good morning. I tried to get up, but flopped back down again on account of the team of muscular blacksmiths hammering vigorously in my head and the cavalcade of infantry tanks driving through my mouth down into my throat.

Goodness knows what Toby had fed me to make me so sick. I'd clearly had a violent reaction to something. Perhaps I've caught a bug? Absolutely not. I strictly forbid myself to catch bugs. Bugs are far too time-consuming.

Someone tapped on the bedroom door. I knew exactly who it was of course. I was still smarting from his abrupt departure the previous afternoon so I turned onto my side, facing away from the door and pretended to be asleep. I heard the door being opened.

'Good morning,' he sang merrily. 'It's another glorious day. I've brought some green tea and dry toast with a little honey for the invalid.'

I waited for the fug. There wasn't any. Forgetting my resolve to feign sleep I said, 'There's no fug'.

'Mm, that's because you're adapting. You'll find it comes and goes. Sit up. Don't let your tea get cold.'

I plumped up the pillow behind me and gingerly leant back on it. I wasn't going to admit to it, but instinctively I acknowledged that weak green tea and toast was the perfect prescription to settle my delicate stomach.

'I've missed the bin men. It was recycling as well this week,' was what I chose to offer as an alternative to 'thank you'.

'Do you mind if I sit on your bed? Or would you prefer me to bring over the chair?'

'Since when did you bother getting my permission? Sit where you like.'

Why am I being so rude?

He handed me the tray and perched on the end of the bed. 'Better to sip the tea slowly; you don't want to be sick again. Now, you gave me a list of questions. I'll try to take them in the order you asked them. Shall we begin?'

'Oh no.' I nearly choked on a mouthful of toast. 'I forgot to shut the rabbits in before I came to bed. I meant to check on them. I hope they're all right. Ben would never forgive me if they've come to any harm.'

'Mildred and Delilah are fine. They're in the run chomping on the hay. I gave them the water you left for them. I don't think they could manage to pour the jug on their own.'

His eyes were sparkling. I couldn't decide whether he was being light-hearted or sarcastic. I settled on light-hearted on the grounds that it was unlikely he'd ever heard of sarcasm, let alone make use of it.

'Ready now?'

'Just one more thing, did you notice if there's any post? It's just that I'm expecting some work to arrive today.'

'I took the liberty of putting it on your desk, my dear. If I might...? Excellent. Thank you. I seem to have given you the impression that I would be visiting you yesterday morning? I must apologise if I misled you. I had intended to leave the timing of our Thursday meeting open. And actually, I was there while you were in the garden with your neighbour, it's just that you weren't aware of me.'

'You were hiding in my garden?'

'Please don't upset yourself. I wasn't hiding, I was observing. I was checking how you were coping with your homework.'

'Homework!' The fug was bounding back, making me feel giddy. 'Ugh, my head's zoned out again!'

'Yes, I rather thought that might be so. Still at least your headache's gone.'

It was true. The fug was a small price to pay, I supposed, compared with the thundering headache and the sore throat.

'Did you say, 'homework'?'

'Yes. I'll come to that in a moment. Now, concerning the help we gave you with your translation–'

'We?'

'Aha yes. It isn't something that is likely to happen again. We made an exception so you can make a start on your retraining programme without any intrusions that might confuse the matter. We also gave you a little shove to get the process going in the evening. You did extremely well with that. We were very encouraged.'

'You do know that none of this is making any sense? I don't know what's happening to me. Yesterday my friend said I was weird.'

'Don't worry, it'll all fall into place shortly and you'll understand perfectly well what is appropriate for you to know. Just go along with it meantime. As for your friend, she will have forgotten all about what was said last night, I promise.

You'll find there's no problem in returning to your yoga class either; any embarrassment you had will have completely slipped their minds. Now, if there are no more questions?'

How could I possibly think of questions with the manic fug reaching full throttle and charging around in my brain?

'Well done. Let's move on then. It's time to set your next homework. Listen carefully please. You'll be given a number of opportunities to perform a selfless act of kindness today. It doesn't need to be anything spectacular; make it something very simple. The person on the receiving end doesn't even necessarily need to be aware of what you've done and you certainly mustn't tell anyone else you've done it. The emphasis here is on "selfless". Some small deed that is entirely for the good of the person you choose, with no obvious reward for yourself. Understand? Good. Now I'll let you get ready for your hairdresser's appointment and I'll be in touch later.'

'Hairdressers? Oh my goodness, it'd completely slipped my mind. I'm going to be appallingly late.'

'No I don't think so. According to your clock it's just coming up to eight thirty and I think you'll find the clock's five minutes fast.'

All the clocks in the house were deliberately set five minutes fast so I'd never be late. I must admit it was doomed to failure as a safety measure though because I always mentally made allowance for the extra few minutes whenever I checked the time.

'It must have stopped. It was eight thirty when I first woke up and that was ages ago.'

'No, I assure you. You even have time to phone Ben before he leaves for school.' He smiled encouragingly. 'You seem surprised. You're overlooking the fact that time has a way of looping and bending. So, I'm really looking forward to seeing how you get on with today's task. Remember to keep it simple. See you later.'

And he left, taking the fug with him and leaving his gentleness and his smile in its place.

The hairdresser's is called The Hairdressers. I can't decide whether the name is a creative stroke of genius or completely idiotic, but it makes for an interesting talking point. I have regular two-monthly appointments with the senior stylist Cheryl, whose own hair creations oscillate from blonde to brunette to black or to a remarkable mixture of all three.

'How's that boy of yours?' she said as she settled me into the shiny swivel chair and tied a black gown around my neck. 'Behaving himself, I hope? Make the most of him now while you can, I say. I swear that on the stroke of midnight on the day of his thirteenth birthday, he'll do just what my four did and turn into a monster. It's true. Unbelievable, but true. I look at my boys sometimes with their dirty clothes and their mess and their testosterone strewn all over the house and I think, "What happened to my little rosy-cheeked cherubs? Where did they go?". Bethany, could you get Mrs Lewis a magazine while I mix her colours please? Filter coffee? Or would we prefer an herbal tisane today?'

The look on my face told Cheryl that a tisane, herbal or otherwise, would not be my refreshment of choice.

'Coffee it is, then. Milk, no sugar? Rightio. Won't be long.'

I thumbed absent-mindedly through Hello! I conceded that teenage boys generally have a reputation for rebellious behaviour when puberty starts kicking in, but Ben, of course, will prove to be the exception. I was confident that I was much too good a parent to allow that to happen. It never occurred to me then how arrogant I was being.

Cheryl arrived with a circular trolley full of the mixed colours and Bethany began opening out mesh pockets, using their sticky edge to hang them around the sides of the trolley.

'Hope you don't mind,' said Cheryl, placing her mobile on the shelf in front of the mirror. 'Only we're not allowed to use the phone here and I'm waiting for the vet to get back to me. I had to take my dog in on the way here this morning because he's eaten his lead. The vet's going to phone and let me know if he needs an operation.'

'Eaten his lead?' Bethany was incredulous. 'Was it leather?'

'No, it was one of those webbing ones. He ate every bit of it. I couldn't believe it.'

'What, all of it?' Bethany exclaimed. 'Sorry but you must admit it's funny.' She put her hand over her mouth to disguise her laughter.

'Not the metal clip, obviously. I'd just put his harness on to take him for his walk when the postie rang with a parcel, so I put the lead down for a moment. The postie and I were chatting for a while, he was telling me about his holiday in Malta, and when I came back there was just the clip and no lead anymore.'

I smiled and nodded supportively as Cheryl went on to describe the details, but I let the words drift in and out of my attention while I busied myself contemplating my homework task and fantasising about rescuing a small child, probably blind or physically disabled, from the path of an oncoming car while the child's mother and bystanders were aghast. I could already see the headlines in the local paper with a photo of myself splashed across the front page (wearing my blue floral dress or possibly my new mustard top if it was just head and shoulders... how fortunate I was having my hair done).

I grudgingly reminded myself that I was supposed to keep the 'kindness' to myself, so I reran the scenario, this time slipping away unobserved from the crowd of cheering onlookers that had gathered.

I revised this, it wasn't so satisfying, and reinstated the headlines and imagined myself telling an admiring TV presenter, 'It was what anyone would've done. I just happened to be in the right place at the right time'. Quietly unassuming. Of course I'd have to tell my GA that I really hadn't wanted the publicity, it was thrust upon me. 'These things circulate quickly in a small town like Hegley. It's how it is, I'm afraid.' And then, of course, there'd be no wrestling with temptation about not telling Jess or Alice or Toby, because they'd read about it in the paper for themselves. When they ask me about it, I'll shrug it off modestly.

'He's chewed things before,' Cheryl was saying, 'slippers, tea towels and cushions, especially cushions. We have to take them upstairs with us at night or they'd be ripped to pieces by the morning. He's always done things like that since we had him. He was a rescue dog. Morning Mrs Radford, how're you? Bethany, could you wash Mrs Radford, please?'

I was Cheryl's sole audience now that Bethany's attention had turned to Mrs Radford's ablutions and was thus obliged to hear the end of the saga without the opportunity to wander off into daydreaming again. It was a problem, in that I had no idea at all how the conversation had moved on, but hoped I'd get the gist and not give myself away. It's a skill in which I am well accomplished – after all I've been practising for years.

'The vet said I should've taken him in within four hours. It might be too late to do anything about it now without an operation. It's already going to cost me a hundred and sixty pounds for the x-ray and sedatives. It could be another thousand if she has to operate.'

'Oh dear,' I said looking suitably shocked and that was clearly the right thing to do.

'It was Tuesday afternoon he did it. I thought it would pass through him. I've had to go through his poop every day, sorry about this, wouldn't normally talk about poop, and I weighed the undigested bits that had come through, but Derek reckons that it wasn't even half of it. He's been very off colour. Buster, that is, not Derek, 'course. Hasn't wanted to eat. Not surprising really.'

I didn't know what on earth to say so was grateful my head was now duly dotted with little plastic envelopes of colour and Cheryl could move on to regale Mrs Radford with the story while the dye worked its miracle. I declined another coffee, intending to use turning the pages of Hello! to disguise my indulgence in further daydreaming of myself in the role of Good Samaritan.

Within minutes I was asleep and didn't rouse until Bethany gently shook me and explained it was time to wash my hair. I was delivered back to Cheryl with my hair towel dried ready for cutting.

'These golden highlights running through your natural brown really do suit you. You wait until it's properly dry, I think you'll be really pleased,' said Cheryl admiring her handiwork. 'Centre parting and keeping it just past your shoulders as usual, are we?'

'Yes, I like to put it in a pony sometimes. Did you get your phone call?'

'No, not yet,' replied the fretting Cheryl, waving her scissors in the air and making eye contact through the mirror. 'I can't make up my mind whether that's good news or bad.' She began snipping and trimming.

I was already drifting off into imaginary deeds of bravery and courage so not paying attention to the rest of Cheryl's concerns. My mindset back then was that day dreams could be so much more gratifying than the real world. I tuned back in again as Cheryl finished blow drying.

'Trouble is,' she was saying while holding up a large hand mirror so that I could see the reflection of the back of my head in the main mirror, 'I completely forgot my lunch. What with one thing and another, I've left it on the kitchen table. I was hoping to nip to the sandwich shop over the road and get something, but with Friday being our busiest day I'll not get time.' I nodded, indicating I was pleased with the cut as Cheryl brushed the stray hairs from my neck and removed the black gown. 'I'll only get fifteen minutes between Mrs Stapleford and Mrs Gamston all day. Even if I did go and get something, I wouldn't get chance to eat it. I'll have to see if Bethany can pop for me. Not very likely, she'll be pretty busy all day too.'

'Oh I am sorry,' I said, my head still full of heroic deeds and thinking: I wish I knew what it is I can do for someone.

I stepped out of The Hairdressers driven to find someone I could heap my benevolence upon. I made my way to the main high street, passing an older woman whose leg was in plaster and who was getting on a bus with a shopping trolley.

Not much happening here, I thought as I walked by the Big Issue seller wearing a brightly coloured jester's hat. The bells jingled as he waved a magazine towards me.

'Good morning. Big Issue.'

I didn't realise at first that he was addressing me, but I don't have time to read magazines.

'Have a nice day,' he called as I headed across the zebra crossing behind a woman with her skirt caught up in her knickers, to Bingham's department store, hoping to find an opportunity there. Maybe there'll be a robber brandishing a gun and demanding that the assistant on the till hand over the money. I did have a moment of hesitation with that one, because it might mean I actually got hurt. But he wouldn't let that happen, would he?

Nevertheless, I had a mental image of the photograph of myself in all the nationals, sitting up in a hospital bed with a bandage around my head. I tried out a few headlines and settled for "Heroine Well on the Way to Recovery Says Doctor". Or would it be consultant? No, surgeon. Surgeon has much more of a ring. I'd have to find a way of making sure Mother saw it.

I went into Bingham's on the ground floor through Cosmetics and Toiletries and found the escalator was, according to a printed sign, Temporarily Out of Order. I remembered there's a lift near to Jewellery and Watches and made my way to it. It was already handily open and waiting. A good sign, I thought.

I stepped into the lift and pressed the first floor button without glancing around. As the door slid closed I noticed a young woman rushing towards me weighed down with a large bag of shopping hanging from her shoulder, a sleeping child in a pushchair and a tearful toddler trailing behind. Oh dear, just a few seconds too late.

There were no emergencies in the carpet showroom, but I did see a rather nice oriental patterned rug that would look perfect in the conservatory. At twelve hundred pounds it was way above my budget, but Who knows? I speculated, if there's a reward for my bravery, well…? Of course, I'll protest that it really is not what I expect or want. I wonder if there might be enough left over to buy something else as well?

I wandered from the hushed whisper of carpets to the grand silence of furniture. Room lookalikes lying in wait for someone to inhabit them. It was deserted, not even an assistant in sight let alone an ailing customer. I passed through soft furnishings carefully stepping over a cushion that had spilled from a shelf so as not to dirty it, and moved on into bedding. I noticed a man paying for a duvet cover and pillowcases, not a colour or design I would have chosen. I was just deciding that this was another unpromising situation when the assistant began dancing alarmingly behind the counter holding the man's wallet aloft as he ambled past me back towards soft furnishings.

'Sir, sir, you left your wallet on the counter… I can't leave the till… Sir… '

I sighed. I could see there would be no opportunity to complete my homework in here, so I took the back stairs down to Stationery and through China, feeling a little despondent and disappointed. My GA had given me the impression there would be several opportunities to help people whereas it looked like no one wanted helping.

I was starting to get impatient. I decided to return to the high street and pop into Costa in case Jess and Alice were still there. Friday is the normal day for the three of us to meet up, but it was probably a bit late by now, unless they'd lingered much longer than usual. I knew I was in danger of another panic attack like the one I'd had a hundred years ago in the kitchen the previous morning. I was not going to let that happen again. Self-control. Breathe. I stopped searching for possible candidates and settled on a quick coffee and a toasted panini instead, before returning home to have a quick whip round with a duster and all-purpose spray before making a start on the work that had arrived earlier.

''Scuse me.'

I turned and saw a young girl wearing a grimy raincoat several sizes too big and grubby white plimsolls without laces, addressing me. I pride myself that I've never been someone who makes rash prejudicial judgements about other people, but to describe this girl as unsavoury would be flattering. She looked unwashed, her hair was lank and greasy, her nails broken and filthy and the overlarge satchel that hung from her shoulder would have been better left on the rubbish tip that it probably came from. She was painfully thin and had dark circles under her eyes.

The girl looked at me and said hesitantly, ''Scuse me. Sorry to trouble you, but I haven't got any money. I haven't had nothing to eat since Tuesday. Would you be able to buy me some food?'

I gulped. This was obviously the deed that had been chosen for me. I hadn't realised it was going to be quite so challenging, but homework is homework and the homework ethic had been drilled into me by Mother and had never lost its grip. I looked at the plush interior of Costa and looked again at the girl. Would we be welcome? Probably not.

'You can come home with me if you like.' I winced, shocked by my rash munificence. 'I'm only ten minutes away. I'll make you an omelette.'

The girl didn't speak. She just nodded shyly.

'I'm parked in the multi-storey. You wait here and I'll pick you up.' I was giving myself a space to digest what I'd just done and hoped the girl would wander off to beg from someone else by the time I returned. I've made the generous offer, surely that will suffice?

'No, it's all right. I'll come with you.'

We walked together towards the car park in an uneasy silence. I think we were both feeling self-conscious. Once in the car I threaded through the town centre and on to the dual carriageway that leads straight home.

'My name's Mel. What's yours?'

'Ruby.'

'Ruby? That's one of them old fogey names. No insult like, it suits you. Your hair looks nice.'

'Thanks. I've just been to the hairdresser's.'

'Thought so. Saw you go in.'

'Really?' I was feeling distinctly wary, starting to suspect I was being manipulated by this Mel who plainly wasn't all she seemed to be on the surface. I glanced at her out of the corner of my eye and felt increasingly apprehensive. I regretted the offer to take her home. It wasn't even what the girl had been asking for or expecting. I could have given her some money or bought her a sandwich. I sensed that I was the one being taken for a ride. I counted my blessings that she would be gone before it was time to fetch Ben. I toyed with the idea of asking Toby to come around for moral support. This was not the act of heroism I'd had in mind; then again at least my GA was going to be impressed.

Mel changed the instant we were inside the house. She switched from being apologetic and humble and vulnerable to being energised and confident and forceful. She hooked the strap of her satchel over a chair and walked around the kitchen picking things up, looking in storage jars and along the shelves. She opened the fridge door and examined the contents, peeked into the conservatory.

'It's lovely, your house, Rubes. Really, really lovely. All these nice things. Wish I lived in a house like this. I want a house like this one day.'

'Come and sit down. Where do you live, Mel?'

'In a squat. In one of them big old derelict houses by The Lawns on Arboretum Avenue. The ones that of been boarded up. They're supposed to of been condemned to build luxury apartments, but the money for them ran out. We get in through a back window.'

'A squat. Oh my goodness. Does your mother know?'

'She gave up on me years ago. I ran away when I was fifteen, I didn't like her boyfriend. He used to... you know... when she wasn't in.'

'That's awful. Didn't you tell her?'

'I tried to, but she wouldn't listen. She didn't believe me. She's a primary school teacher,' she said brusquely, as if being a primary school teacher explained her mother's inability to pay her any attention.

'How old are you?'

'Twenty.'

'How old are you really?'

'Eighteen. Oh, alright, sixteen.'

'Shouldn't you be at school? You should contact your mother; let her know you're okay. She must be worried about you. Think about it, mm? Do you share the squat with anyone else?'

'Yeh. There's ten of us sometimes. People come and go, you know the sort of thing, how it is. My boyfriend, Ed, he's usually around pretty much all the time. Haven't seen him for three days though, since the food and the money ran out. Think he might be lying dead somewhere. He's a druggie. They all are – 'cept me, of course.'

I had the distinct impression I should be selective about what I chose to believe of Mel's story. As a veteran liar myself, I could spot another person's lies a mile off. Mel's lies didn't fall into the same category as mine though. I hated myself for doing it, but my lies were mostly a knee jerk reaction to cover my feelings of inferiority and inadequacy or about wanting to impress, to live up to the high expectations set by Mother. It dawned on me I'd not properly understood why I'd been so predisposed to distorting and embellishing the truth before. I'd rationalised it to myself as laziness or lack of character, but presented with Mel's apparent inventive use of whatever story would most reward her, I could appreciate my own motives better.

I always castigated and criticised myself when I resorted to lies, felt as if I was worthless and contemptible. I resolved to be more accepting and acknowledge where my compulsion to lie was coming from. Funny that, that there are different shades of lying. It seemed to me that Mel was using lies as a means of coercion and exploitation. A different ball game entirely. I knew instinctively not to trust her. Oh yes, young lady, the sooner we get this over with, the better.

'I'm about to dish up. Would you like to wash your hands first? The cloakroom's just through there on the left.'

I watched Mel head towards the cloakroom and checked she came straight back into the kitchen. I placed an omelette and salad on the table for her and sat opposite with a cup of tea.

'What can I get you to drink?'

'A beer would be good.'

'Beer? Oh, no, I don't really drink alcohol much. I meant a hot drink or some squash perhaps?'

'Don't you have some vodka or something?'

Alarm bells were clanging. 'I might have some sherry left from Christmas if you'd like a small glass of that?' Why didn't I just say no?

'Never had sherry. I'll give it a go though. Is there any more bread?'

I dutifully supplied the girl with two more slices of bread and a hunk of cheddar. I found the almost full bottle of sherry, covered in dust, on a shelf in the utility room and poured out a small glass.

'I'm sorry to rush you,' I said, trying to appear composed, but growing gradually more uneasy, 'I need to go out again soon. I'm... er... I've arranged to meet a friend, then I have to pick my son up from school.'

'Oh yeah. Your son. Called Ben isn't he? I've seen you with him in The Lawns.' I clenched my teeth to stop myself from gasping. 'He's got one of them kites that make a whistling noise. Nice little lad. Always happy.'

'So, shall I give you a lift somewhere then?'

'No, no, the squat's only round the corner. I'll go and see if Ed's back yet. Thanks for the dinner. It was lovely.' She extended her hand to be shaken as if we were two executives who'd just completed a successful business deal.

I was flustered. 'Here, take these for later if you like.' I pushed an unopened packet of chocolate biscuits and a bag of peanuts into her satchel. I let her out by the front door and watched as she crossed the drive to the street, running her fingers along the side of my car as she passed it.

I followed her to the pavement. 'Bye.'

'See ya,' she replied without looking back.

I didn't move from the spot until Mel turned the corner and was out of sight. I shuddered. When I returned to the kitchen and cleared the table I saw the bottle of sherry had gone.

GA's words came back to me: "Some small deed... make it something simple." I'd been trying too hard. Again. And it led me into a situation I couldn't cope with. Again.

Sod it, I thought.

I'd already driven halfway to picking up Ben from school before I remembered my intention to walk across The Lawns. However, the carefree image of Ben and I, playful and frolicking as we walked towards the south gate was tainted now. Mel had said she'd seen us in The Lawns together and she knew he's called Ben. There was something disturbing about that. It was probably better to continue to make the journey by car for the rest of the term – there was anyway only a week left before the summer holidays. And I reasoned that perhaps Ben wouldn't mind flying his kite in the garden in future.

The children came streaming out of school clutching white envelopes containing their annual school reports.

'Mr Gupta said to tell you I owe him a tenner for this.' Ben grinned as he handed over his envelope.

'Well done, I'm really proud of you.'

'Aw, Mummy, you haven't even opened it yet, how do you know you're proud of me?'

'Because there's such a lot to be proud of. Did you have a good time at Jake's?'

And while he excitedly recounted his delight with the PlayStation game and the barbecue, I reminded myself of how fiercely proud I am of my golden boy with his spiky hair which, like his dad's, refuses to lie flat. I already knew his school report would be glowing, but it wasn't the report that made me proud. It was him. Ben. My son. My darling boy.

I opened the report whilst the pasta was simmering. Ben had "exceeded the expected level for his age band" for all criteria. The words "accomplished", "accurate", "innovative", "inventive", "thoughtful", "considered" and "excellent" shouted from the pages of the individual subject reports, but it was what his teacher had written in his general comments that surprised me most: "*It has been my great privilege to have made a small contribution to Ben's school life this year. He has that rare ability to bring joy to all he touches. His wit, honesty and integrity are irrepressible. It is humbling to meet such strength of character in one so young.*"

I wasn't entirely sure how to react to that. It seemed a bit mawkish for a primary school teacher to make such comments on a child's report. It's generally acknowledged that Deepak Gupta is an inspirational teacher with a well-deserved reputation for helping his pupils to find the best of themselves, but "honesty" and "integrity" and "humbling", especially "humbling", seemed over the top and somehow inappropriate. I toyed with the idea of asking Ben what he thought of it. I could hear him on the landline in the hallway speaking to Mother. In French, of course. I leant on the doorframe listening to the end of the conversation, piecing together from his contributions what Mother must be saying to him.

'Bien sûr, Mémé, de temps en temps nous dégustons les plats français.....oh, pardonne-moi Mémé, je plaisante......j'ai pensé que c'était drôle......Mais oui, bien sur je te comprends. On parle rarement l'allemand. Maman doit toujours m'aider quand je l'oublie, mais, par contre, j'apprends beaucoup de vocabulaire en italien!.....Oui, oui, ça aussi, je t'ai dit pour te faire rigoler. Je rigole......Au revoir. Je t'embrasse..."

'She wants to know if we're remembering to practise French conversation, yes?'

'You guessed. She's told me to write her a long letter in French in the holidays. You'll have to help me, okay? She'll make me do the corrections if I get anything wrong. It's not funny, Mummy, stop laughing.' But he was laughing too. 'She's done it before.'

'And did she ask how you're getting on with German?'

'That too.' He rolled his eyes playfully.

'I wasn't much older than you when we had language weekends. On Saturdays we spoke only in French and then on Sundays we spoke in German. Every weekend she was at home, no exceptions, for years.'

'We're not going to do that are we, Mummy?'

'No, not unless you decide you want to. I used to enjoy it, actually. Eventually it was second nature. When I went back to school on Mondays and heard everyone speaking in English, I found I was automatically translating what they were saying into French and German.'

We sat and ate.

'Ben, if you don't want to learn languages you don't have to. Your spoken French is already fluent. We can leave it until you're older if you'd prefer?'

'No, I love it, Mummy. I want to learn to speak German and Italian and Spanish too, like you.'

I grinned. 'Another thing I've been thinking about is Jacqui and your piano lessons. You've been having them for two years now, that's long enough to know whether you like playing or not. I know you only practise because I make you. Sorry if I've been forcing you to do something you don't enjoy. How about I phone Jacqui and say we're going to stop them for a while?'

'What, stop my piano lessons? Then what would I have to moan about? I guess I'd better carry on just so's I have something to chunter about every now and then.'

'Chunter?'

'Yep, that's what Ungrampa says he's doing when he's talking to his fish and his plants and his hens. He says he's just chuntering. It's a great word, isn't it?'

"Joy to all he touches" resonated in my head. Sometimes, there is something about my son that's humbling. *I wish you could see him, Paul, you'd be proud of him too.*

The phone rang. It was Adrian.

'Hello Ruby, just checking you haven't forgotten the Singathon tomorrow?'

I had forgotten. 'Of course not. Remind me what time you need me to be there.'

'We're the final act so it's about three fifteen for three thirty. It finishes at four. Have you seen the weather forecast? It's rain, rain and rain all day. Did you manage to get any sponsorship?'

'Spon... oh yes, twenty pounds.' *Why am I doing this, especially after all my resolve just a few hours ago?* Why couldn't I just admit, 'Sorry, I'd clean forgotten about the Singathon and I don't have any sponsors'? Now I would have to dig into my pocket for twenty pounds and falsify names on the sponsorship form.

'Well done, Ruby.' Adrian sounded impressed. 'Between you and me, I think there's one or two of our number that haven't bothered. See you tomorrow then. Hopefully there'll be a good turnout.'

'Adrian?' said Ben when I hung up.

'Mm. It's the Singathon tomorrow. I forgot all about it.'

'What am I going to do with you?'

He took me by the hand, led me like a recalcitrant puppy to the weekly planner and pointed to the date. 'Saturday 13th. Singathon. Church of the Immaculate Conception, 15:30 to 16:00. It's all there, Mother Dearest.' He folded his arms and tapped his foot whilst he sighed and shook his head with a long-suffering pained expression on his face.

How the roles had reversed. How many times have I repeated this ceremony with Ben when he's not registered a pending appointment? I had a sudden insight into how farcical the behaviour was; even Ben saw it as ripe for teasing me with.

I kissed the top of his head. 'Maybe this is something else we should dump. What do you reckon?' I said tapping the planner. 'Stick a picture on the wall instead.'

Ben's gently mocking humour was a sobering wake-up call to the absurdity of exactly how rigid and onerous my timetabling was, how much I limited our potential for spontaneity and for just being. I felt a definite shift in perspective. I was beginning to realise how complicated and difficult I made our lives in my efforts to compartmentalise and organise and structure and shape and mould. Instead of the planning existing to help us remember dates and events, through my obsession – because I see now that's what it amounts to – with order, Ben and I were fragmented into behaving as if we existed to facilitate the planning.

'Wow, Mummy! What's going on? Why all these changes all of a sudden?'

'Just because,' I said cheerfully. 'And this is just the start.'

'Do I have to come to this Singathon thingy or can I go round to Ungrampa's to see the chicks?'

I had a mental image of my soon to be ten years old son surrounded by nubile bikini-clad young girls plying him with cocktails and hanging onto his every word.

'Chicks?'

'Yep. Ungrampa thinks they'll hatch today or tomorrow. I'd love to see one hatching.'

'We'll need to check that he's going to be in first. We'll give him a ring after your swimming lesson in the morning.'

We spent the evening watching a Laurel and Hardy movie (Ben's default favourite) whilst I caught up with the ironing. I settled him in bed and left him to read a couple of chapters of his newest Michael Morpurgo, then settled down to start work on the commission that had arrived in the post earlier. It was still untouched on my desk where my GA had left it.

In barely three days my life had been turned upside down. It was hard to take in. Had I actually accepted the outrageous idea that this man genuinely existed and was my Guardian Angel then? Was I really so gullible? What other possible explanation could there be for what was happening? And why? I considered the events so far from finding him in the kitchen, and the mixed emotions that triggered, to my panic attack the following morning when he didn't turn up when I expected him and then the exhilaration of being in the garden with Toby.

Was it Toby that had changed or was it me? The simple meal we shared in his garden later in the evening was the first time in all the years of knowing him that he'd confided something of his life to me. I sensed a great underlying sadness in him. A sadness I'd not previously recognised. Was his love of growing things to compensate for the emptiness and regret inside him? I vowed to find ways of repaying his years of kindness and of showing how much I'd come to appreciate him.

My thoughts drifted to the yoga class where the euphoria of the morning had freed me from my usual self-imposed insecurities and inhibitions. The penny was starting to drop.

I was shocked by my reaction to seeing my GA looking in through the window. Why had I been so angry? Why had I felt such rage? And then in the car and again that morning? I cringed when I realised how unbelievably rude and dismissive I'd been towards him. I prided myself that I was polite and respectful. I didn't remember ever speaking to anyone like that before in my entire life. He seemed to bring out the worst in me. And, come to think of it, why had I been so sick? I was left with none of the general side effects I might have expected after eating something that disagreed with me. I was clearly not coming down with a virus.

Then finally there was the episode with Mel. What of Mel? What was it about Mel that made me shudder?

At ten thirty I turned off the lights and went up to bed; the envelope containing my next commission still on my desk unopened.

What a peculiar day it had been.

I dreamt I was painting a wall white. Just as with the speedboat nightmare, I was totally immersed in the dream. I knew I needed to get the wall painted, but there was no urgency. My strokes were slow and rhythmic. I could smell the fumes from the paint reaching into my sinuses and could feel the pressure of the paint roller on the plastered surface as the glistening white oozed without the need to be replenished. There was no beginning or end to the wall. I was totally absorbed in the task as I progressed to each new area to be covered. My only motivation was to ensure I'd left no streaks or gaps, with no thoughts about what I'd already completed or what there was still to do.

Saturday 13 July

As the weather forecast predicted, a strong south westerly gale blew rain against the windows of the Hegley neighbourhood most of Friday night, but by Saturday morning the storm had spent its fury and the wind had dropped, though the rain was set in for the duration. A tiresome drizzle punctuated with heavy showers with the tantalising promise of 'dry later'.

The day got off to a good start for Ben; he swam twenty-five lengths at his swimming class and became the proud recipient of his thousand metre certificate. He couldn't wait to tell Toby. And, as usual, Toby was more than happy for Ben to spend the afternoon with him. Three chicks had hatched already and four more were imminent. Toby proposed that Ben should go around straight after an early lunch to give me time to get a couple of hours' work done before I went out and he offered to sponsor the Singathon for three pounds.

I set off for the church, brandishing my brolly, just before three o'clock. It's barely more than ten minutes' walk along Lawns Road; the opposite side of The Lawns from Mel's squat on Arboretum Avenue.

The hall belonging to the Church of the Immaculate Conception is where Ben's Cubs and my weekly choir meetings are held. I'd been filled in on the details. The car park was in urgent need of resurfacing and the Singathon was one of a number of "exciting ventures" to raise enough money to pay for the work to be done. However, it had become apparent that car park resurfacing isn't a sexy cause in the way that undernourished children in Africa or rescued donkeys, say, might inspire Mr and Mrs Public to part with their hard-earned cash, so thus far the fundraising had been an uphill struggle without much conspicuous success. Consequently a lot of hopes were pinned on this event.

The plan was to kick off at eleven with the Immaculate Conception choir making a suitable first contribution, followed by various other local choirs and singers who'd been appointed to perform throughout the day. Adrian's choir, Many Voices, was chosen to be the final act, with a medley of rousing sea shanties inviting audience participation. I've always loved singing and the prospect of an appreciative and responsive audience was something I eagerly looked forward to. It was generally considered by the organisers, I'd been told, to be a fitting highlight to end the day's event.

Adrian saw me hovering and beckoned me over to where the choir was allocated to sit. 'So glad you could make it,' he whispered as he handed me a running order. 'We're going to have to sing acapella as Gareth's forgotten his accordion.' His outrage and frustration with the unfortunate Gareth, while not apparent in his choice of words, was abundantly evident in the sardonic way he delivered them.

There was a good crowd seated in the front pews and a few others scattered here and there. A young boy of about 12 or 13 was part way through his rendition of Where is Love from Oliver. It was painful. Before his voice had started to break he had been a wonderful treble according to Adrian, called upon across the county and beyond to sing to the pleasure and enchantment of his many admirers. There had been talk of him recording a CD with a compilation of his favourite pieces, apparently. Hearing him struggle through this particular song though, never quite sure how his voice would sound, was agony. Agony for the poor lad's own comfort. Agony for the audience. There was rapturous applause when the song came to an end – I suspect more out of gratitude that the ordeal was over than in appreciation of the performance.

The boy didn't move. He waited for the applause to die down and then announced his final offering was "Jerusalem". The audience notably shrank a little lower into the pews as we gritted our teeth in readiness. By the time he reached the final bars the reassuring smiles on our faces had taken on a fixed grimace of hysteria. The general relief as he took his final bow was palpable.

'William Blake must be turning his grave,' Adrian whispered.

Four particularly serious and intent fifty-something, bespectacled ladies made their way haltingly to the platform as if they were about to be hanged, drawn and quartered. They looked terrified. They hadn't had a chance to practise with Malcolm the pianist they explained and craved the audience's forbearance. Meanwhile, Malcolm had their music thrust before him at the point when they were ready to start singing. He was reputedly an ebullient pianist, but sight reading was not one of his strong points. They did not get off to a good start. It might have been more successful if the singers and the accompanist had been in the same key. The song was a dirge, a sixteen verse dirge, entitled 'How Oft I Have Wandered', written by the ladies themselves especially for the occasion. They gripped their song sheets as if their lives depended on them and seemed to be oblivious of the fact that they were meant to be performing to an audience.

'Can we just take the chorus again, please?' requested the tallest of the quartet, interrupting the proceedings. She was dressed in an unseasonal tweed suit, fluorescent orange ankle socks and heavy brogues. Her glasses, dutifully resting on the end of her nose, were attached to a long silver chain around her neck. She appeared to be in charge.

'I think we were a little flat there if you don't mind me saying, Meredith. And Rosemary, we forgot the harmony on "sweet rivers of honey", hmm? Malcolm, can you give the intro again please? I think we'll start from verse three.'

When it came to a merciful end, the ladies were beside themselves, bobbing and hugging and shaking hands with Malcolm. 'Thank you. Thank you so much for giving us this amazing opportunity.'

Adrian stood to assemble Many Voices, but was first pressed into taking photographs of the ladies from several angles posing as if singing with and without Malcolm in shot. Adrian was, as always, obliging and patient and deferred signalling to us to take our places until his photographic services were dispensed with. The ladies took their leave in a flurry of rapturous exhilaration.

Adrian expressed his gratitude that so many of us had made the effort to turn up – almost a full turn out. Eighteen strong, we spilled across the platform.

'Take note of what we've just seen,' he whispered. 'Don't look down at the words, make eye contact, smile and sing with gusto. Let's make this a performance our audience will remember. Leave them wanting more.'

We, of course, could see what Adrian could not. He was facing us with his back to the pews. The treble had left, taking the majority of the spectators with him. Our choir had been most of the audience for the choral ladies. Once we moved from our seats to the platform the only audience that remained were two old biddies who started to get up to go, but then clearly felt obliged to stay out of politeness because without them, apart from a man sitting at the back who'd almost certainly only come in to shelter from the rain and then fallen into a deep sleep, the pews would be empty.

Assuming his professional choirmaster persona ready to introduce the choir and announce the jolly entertainment to follow, the smiling Adrian turned to address the audience.

'Ah!' he said. 'Oh I see.' As he turned back to face us, I noticed the two old biddies seize their opportunity and make a hurried exit. 'What does everyone think?' he said.

There was a gnashing of teeth, recriminations, indecision and consternation.

'Ruby?' said a startled Adrian, seeing me waving eagerly.

'Oh let's sing,' I said. 'Let's sing, sing, sing.'

GA was standing on the middle of the central pew three rows from the front, rubbing his hands with glee, impatient to begin. 'Come on. I love a good sing song. I'll join in,' he said.

The rest of the choir appeared surprisingly reluctant. They're used to me being quiet and reserved, but I threw myself into the moment, fervently belting out the songs as if I was playing to a packed house.

'Join in the chorus!' I called out, aspiring but failing, to wake the man snoring in the furthest reaches. GA, on the other hand, rose to the occasion, singing enthusiastically, running up and down the pew and joining in with the actions. 'Way, haul away… Put him in the long boat till he's sober… Cockles and muscles, alive, alive oh…'

My eagerness was contagious and little by little my colleagues were drawn in until they too filled the church with the sounds of the sea shanties. Quite apart from anything else the acoustics were amazing. We couldn't have been more eager if we'd been singing to a cheering crowd at the last night of the Proms.

At the end of the set there was a momentary lull. Still full of euphoria I turned to my fellow choir members expecting them to feel the same. They were floundering in a tidal wave of embarrassment and avoided eye contact. Adrian hurriedly thanked us all for coming as he made his escape. No one, it seemed, wanted to stop and chat. They were all equally bent on leaving as soon as possible.

'Bye, see you Wednesday,' they called out, leaving me wondering why they were so reticent, and dashed out before I could reply.

I turned to GA expectantly.

'I did enjoy that. Congratulations. I think your friends might have been a little taken aback by your zeal. You do realise that they couldn't see or hear me?'

'You mean…?'

'Yes, I'm afraid so.'

I groaned inwardly. 'Did they hear me tell you to join in the chorus?'

He nodded. 'Not to worry. They probably won't remember anyway. And our friend is likely to go on sleeping soundly until someone comes to lock up. It's stopped raining and the sun's come out again. Might I walk you home?'

'I'd like that,' I heard myself reply. 'The side door goes straight onto Lawns Road and then we won't have to walk round.'

He indicated for me to lead the way. 'An excellent idea. Would you be so good as to hold the door open for me?'

I opened the door and held it while he walked through.

'Thank you so much for your kindness,' he said and I felt his smile permeate every cell of my body.

It was glorious to be out in the sparkling sunshine after the heavy downpour. The air was wonderfully fresh and clear. He pointed out the perfect rainbow arching the sky across The Lawns. I noticed the raindrops on the clematis and the rhododendrons glistening in the sun. All was well with my world. I felt contented and serene. Even though the Singathon had been a shambles, I'd loved every minute of it. I felt completely free and uninhibited; no wonder the other choir members seemed so taken aback.

'You see the elderly gentleman walking towards us with his dog?' GA asked.

'Yes, of course.'

'He can't see me, you understand. Why don't you say something to him?'

'What? What shall I say?'

'You'll think of something, I'm sure. Start with a smile.'

'Hello,' I said as the man drew closer, 'I was just looking at the rainbow over The Lawns. Isn't it beautiful?'

The man stopped. He didn't look the type to be communicative, as if he wasn't used to being noticed by other people.

'Indeed it is. Indeed it is.'

'Is this your dog? Isn't he gorgeous? D'you mind if I stroke him?'

The little Yorkie pulled at his lead, eager to be cosseted. I bent down close and he put his front paws on my knees.

'Oh dear, I'm afraid he'll have dirty paws.'

'No worries. It'll brush off when it dries.'

'He can take any amount of that,' the old man chuckled. 'He loves being fussed.'

'What do you call him?'

'Arnold.'

'Hello, Arnold. Hello, boy. Well, aren't you a sweetie? Yes, you are. Yes, you are.'

'Say hello, Arnold. Show the lady.' The dog looked up at his owner and then raised himself on to his back legs and held out a front paw to me. 'Go on, shake it,' the man said.

I took the dog's paw in my hand. 'How do you do, Arnold? Nice to meet you.' We both laughed. 'And it's nice to meet you too,' I said as I stood up again. 'My name's Ruby. Do you live around here?'

'I used to, but we moved to Teignmouth when I retired. We're just visiting my daughter for a couple of weeks. This is her house here. I took Arnold round The Lawns to get some fresh air after being cooped in by all that rain. I'm George, by the way. Very nice to meet you, Ruby.' He raised his hat.

'Take care,' I said.

'Bye,' he replied turning into his daughter's front gate followed by the scampering Arnold wagging his tail.

As I continued home, I was still smiling. I felt a tug at my arm. It was GA. 'Oh sorry, I thought you'd gone.'

He fell into step with me. 'That was another act of kindness. How did it feel?'

'Delightful actually. He's such a lovely man and Arnold's a great little chap.'

Just ahead of us a muddy ball bounced over The Lawns' railings and started rolling down the incline towards us. I scooped it up, regardless of the mud, and threw it towards the gaggle of children looking through the railings in dismay as their game was about to come to an abrupt end.

'Catch!'

'Cheers,' said the lanky, loose-limbed youth who caught it and the children bounded off to resume their game.

'You're getting good at this kindness business.' GA looked delighted.

'Okay, I get it,' I said with a broad grin despite my embarrassment. 'It's not about grand gestures. I missed the point a bit with Mel and went over the top. I can see that now.'

'The trick is to keep it simple. Just a smile and a good morning as you pass a stranger in the street can be enough. No need to try too hard.'

'Would you like to come in for a cup of tea?' I felt a flash of shyness, my old self-consciousness raising its head. 'I'd really like you to. Please?' I babbled.

'Thank you,' he replied graciously. 'I'd love to.'

We walked the short distance to the house chuckling about the choir's reaction at the Singathon.

As we settled in the kitchen, Ben knocked at the French windows of the conservatory to be let in. He'd seen me arrive home.

'Hello, darling, have you had a lovely time? Thanks, Toby,' I called as Toby went back through the gate into his own garden. He took his vacant briarwood pipe from his lips, held it up to me in recognition and then popped it back into his mouth as he disappeared behind the hedge.

'Yep. Ungrampa helped me clean out Mildred and Delilah after it stopped raining. I won't have to do it in the morning now. There's seven chicks hatched. You must go over and see them, they're so cute. What's for tea?' He headed for the kitchen. 'Oh hi, Cameron, I didn't know you were here today.'

'Camero…? You can see him?'

'Yes, of course, silly. Can we have pizza? What's the matter, Mummy? You look really surprised. Why are you staring?' He looked at "Cameron" to see if he was in on whatever the joke was about. "Cameron" winked.

'I guess I'm learning not to be surprised by anything these days. Yes, we can have pizza, why not? You can go and play if you want to. I'll call you when it's ready.'

'Can I go on the Xbox?'

'How did I know that was coming? Go on then, before I change my mind.'

I waited until Ben had gone into the lounge, poured out two mugs of tea, set one down on the table for "Cameron" and the other for myself. I sat down and began sipping my drink.

I waited.

No response.

'Cameron?' I said eventually. 'What kind of a name is "Cameron" for an angel? No, don't answer! I'm sure I wouldn't understand if you did.' I noticed that his continual smiling had left permanent laughter lines grooved into his face. He had a warm friendly face. A face you could trust. 'How come Ben can see you?'

'Ben and I have been friends for a very long time. I think he probably assumed you knew.'

'This just gets weirder by the minute. Are you his Guardian Angel too then?'

'Not exactly.'

I paused expectantly. He was comfortable with that and concentrated on sipping the hot tea.

'You're not going to explain, are you?'

'It'll all become clear to you in good time, my dear. Cameron is Ben's name for me and, of course, he doesn't see me in quite the same way as you do.'

'You mean you can change your name and what you look like?'

'Yes, that's quite correct.'

'Then how does Ben see you?'

'He sees me as a few years older than himself. We've grown up together, if you see what I mean.'

'So why am I seeing you as a silver-haired balding old man who always wears a suit and tie however hot the weather?'

'That's how you're choosing to see me. I'm your projection of what you think I should look like.'

I burst into laughter. 'Danny DeVito. That's who you remind me of, Danny DeVito. In a suit. It's been bugging me ever since I first saw you at the garden centre. I knew you reminded me of someone.'

'Mr DeVito might be a little upset by how many years you've chosen to age him.'

I was still laughing. 'Danny DeVito with a posh English accent. Just imagine. Why on earth would I choose to see you as Danny DeVito?'

'No doubt there'll be good reason somewhere in the recesses of your mind.'

I struggled with the notion and drew a blank. 'So do I call you Danny or do I call you Cameron?'

'That's entirely up to you. I'm sure Ben won't mind you using his name for me. It'll probably make things a little less confusing for the two of you if you do.'

'Cameron it is then. Funny, I hadn't thought of you as having a name. Sorry, that sounds rude.' He smiled. 'So what's your real name?'

'I'm happy to be called Cameron. I rather like it.'

Mysterious as ever, I thought. 'Does Ben know that not everyone can see you?'

'He isn't always aware of us when we're around, just like you aren't. We have a way of dipping in and out of people's lives every now and then.'

'What do you mean, dipping in and out?'

'Oh sometimes it's useful to bring clarity to a particular situation. We help people think through things that might be bothering them. You look surprised.'

'No one's ever said anything to me about it before. Is it a big secret that they don't tell other people?'

'Who have you told about meeting me?' His smile wrapped around me like a mischievous bubble.

'Um. I haven't… Not sure who I'd tell, actually.'

'No, we're not a big secret. People just don't remember usually – unless it would be good for them to do so. We have a way of putting people at ease so they can speak to us openly without having to question why we're there or who we are.'

'I'm not sure I'm happy with that. That sounds like mind control.'

'Not at all. We never take away free will. We wouldn't have the ability to do so even in the unlikely case of us wanting to. And we only ever respond to a direct invitation such as your own.'

'I see.' I let that sink in for a moment. 'So that's what the fug's about?'

He laughed. 'Everyone's different. There's no one prescription fits all.'

'How does Ben figure in all of this? Why does he need to know you?'

'Ben understands more than most. He knows instinctively that he can trust me, because I've always been a part of his life. Do say cheerio to him for me. I know you have work you must do in the next few days but keep up with your acts of kindness and remember…'

I laughed, 'To keep them simple?'

'Absolutely. With that I'll leave you with your new homework. No need to look so worried. It will require thoughtful consideration, yes, but it too is simple. Pay attention to your dreams. The changes you want to make in your life come through you, not to you, but your dreams can sometimes be a useful guide.'

I wasn't sure how to react. He smiled and I bathed in its warmth, my anxiety already forgotten. I knew I was in safe hands.

This time he waited for me to show him to the front door and let him out.

'Just let me know when you want to wear something more casual,' I called after him as he turned to wave.

His smile was catching. I was positively glowing. I just couldn't help myself.

The Dublin company who commissioned the translation of the German manual I had just mysteriously completed, is setting up new premises in Mainz and now wanted their current contracts of employment and employee handbook updating into German. It's a similar task to other commissions I've completed many times. It requires little specialist knowledge of technical terms or procedures, so only minimum research for checking vocabulary. Work that is undemanding to translate, but lengthy and time-consuming. This kind of assignment is my bread and butter and therefore dependent on a hundred per cent accuracy. The French agency I work for will only continue to put work my way if I'm meticulous and punctual.

It's bittersweet, but as a result of Paul's early death I'm financially secure. His life assurance policy paid off the mortgage outright, I also received a large lump sum in compensation after the accident and a death in service payment and modest monthly pension from the Fire Service. My translation business and my part time teaching more than cover my monthly expenses.

My plan before Paul was killed had been to set up a language school, but when Ben was eighteen months I decided to redesign the house so I can work from home. That's how I got to know Alice better and how I first met Jess. I knew Alice and another friend, Jenny, both five years younger than me, from playgroup. They were at school together. Our sons Ben, Jake and Owen are also the same age and are now in the same class at school. I asked around at playgroup if anyone could recommend a good builder. Alice told me her husband, Pete, is joint owner of a property development company with Jess's partner, Dom. Pete is Jess's younger brother so Alice and Jess are more or less sisters-in-law.

I invited myself to their houses to check the company would do a good job. Dom helped me with the layout and Jess gave me the benefit of her advice too. If I say so myself, what they've done to the house is terrific. They converted the old dining room into an office, then extended out into the garden so that I now have a bigger kitchen, a utility room with a downstairs toilet accessed from under the stairs and a conservatory with decking outside. It cost me a small fortune, but it was worth every penny.

The work took getting on for a year because of getting planning permission. Alice and Jess used to visit sometimes to see the changes as they were developing and we've been close friends ever since. We meet up for coffee and a chat and maybe shop for clothes or shoes or cosmetics or whatever on Friday mornings. Of course, I'm talking about a time – was it really only two weeks ago? – when I believed I had to rationalise spending time with them to quieten Mother's admonishing voice in my head. Her mantra was that work should take priority, so I didn't mention it to her. Nevertheless, somewhere in my gut I felt guilty, as if I didn't deserve to have friends. I knew it was irrational, but somehow...

The downside of teaching a few hours a week at Hegley Community Academy in term time and, more particularly, my translation business was that I mostly had tight deadlines that involved me working intensively every few days. As it happens, there was no urgency as far as the agency was concerned for the completion of the employee handbook, but I was expecting the German Meaty Goodness dog biscuits to arrive on the eighteenth so I needed to finish the Dublin commission first.

I consoled myself that Ben was used to my erratic hours and could be relied upon to entertain himself when need be. I always built in time between work schedules, when I could, to give him my undivided attention and thought him happy to accept how it was. Alice said it troubled her sometimes that I took his co-operation for granted. I reasoned that her picture-perfect life with Pete meant she didn't understand how hard it was for me as a single parent. Jess said I might want to think about how difficult a less amenable child might make the situation. I trusted they both meant well, but I convinced myself that my arrangements for Ben were always my first priority. Whatever others might be thinking, I believed that I never compromised his wellbeing for the sake of one of my activities or work. That said, I fully intended to honour the big changes I'd hinted at to make our lives less prescribed. A little adjustment here, some minor rescheduling there, I'd soon show Cameron – Cameron! Really? – I was responsive and receptive. Was that what he meant about the changes coming through me and not to me? I guessed it must be.

I stood in front of the planner for the week ahead to see where I might make a start in changing the routine to make it less demanding. It was an undertaking needing to be completed systematically and methodically, of course.

Every morning, afternoon and evening of every day was ear-marked with activities. Not joint activities with myself and Ben spending time together I realised with some alarm, but each of us with separate engagements. I'd never looked at it that way before. Worse still, seeing it as a whole, rather than the individual commitments, highlighted how often I relied on other people to chaperone Ben, when the timings overlapped.

Toby picked up Ben from Cubs on Monday evenings twice a month so I could go to PTA and School Governors' meetings. The meeting that coming Monday was particularly important because it was the last before the school summer fair on the following afternoon.

On Tuesday evenings Ben had Badgers from six until seven thirty and I had my Spanish Intermediate Conversation class from six thirty until nine. I enjoy teaching and my students are keen and hard-working. Most of my improvers have been coming to my daytime French classes on Mondays for three years and I have a good relationship with them. At their request, the Academy has set up a new course for September in Advanced French.

Unfortunately, the Community Academy is in the opposite direction from the St John Ambulance Hall so I had to rely on Theresa, one of the youth leaders, to pick him up and return him home again. Toby came over and waited for him and then stayed with him until I got back. In a way it was a perfect arrangement because Ben and I were both out on the same night. It was a pity I wasn't able to be at the ceremony when Ben received his prestigious Super Badger Award, but Theresa took photos for me. I felt slightly intimidated by Theresa and more than a little embarrassed at having to rely on her, especially as it was Theresa who'd invited me to join the Friends of the Hegley Lawns Pavilion Working Party.

I was mostly available to take Ben to his karate class from five until six at the Lakeside Centre on Wednesdays – I was able to catch up with my emails in the internet café – but we did have to rush back in time for choir. Toby stepped in to babysit again. My goodness, I relied on him more than I realised, but I recorded the gardening programmes for him to watch after Ben went up to bed.

I was about to turn my attention to Thursdays when the strangest thing happened. There was a strident chemical smell coming from the planner and white paint began spreading itself across the surface covering the words. I watched as they disappeared a stroke at a time. Incredulity is an odd sensation, difficult to describe. I stared with eyes open wide. I think I must have stopped breathing, stopped thinking. The busyness of my "systematic and methodical" intentions dropped away. I dabbed at the planner and felt the wetness. My fingerprint gazed back at me and there was paint on the end of my finger.

I don't really remember much about the rest of the afternoon; cooking dinner, eating, clearing the kitchen. Ben gave me a hug and said I looked tired. Pressing translation untouched, we played Scrabble all evening. The last time we'd played had been when Mother was here at Christmas.

I worked from when Ben was settled in bed just after eight, until I could no longer keep my eyes open at just gone two. I thought I'd go straight to sleep but instead lay churning over what had happened. I had deliberately avoided looking at the planner all evening, but curiosity impelled me to check before I went up to bed. The paint-over was gone. The timetable stared back at me; all the ridiculous scheduling returned. I picked up the eraser and wiped the board clean. I wrote SMILE in huge letters. It was such a good feeling.

Maybe that was the point of my dream of painting a wall the night before? Perhaps it was showing me symbolically that

I could "clear the slate", start afresh. I remembered how I was feeling in the dream whilst I was painting: Unhurried, focused, doing the work I had to do and knowing that I was doing it well with no rush to complete it.

Yay! I get it. Thank you, Cameron.

Sunday 14 July

Feeling surprisingly fresh and revived considering how little sleep I'd had, I began working again before seven the following day. On Ben's insistence I went with him to see the chicks midmorning. I was pleased I did because, as Ben had said, they were very cute. I'd have liked to have dawdled over lunch with him – I just shoved a ready-made lasagne out of the freezer into the oven for speed – but the translation was taking longer than I'd anticipated because I'd left it so long before making a start and, to be honest, I found it boring. I'm never usually bored when I'm working.

Thankfully, Ben was perfectly happy to amuse himself in the garden, popping in every now and then without disturbing me to get himself a glass of squash or an apple. It was suddenly gone seven and we'd had nothing to eat since the lasagne at one o'clock. I went on a hunt for him and found him curled up with his Michael Morpurgo on the sofa.

'Sorry, darling. I'd no idea it was so late, you must be starving. Can I get you some beans on toast or something?'

'No worries, Mummy. I had the rest of the quiche from yesterday lunch with some of Ungrampa's salad leaves and a tomato. I put some on a plate for you too. And I filled the dishwasher. I practised the Chopin Nocturne for nearly an hour. Did you hear me?' I was ashamed to admit I hadn't, even though he'd been in the next room. 'I know it off by heart now.'

'You're such a good kid, Ben. You're a gem, do you know?'

'I know. I'm priceless. Every home should have one. Can I play it for you?'

'Please, I'd like that.'

'Lady and no gentlemen, may I present the Chopin Nocturne in E minor, opus 72 number one?' said Ben, standing to attention then bowing.

He took his place on the piano stool, linked his fingers with his palms turned away from him and stretched out his arms in time-honoured tradition.

I applauded appreciatively, but before he'd stumbled through more than four bars I was cursing myself for accepting Meaty Goodness. The Dublin commission was more than enough work for one week. Realising that Ben had finished playing and was waiting for my response, I applauded again and planted a kiss on his forehead.

'Brilliant. Absolutely brilliant. Well done, Ben. Much better than I could do at your age. I'll run your bath for you, then it's straight to bed.'

I thought I might be able to squeeze in another four hours after Ben went to bed, considerably later than his usual eight o'clock, but the phone rang before I'd even switched on the computer.

'Hello Ruby. How are you? How did Ben get on with his 1000 metres? That seems an awfully long way for a little boy to swim.'

'Oh Mother, hello. Is everything okay? You don't usually ring on… Yes, yes he passed with time to spare. He did brilliantly well. His teacher's really pleased with him. He's moving up into the silver caps next term. I'd love to chat, but I have a huge commission I'm chasing to get done.'

'This won't take long. I need you to go to your grandfather's open day next Saturday.'

'Next Saturday? You haven't mentioned it before.'

'His nursing home is having an open day and I think Dad should have someone from the family there to support him, that's all. It's from two until five, but you don't need to stay the whole time. Your Uncle Kenneth's going to visit his in-laws in Ireland and I'm going to Turkey.'

'You didn't tell me you're going to Turkey.'

'No, it's spur of the moment. We booked yesterday morning on impulse. We saw it advertised in the travel agent's window when we were walking by and we thought, well why not? We're going to Marmaris for two weeks next Saturday.'

'I think you might get a shock in Marmaris, Mother. Don't young people go there for the night life?'

'Probably. We're staying in a very plush hotel in a place called Icmeler, just outside Marmaris.'

'Are you going with Delia?'

'No. As a matter of fact I'm going with Andrew.'

'Oh my goodness, Mother. You have a boyfriend? You kept that one quiet.'

'Hardly a boyfriend, he's my gentleman friend. I've known him for some time. I introduced you at Robert's wedding, surely you remember?'

'Oh, um. Of course. How silly of me,' I said, trying to sound convincing.

'We've been doing Ofsted inspections together for a couple of years now. It's only fairly recently that we've been seeing each other though.'

'I'm really pleased for you, Mother. It must be quite serious if you're going on holiday with him?'

'Well, put it this way, I said yes when he asked me to marry him.'

I did try to work after I put the phone down. I wasn't sure how I felt about Mother remarrying after all this time. It's thirty-five years since my father left us for someone else and I can't remember Mother even being interested in having another relationship in all that time. It was disquieting.

I decided to get an early night and then get up at five and work through to eight. Ben always gets himself up at seven-thirty and I could rely on him to get himself some cereal and toast. He'd done so on several occasions before.

Monday 15 July

It was almost seven before I woke, I slept right through the alarm, so I only managed an hour of translating after all and I made little headway. It was a bit of a scramble getting Ben to school on time. We were halfway there when we realised we'd forgotten his PE kit so I had to turn around and go back for it. Worse still, I'd forgotten to wash it.

Later, at the end of my French classes at the Academy, both of the groups gave me a card and flowers. It was the last day of the summer term. I feigned appreciative surprise as I always do at this annual event, not because of indifference, rather because I was embarrassed. When I said, 'You shouldn't have,' I really meant it. I intended to take in cream cakes to share, another annual ritual, but I completely forgot. My catalogue of ineptitude and incompetence was accruing alarmingly. If only I'd written my usual list then neither the PE kit fiasco nor the cream cake debacle would have happened.

Cakes. That was something else that had slipped my mind. I needed to get a grip on myself. Ditching the planner had been a rash decision that I hadn't properly thought through. I was letting myself down. I sighed.

Tuesday was going to be much busier than normal. There would be no few hours to snatch for translation as Alice and I had cakes to bake. We were running the cake stall, for the third year in a row, at the school summer fair. It was going to be tight after the fair to get Ben fed and changed into his Badger uniform ready for Theresa to collect him at half five. The summer fair was from three until five. As it was I wouldn't be able to stay and help clear up as he would have only twenty minutes at home. It was a good job Alice was so understanding. And a good job too that it was the last week of Tuesday activities for a while. I made a mental note to remind myself to rethink Tuesdays for the autumn term.

Fortunately there's a petrol station with an express supermarket on the way to picking up Ben from school. I rushed in and bought the forgotten butter and sugar we'd need for the cakes, cursing that it cost far more than it would have done if I'd got them from my regular supermarket. Then I remembered why my usual Wednesday shop was cut short the previous week and I'd left without getting everything on my list: Cameron and the frozen peas.

There was no doubt about it, something decidedly odd was unfolding. It was as if a force stronger than me was creating chaos and mayhem. I was no longer sure of my parameters. Despite my frustration, I found myself smiling. After all that happened the previous day and my insight into my crazy programming and my resolve to bring more balance into our lives, I'd let myself lapse back into the old mind-set again already. My exasperation melted. I decided the urgency, and the pressure that goes with that, to complete the translation could go to hell. I would just have to tell Dominique I needed more time.

I checked my emails when I arrived back home from the governors' meeting and said goodnight to Toby. There was one from Dominique, suggesting I should delay working further on the Dublin commission as the company were making some amendments. They'll get back to me in September. Meanwhile, they would pay the agreed rate for the hours I'd already worked. I was to submit the work I'd completed to the company and an invoice with my hours to the office.

Synchronicity, perhaps?

Tuesday 16 July

Alice organised our morning's cake making within ten minutes of arriving at my house after dropping Jake off at school. Muffin tins, spoons and bowls methodically laid out, oven on, electric mixer primed, ingredients assembled and coffee refused, she was ready to start.

'We'll keep to batches of twenty-four. It never works trying to mix too much at once. I think we should just about get two trays at a time in your oven.'

I could see that Alice's whole approach to cake making was subtly more co-ordinated and efficient since she'd started planning to transform what once was her hobby into a professional business. The batter was creamed like clockwork, leaving me feeling vaguely redundant.

'What would you like me to do?' I asked hesitantly.

'Um, well how about you whisk the eggs? Four should be enough, put a tablespoon of milk in with them and don't overbeat them. At least we don't have to worry about using warm ingredients on a day like today, the butter's pretty much liquid already.'

'Put milk in with the eggs and not with the flour?'

'Yep. It works, trust me, and I mix a little spelt flour in with the self-raising too. It makes for a tastier sponge. I'll probably have to kill you now I've given my trade secrets away! Don't bother measuring, I judge the amounts by eye, by feel, these days. The temperature affects the consistency.'

I was relegated to putting paper cases into muffin tins, whisking eggs, taking the cooked cakes – first sanctioned as ready by Alice – out of the oven and transferring them to cooling racks. Whilst Alice glowed with competence and efficiency, I became the eager toddler given marginal tasks so I could feel useful. I found that really rather pleasing and was happy to watch in awe as my friend weaved her cake magic.

'My mother's getting married,' I said as Alice turned off the deafening conversation-killer rasping of the food mixer and began to fold in flour by hand.

'Really? Congratulations. Oh! You're not pleased about it?'

'Well… yes… no… I'm not sure to tell you the truth. It's such a shock. I didn't even know she was seeing someone. She's sixty-four.'

'That's okay, isn't it? Lots of people have second marriages in their fifties or sixties, in their seventies, nowadays.'

'But I don't know anything about him. I just know his name's Andrew and they work together sometimes.'

'It's taken you by surprise, that's all.'

'I can't imagine her living with someone else, being married. I'm not convinced it's right for her.'

'Ruby, I see where you're coming from, but don't you think you're worrying unnecessarily, if you've never even met him…? I expect he's really nice and your mum will have someone to look after her. Right, that should do. I'm ready to get the batter into the cases now; then you can you pop them into– '

'I feel like she's let me down a bit.'

'How do you mean?'

I didn't know what I meant. My words had taken me by surprise, I'd no idea what was behind them. I studied the oven door; wielding the newly filled tin tantalisingly close to its destination. 'It sounds stupid, doesn't it?' I said, swinging the door open, 'but who will I have to look after me?' I thrust the tin onto the shelf and turned to take the second tin from Alice. 'There's always just been the two of us. Me and Mother.'

'And Ben.'

I was aware I wasn't making sense. I ought to be pleased for Mother. The churning in the pit of my stomach was irrational. I wanted to cry. Silly impetuous tears of a stubborn child who couldn't have her own way. I slid the second tin into the oven and closed the door. 'And Ben, yes, of course, Ben,' I said, somewhat deflated.

Alice was already filling the mixer bowl with melting butter and caster sugar. 'But?'

'But that's not what I mean exactly. It's… she's not going to have time for me anymore now is she? She's going to Turkey on Saturday for two weeks with this, this…'

'Andrew.' Alice laughed.

'Yes, Andrew. It's a slippery slope.' I said grinning.

Alice was ready to restart the mixer. She hovered with her finger on the switch. 'You just need to get used to the idea, you'll see. I'm sure that if your mum is happier, then you'll be happier too.' She flicked the switch, drowning out the possibility of further conversation.

Whatever it was that was fidgeting and struggling to be given voice continued to mull over in my head as I dutifully broke the next round of eggs into a bowl and whisked them.

'It's alright for you, you've got Pete. Who've I got?' I said as soon as the mixing machine was silenced.

'Oh Ruby. Lots of women are single mothers. My sister Lucy's divorced and she has two chil–'

'Ben has no male role model in his life. How is he going to learn how to grow into a man? I can't teach him. There's no one.'

'Didn't you tell me you have a step brother?'

'He lives in America.'

'Go to America and visit. Take Ben to meet your dad and your brother and sisters, they're his family too. It would be good for him to get to know them.'

'I can't.'

'Can't?'

'I don't know them myself. Besides, Mother would never forgive me. I have my cousin, Robert. He's a bit older than me, but he's the last person I would want Ben to learn from. I never felt comfortable with him, not even when we were growing up. He was really mean to me when there were no adults around.'

'Some kids are like that. They grow out of it.'

'He used to say horrible things about my dad leaving us because I was ugly and stupid.'

'Oh that sort. No, I can't imagine Ben learning anything from someone like that either.'

'He's even worse now, according to Mother. I hardly ever see him these days. He works in the dog-eat-dog world of commerce, I'm not sure what it is he does exactly, something to do with BT, but you can bet your life he's good at it. He was a genius at maths.'

'Wasn't it his wedding you went to a couple of weeks ago?'

'Yes, him. After all that anguish about choosing the bloody coffee machine – do you remember? – I never even got a thank you for it. Plus ça change.'

'Hashtag male chauvinist. Perhaps you should introduce him to Jess. She likes a challenge,' Alice offered.

I laughed. 'Can you imagine? Clash of the Titans. Where Egos Dare.'

'She'd have him sorted in no time. He'd end up on his knees whimpering.' Alice roared with laughter.

'She can be une femme formidable when she gets her teeth into something.' I joined in the laughter, but felt a prick of conscience about poking fun at Jess.

'Whatever une femme formidable means.' Alice rolled her eyes playfully.

'I don't suppose I'll see him again until Mother's wedding now. My God, Mother getting married. The thought of it brings me out in a rash. Do you think they… you know?'

'Ruby. Behave. Don't go there. Of course they bloody do. And good luck to her; she's got how many years to make up?' We erupted into a fit of giggles.

With the last batch of muffins in the oven we turned our attention to icing and decorating. Alice fixed a nozzle to the icing bag, added the freshly made icing and pointed it at the waiting buns.

'Do you want to have a go at this? I'll show you how.' She deftly squirted a towering swirl.

'Perhaps another time, when it doesn't matter so much.'

Alice chuckled and repeated the swirl on another dozen cakes in a matter of seconds, each one as precise as the last.

'I'll do the washing up,' I said in admiration and left the icing and toppings to the expert.

Alice was good company and, after all, cake making is her forte, so although it wasn't the ideal activity for such a hot day we produced a tempting assortment; worthy of a place in any stylish cake shop. We even had time for a quick snack before we set off in Alice's car just after two to start setting up.

Hegley Lawns Primary School prides itself on its reputation for excellence in pupil achievement and in the range of activities it offers. The annual summer fair was a whole year in the planning and this year those of us in the PTA had surpassed ourselves by organising a street dance display by The Dynamos, an inner city all boys dance group that had recently won the West Country Championship. To be strictly honest, our first choice had been a display by the Red Arrows or failing that hot air balloon rides, but those had both turned out to be somewhat financially overambitious.

The school gates were unlocked at two forty-five, half an hour earlier than usual, and parents and friends surged onto the playing field ready to experience the pleasures on offer and to spend lots of money in support of funds for future projects. The weather was glorious and all Alice and I needed to make our efforts worthwhile was to sell a hundred and ninety two cupcakes for a pound each plus the takings from the shortbread and flapjacks that Alice had previously made. Our assigned table top was someone's round plastic garden table on loan for the occasion, its large parasol fixed through the centre to protect the delicacies from the sun. Boxes to put the goodies in had been donated by Alice's husband, Pete, who had taken the afternoon off from work to run the hoopla.

Ben and Jake were entrusted with five pounds each to spend and told they could keep any change. They headed straight for the much anticipated and talked about remote control car circuit, bypassing their previous favourite, the bouncy castle, because they considered themselves too old for such childish pleasures now. After all, they are about to move up into Year 6 and be the big fish in the small pond. They had the afternoon mapped out and their itinerary was equal in detail to anything I might have planned.

The sale of cakes started slowly, but steadily enough to promise a good return. It helped that we were positioned right next to the raffle ticket table, which already had a queue waiting to be served. The raffle prizes were particularly abundant and tempting this year; boosted by a local toy store who donated their overstocked items. I was enjoying myself. It was a beautiful, sunny day. There was a happy carefree atmosphere and a general air of bonhomie. We checked from time to time to see where our sons were, but were confident that all would be well.

'Who's that with the boys?' Alice said. 'I've seen her hanging about before.'

Mel was talking to Ben and Jake. A very different Mel from Friday morning. Her hair was scraped back into a bun and she was wearing a long spotty summer dress. The same old plimsolls were on her feet, however, and the tatty satchel hung from her shoulder. Ben was showing her something and she seemed intent on what he was saying.

'It's Mel,' I mumbled, trying not to panic, struggling not to lose the feeling of wellbeing, but the gnawing anxiety in the pit of my stomach was difficult to ignore. 'I'll just be a moment,' I said and left Alice to attend to the threesome who were deciding which cakes to choose.

By the time I had crossed to where Ben and Jake were, Mel had completely disappeared.

'Are you having a good time, boys? I take it you're giving the face painting a miss?' I forced a not-very-convincing laugh when the boys grimaced at the prospect. 'Who was that I saw you talking to? What was she talking to you about?'

'She wanted to know what we'd won in the lucky dip,' offered Jake. 'We both got a bag of marbles. They're not the ordinary kind; they're supposed to be an alien force. Bit of a con if you ask me.' He held out the open bag for me to inspect.

'We've seen her before. Do you remember,' Ben said to Jake, 'when your daddy took us to The Lawns to play French cricket a couple of Sundays ago?'

'I remember playing cricket. I beat you. I'm not likely to forget that.'

'Only because you cheated,' Ben countered laughing. Jake raised his eyebrows in mock indignation. 'Yes, you know you did. You ask Owen.'

'Whatever,' Jake retorted, playfully dismissing the matter.

'We were queuing at the cafe for ice lollies and she was arguing with that guy?'

'Oh yes, I do remember that. Are you sure it's the same girl? She had that humungously dirty coat on and she looked dead scruffy. I remember they were yelling and swearing and the man with the two toddlers asked them to move on.'

'Yes, it was the same girl, definitely.' Ben turned to his attention to me. 'She said her name's Mel and she says she knows you, Mummy.'

'She what? No, not really. I met her in town on Friday and she introduced herself; that was all. I wonder why she's here.'

'There's lots of local people here that have nothing to do with school. Mr Gupta says The Dynamos are expected to draw a big crowd. We've all got to be on our best behaviour because we're "ambassadors for the school".'

'Teachers always say that stuff,' said Jake wisely.

Ben laughed, nodding. 'All the school is being kept locked for security except the dining room and toilets so you don't need to worry about anybody stealing anything. Would you like us to get you both a cuppa and bring it across? Our treat.'

I was grateful that Ben had misjudged my motive for concern. 'Yes, thank you, I think we'd both appreciate that.'

'Sorry about that, Alice,' I said when I got back to the cake stall. 'The boys are treating us to cups of tea.'

'Doesn't someone usually bring refreshments for the volunteers?'

'Normally yes, but it's one of the things we cut back on this year. We decided that no one minds paying because it's for a good cause.'

'I'm not sure I agree with that. It's a small appreciation of the effort we're making.'

'I'll pass that on.' I said, not admitting that it had been my idea and had had a mixed reception from other members of the PTA committee for the very reason that Alice had expressed. 'We can still claim for the cost of our ingredients though.'

A boy I vaguely recognised as being in Ben's class came over with the teas. His look of studied concentration as he balanced the tray said this wasn't something he did regularly.

'These are from Ben and Jake,' he said. The tray was swimming with tea slops. 'They've gone to help Jake's daddy with the hoopla for half an hour.'

'Thank you, Harry,' said Alice, taking the drinks from him. 'Are any of your family able to be here with you this year?'

'My Aunty Emma's coming, but she can't get here until four. She has to pick my cousin Bertie up from nursery first.'

'Great. Bring her over and introduce us. You can choose a cake if you like.'

He walked off happily munching his smiley face cupcake. When the next rush of customers had gone, I said to Alice, 'What made you give that boy Harry a cake?'

'That was the Harry. You know, Harry.'

'Am I supposed to know something about him?'

'Surely Ben told you? Harry was the one who was being bullied.'

I smiled trying to look casual. 'Ohhh, that Harry.'

'Ruby, sometimes... Harry used to be really shy and withdrawn. You wouldn't think it to see him now, would you? Neither of his parents ever turn up to any school events and some of the other kids made sport out of teasing him. It's such a blessing he's in Mr Gupta's class. You know Mr G never lets something like that go unchallenged.'

'No, I suppose he doesn't.' I attempted a misplaced light-hearted titter. 'What was it he did again?'

'He told the class a true story about a twelve-year-old girl who killed herself because she was being bullied at school. Yes, exactly. He didn't pull any punches. Then, he showed them a recording of her mother describing how her daughter had suffered. I so admire him for having the guts to do that. There wasn't a single kid in the class that wasn't moved by it. Most teachers wouldn't dare to do that, especially when he had a room full of girls – and I'm not being sexist here, it was mostly girls – who were actually weeping. Can you imagine how some of the parents – we both know who I'm talking about – would have reacted if he hadn't handled it sensitively? He was opening a can of worms.'

A man thought he was going to be able to walk past the cake table on his way to the raffle tickets without stopping to buy cakes. Not if Alice could help it, he wasn't.

'They're all one pound each. Made freshly this morning.'

He ended up offering to buy four, but didn't have the right change and so bought five. Honour was satisfied.

'I've just realised who he is,' Alice confessed when he'd moved on. 'His wife isn't going to be very pleased. She was the woman who did exactly the same thing earlier. Oh well. They'll enjoy them. Perhaps they'll come back for more.'

She laughed and then returned to the story about Harry. 'He, Mr Gupta, carefully explained to the children that he knew he was taking a risk telling them the story. Said he'd only decided to do so because he trusted them and respected them to understand why he was doing it. Surely you got the letter he sent home explaining it all and asking for our support first?'

She stared at me, almost accusatory. I think she was having a dig. It made me feel uncomfortable.

'You were there when we were talking about it the next morning…? There was you, me, Jenny and Rachael? We were standing next to the garden by the new portable classrooms?'

I neither remembered the conversation nor the letter. Maybe it was one of those letters I hadn't bothered to read properly because I presumed that if it was anything significant, it would have come up at a governors' meeting.

'He did a drama lesson with them about the difference between what's fun and what's bullying and where to draw the line. Jake was really inspired by it. He told us all about what Mr Gupta said were the… what did he call them?… the "learning outcomes". Then they had to write about what they'd learned personally. I think what they wrote is still on the wall in the classroom. Didn't you notice at parents' evening? Most of us were reading them. Everyone was gobsmacked how perceptive and aware the children were. I think we all underestimated the children's ability to understand.'

I nodded, but said nothing.

'Anyway, Mr G has revised the school anti-bullying policy. He calls it "Trust and Respect". He did an assembly about it.

There's a box the children can put a note in if they're unhappy about the way someone's treating them.'

Alice had to break off as we had another trickle of customers, but returned to the subject as soon as there was another lull.

'Where were we?'

'Mr Gupta's anti-bullying policy?'

'You should talk to Ben about it, yes? He's one of the star players. He and Jake, and Hannah and Holly from Year 6, are the anti-bullying counsellors. If anyone is being bullied they can ask to have a face-to-face meeting with the person responsible, and the four counsellors sit in to moderate. Sort of thing Jess would come up with, eh? Right up her street.'

'Mmm,' I managed to respond.

'It's been going on all term; it's a great success, apparently. I can't believe it hasn't been discussed at the governors' meetings..?' She paused, clearly waiting for a reply. I gave a half-hearted nod. 'The whole thing is about making the children responsible for their own behaviour and getting them to see how the choices they make affect other people. It also teaches the ones being bullied to ditch any victim behaviour and learn to speak up for themselves.'

'Yes, well come to think of it, I do remember something about an anti-bullying policy.'

I was ruffled. I vaguely recalled that there had been an entire meeting devoted to the subject some months before, but I had no recollection at all of what was discussed or decided. It must have been one of those times when I had other things on my mind and I'd drifted into my own thoughts. I guess I did that quite a lot. Well, sometimes reality was daunting. Fantasies were generally reassuring and comforting. They gave me the opportunity to appear to be in charge with none of the challenges that real life presented.

My phone rang. 'It's my neighbour. What on earth can he want? I asked him if he wanted to come and he said he didn't... Hi Toby, anything wrong?'

I felt as if I'd stumbled into another nightmare as his words washed over me. I ended the call without replying.

'I have to go home. Someone's broken in. Toby's called the police because they're still in the house right now. Toby was in my garden and he saw them through the kitchen window, so he's gone back into his own garden until the police arrive.'

There was a ringing in my ears, my vision was blurred and my mouth went dry. I could feel my heart thundering. I was going to have to walk home; I'd come in Alice's car and Alice would have to stay at the fair. I'd arranged for Jenny to give me and Ben a lift home, but not until five o'clock. *What about Ben? What about Badgers? What about clearing up? I'll miss the Dynamos' display. How come the thief wasn't been put off by seeing my car outside? What if Toby's made a mistake? Why wasn't Cameron there to guard me? Isn't that what Guardian Angels are supposed to do? Guard?*

'You go, Ruby, I'll sort everything out here and bring Ben home. Try not to worry; I bet there'll be a simple explanation. No point in panicking before you have all the facts.'

'Theresa's coming to take Ben to Badgers at half five and I'm teaching tonight.'

'Don't worry about any of that now. Just breathe deeply and focus. Take a shortcut through The Lawns and calm yourself. Phone me as soon as you can. You can do this, Ruby, you'll be fine. Just don't go in the house before the police arrive. Promise me.'

I decided on the shortcut option through The Lawns regardless of whether I was likely to bump into the dreaded Mel. I'd cross that bridge if it happened. It was fortunate that no one was around to hear me yelling frantically, 'Cameron? Cameron? I know you're here. Stop hiding. Show yourself now. I said, "now". I'm desperate. Pleeeeeeeease.'

My attempts to take Alice's advice and stay calm weren't entirely successful. My head was pounding and my heart racing. The thoughts teeming through my mind were random and on overload. By the time I left The Lawns, hot and out of breath, by the south gate and headed the short distance to the turning for my road I was convinced Toby was lying bleeding in the garden and the thief was waiting for me brandishing a kitchen knife. No thoughts of bravery or heroism played any part in this mental image.

I rounded the corner and saw a police car parked outside my house facing the opposite direction. I could tell someone was sitting in the back, but it wasn't until I approached my driveway that I could make out that the person was Mel. There was a policewoman sitting in the driver's seat. They were evidently deep in conversation and gave no indication that they had noticed me. I felt a wave of relief.

I swallowed and stood taller. I could handle this. I took a deep breath in and let the panic ebb away on the out breath. Mel was just a kid and the police had apprehended her. Trust Alice. As usual her common sense had prevailed; she'd said there could be a simple explanation and there was. With hindsight I should have guessed Mel would have something to do with it.

Toby was waiting for me in the porch. He was clearly agitated and upset. I felt moved to reassure him. There was a turn-up for the books. I'm usually the one in need of consolation.

'There's a policeman in the kitchen waiting to speak to you. Hope I did the right thing? Sorry if… She says she's your lodger, only I didn't know, thought someone had broken in, she has her own key. You never said. Ben never– '

'No, she isn't a lodger, but I recognise her. You did the right thing, Toby. I'm grateful, thank you. Don't worry about it, I can handle it from here.'

I was surprised by my composure. I could see by his expression that Toby was impressed that I was taking charge. Only minutes before I'd been in the throes of yet another out-of-control panic attack. Moreover, I was able to be gentle with myself about that. When I greeted the police constable I was actually smiling and thanked him for coming. He was, I noted, very good looking and about the same age as me. I noticed that his whole face lit up when he spoke and he had the most gorgeous brown twinkling eyes and long sweeping dark lashes.

'I'm PC Gabrielli. We have a few questions Mrs Lewis, if that's okay?'

'Ah, Gabrielli. Un vero cognome italiano. Voi siete italiano?'

'Erm, I think you're asking me if I'm Italian? No, not me, my grandparents. I never learned much Italian I'm afraid. I always meant to, but never got around to it.'

'Ah. Well, as a matter of fact, I teach Italian. I could give you some lessons.'

He seemed a little embarrassed. I liked that, it meant he was unpretentious, not someone who was full of his own self-importance.

'Er, I need to ask you if you know Mela Kaczmarek?'

I brought myself sharply back to the present and reminded myself that this situation was not something I could drift away from. I briefly explained a carefully edited version of the previous week's meeting.

'I realise with hindsight that it was a reckless thing to do. It would have been better if I'd just bought her some fish and chips or a sandwich or something.'

'The young lady claims to be moving in as a lodger at your invitation. She let herself in with this front door key.'

I checked in the downstairs cloakroom. Inevitably, I found the spare key was missing from its hook. The police officer suggested I might want to check out my bedroom. He explained that when they had arrived the front door was unlocked and they'd found Mel having a shower in the ensuite. We left Toby waiting in the kitchen and went upstairs. The drawers were open and my wardrobe had been more or less emptied with clothes scattered over my bed and on the floor.

'I didn't leave the room like this.'

'We thought you probably didn't, but we needed to check.'

'I noticed she's wearing one of my jackets. Can I look around and see if she's taken anything else?'

My jewellery was as I'd left it in the middle drawer of my dressing table. The drawer was open, but nothing appeared to be missing or disturbed.

'What happens now?'

'Well, as she's someone you know, that depends on whether you wish to press charges.'

'No, probably not. That wouldn't help her in the long run, would it? She told me she ran away from home and she lives in a squat with drug addicts. She's only sixteen. Can't you phone her mother? She must be frantic to know what's happened to her.'

'We can't do that, I'm afraid, she's actually eighteen. We will advise her to contact home, but she has to make her own decision. I expect she will be cautioned.'

'Then tell her that I won't press charges on the condition that she phones her mother.'

I said most emphatically that I definitely didn't want back the green cotton jacket Mel had taken. Neither did I want to speak to her. I was almost glad this episode happened because I wouldn't need to worry any more that Mel might be bothering me again.

PC Gabrielli left me a card with a number to call if I needed to contact him in the future.

How very tempting.

As the police car was driving away, with Mel still in it, Theresa and Alice arrived just a few moments apart. It was agreed that Ben would hurriedly change into his Badger uniform while I found something he could eat in Alice's car as she drove him to Badgers a few minutes late. Alice was my saviour once more. I needed to leave almost immediately for my Spanish class and Theresa had to go straight away because she had to unlock the St John hall.

Ben settled in the back of Alice's car with a sandwich and I gave Alice the flowers my class had given me as a thank you. It was the least I could do, especially when Ben unexpectedly presented me with a somewhat lopsided handmade grapefruit and lemongrass candle.

'You won this in the raffle, Mummy,' he said.

By the time I arrived home from my Spanish class, armed with yet another card and this time a now, at my insistence, half-eaten box of chocolates, the incident with Mel was a crisis that was resolved as far as I was concerned. I felt ambivalent about it. On one hand I was astonished by Mel's impertinence, whilst on the other I no longer thought of her as being a threat. Being apprehended by the police and driven away in a police car would surely be enough of a warning for her to know that she would not be able to get away with anything like that again?

Yes, I felt confident, Mel would go out of her way to keep her distance now. I was satisfied I'd done the right thing in not pressing charges. That in itself would be enough of a deterrent to stop her from risking potential police proceedings in the future. The girl would be grateful I'd taken no action, get in contact with her mother and in all probability return home and reconcile their relationship. It had been stressful for a while but it had all turned out satisfactorily in the end and I could draw a line under the whole unpleasant episode.

I let myself into the house. There were no lights on and I couldn't hear the television. Toby was sitting in semi-darkness in the lounge.

'Toby? You're not watching your gardening programmes. Is it alright if I put the lamps on and draw the curtains?'

I could see from his demeanour that he wasn't happy. He'd obviously been churning something over and it was clear that I was the cause of the something, but I couldn't think why.

'Is everything ok?'

'I'll be off,' he said and made a move to stand up.

'Please Toby, I can see you're upset with me. What've I done?'

He continued to sit, clearly wanting to say something, but not able to find the words. I hadn't considered that he might be upset by what had happened. My head had been full of my evening class and I hadn't thought about him at all. I remembered how anxious he'd been when I arrived home from the fair, yet I'd rushed out just assuming he'd be there to look after Ben, without pausing to check that he had recovered from his ordeal. I realised then that he'd left while I was upstairs with the policeman. I'd been in such a rush I hadn't even noticed.

I was poised to deliver my spurious, insincere excuses. He was clearly expecting to hear them. I sat on the other end of the sofa and took a deep breath. 'Toby,' I began, 'I don't know what to say to you except please, please forgive me.'

Something about the expression on his face and the resignation in his manner stopped me in my tracks.

'I've been incredibly selfish, haven't I? I won't insult you by making excuses. The truth is I was completely tied up in getting Ben to Badgers and getting myself to my class and you went clean out of my head. It's completely indefensible. I can only apologise.'

I searched his face for a response, but he remained implacable.

'I know that's not enough,' I ventured hesitantly. 'It isn't the first time I've taken you for granted. I realise that now.'

He didn't speak, but he looked at me directly in the eyes and I unselfconsciously returned his gaze. I was scarcely aware of doing so, so intent was I on what I was trying to say. 'When you showed me around the gardens last Thursday and then when we spent the evening together something changed. I realised, all these years, I've been… exploiting you.'

"Exploiting" is such a harsh word and he didn't dispute it; in fact he nodded in agreement.

I felt tears beginning to prick at my eyes, but I didn't want self-pity, I wanted to make amends to Toby and I fought them back. 'I want to make you a promise that I won't ever disrespect you again… I'll try not to. I'll make a real effort to try not to. I'd already decided that I wouldn't and then I've behaved like this. I really am so very sorry.'

I fell silent and he didn't reply. We continued to sit in silence for several minutes.

'Thank you,' he said finally and got up to leave. 'I'll say goodnight.'

He headed towards the French windows in the conservatory. I followed him, at a loss what to say. He didn't speak or look at me, but opened the door and stepped onto the decking.

'Goodnight,' I said, turning the outside light on for him. 'I'm going to the supermarket tomorrow morning if you need anything picking up?'

He still didn't acknowledge me, he just continued towards the gate into his garden. He didn't turn and wave. I knew I'd hurt him very deeply.

Cameron was waiting for me in the lounge. He didn't speak, he just opened his arms to me and held me as if comforting a small child while I sobbed and sobbed and sobbed.

Wednesday 17 July

'Ungrampa wasn't here when I got back from Badgers last night,' Ben said at breakfast. 'Theresa had to knock on his door and ask him to come round. He thought I'd gone to stay at Jake's house.'

'Why would he think that?'

'Because he saw me get into Jake's mummy's car. Would you mind turning the radio off and sitting down and talking about this with me please, Mummy? I think it's really important.'

I was a little taken aback that Ben was being quite so forthright. This was a side to my son I hadn't met before. However, I turned off the radio, stopped emptying the dishwasher and sat across the table from him. He was clearly troubled. I'd been too preoccupied with my own thoughts to notice Ben was preoccupied as well.

'I didn't realise, Ben. I could see he was upset when I got home last night. I think I hurt his feelings because I didn't go round before I left for the Academy to thank him for calling the police. I should have spoken to him first. I tried to apologise when I got home, but I didn't make a very good job of it.'

'He told me the burglar was still in the house when the police arrived and she pretended to be our lodger. He heard you tell the policeman that we don't have a lodger and that our spare key had gone missing and then the policeman took you to check upstairs. He said you were gone for ages and he felt awkward so he went back home. He didn't know what was happening. He expected you to go round and explain. He saw the police drive off and then you left when I did, so he thought you had to go to the police station and I'd gone to stay with Jake.'

'Oh my goodness, of course, he didn't know I won't be pressing charges.'

'We ought to have gone round to tell him, even if it'd made us late. It wasn't fair of us to leave him worrying. It was horrible for him having to call the police and he was really, really worried about you, Mummy.'

'It wasn't up to you, Ben. I should have spoken to him,' I said quietly, almost to myself. I could see how Toby must have felt. He'd been anxious about me all evening, and I hadn't even given him a thought.

'He wanted to know what'd happened, but I only knew what Jake's mummy told me on the way home from school. She didn't seem to know very much either.'

I outlined the gist of the story to him. He listened carefully without comment.

'I don't know how to put things right with Ungrampa. I've made a mess of everything, Ben. I'm so sorry, I've let you down and I've let Ungrampa down. I was concerned because it was your last time at Badgers and my Spanish class was breaking up for the summer. Like you said, it wouldn't have mattered if I'd been a few minutes late. My students would've understood. I could have easily phoned ahead and let them know. I wish I'd put you and Ungrampa first, I really do.'

'Yes,' said Ben deeply troubled, 'I wish you had too.'

I saw he wasn't being critical, he wasn't being judgmental and he wasn't putting me down. He was simply agreeing with me. Remorse throbbed in my throat and across my shoulders. I felt ashamed that, yet again, I'd been so tied up in myself I'd never even considered how Toby was feeling.

The post arrived before we set off for school. There was a handwritten envelope with a local postmark. I didn't recognise the handwriting, so I left it on my desk to open later. It was probably another advert for something or someone wanting a donation. There was also a card for Ben from Mother, congratulating him on his swimming award and enclosing a £5 note. It wasn't enough to lift his mood, but he said he would phone her and thank her later.

I suggested we might walk together through The Lawns to school and Ben thought that was a good idea – it was going to be another scorcher of a day – then I remembered I needed to call at the supermarket on the way home so we would have to go in the car. We agreed to go through The Lawns on the way home again.

We said very little on the journey and we parted in a sombre mood.

'Love you,' he said as he got out of the car.

'Dots and spots?'

'Oodles and spoodles. See you at home time. Hope you manage to get your work finished.'

I parked in my usual spot at the supermarket, took the key out of the ignition, but remained in my seat. I had no shopping list, I hadn't checked the fridge or the food cupboard and I couldn't bring to mind what I needed to buy. The yawning heaviness inside me had just grown weightier after my conversation with my son. I couldn't focus or concentrate.

Cameron tapped on the window. I was glad to see him.

He was still smiling but not his usual jovial, good-humoured smile, more an empathic, supportive smile. 'Would you like to talk?'

I nodded and he crossed to the passenger side and got in beside me.

'How strange, I'm starting to feel the fug again. I thought I was over that now.' My voice was flat and expressionless.

'You only feel it when you're fighting. You don't need it when you're open and happy.' He pulled the visor down to shield his eyes from the blaring sun.

'That makes sense I suppose, but I'm not fighting now... I am fighting though, aren't I? A different kind of fighting. I'm fighting me.' I took a deep breath. 'I'm a horrible person, Cameron. I never realised how selfish and self-centred I've been. I'm really horrible. I let people down all the time and I use them, even my friends. I don't mean to, I try really hard. I work hours and hours, often until two or three in the morning to meet all the deadlines. I check and recheck the work so I don't make mistakes. I take on more work than I can cope with, sometimes when I don't need to, and then I have to rely on other people to take care of Ben so I can get it finished. I see it all now.'

I ran my fingers through my hair over the top of my head, then let them rest on the back of my neck. 'When I realised how much I hurt Toby last night, something just switched in my brain, but even then it took Ben to show me I still hadn't really understood what Toby was so upset about... I've ruined everything.'

I let my hands drop back into my lap and began fidgeting with my wedding ring. 'Ben really loves Toby, you know. He even calls him Ungrampa because he's as close to him as he would be to a real grandad. Let's face it, Ben's never even met either of his real grandads. What have I done? How can I show them all I've changed, Alice and Toby and Ben? Help me, please, help me. I'll do whatever I can to make it right.'

'I'm sure you will and I'm equally sure that Alice and Toby and Ben will be aware of your intent.'

'Do you think it will make a difference?'

'That really is dependent on them. It's their choice.' He mopped his forehead with his handkerchief.

'It's all such a mess. I can't deal with it. I'm supposed to go to choir this evening. I don't know whether Toby will still look after Ben or not. I don't suppose you...?'

'No, my dear, I don't suppose I would.'

'No, I thought not. It's probably for the best. I'll have to ring Adrian and tell him.'

He didn't reply.

'Are you here to give me another homework?'

'That was your homework,' he said, pulling at the neck of his shirt. 'Your homework was to consider other people's viewpoints. Not everyone has the same perspective as you do and sometimes what you say and do affects them adversely.'

'But I never mean to hurt anyone.'

'Yet that is what you often do.'

'Ouch.'

'It's very hot in here. Would you open the windows to let some air in please?'

The temperature on the dashboard was reading thirty-two degrees. I was wearing a thin strappy summer dress and felt unpleasantly clammy. For some reason I wasn't conscious of, I'd dressed Cameron in a three piece suit and tie again. There were beads of perspiration on his forehead and he was clearly physically distressed and uncomfortable.

'I'm so sorry. I've done it again haven't I?'

'I'm going to leave you to do your shopping now,' he said as he opened the car door. 'Remember to continue with the small acts of kindness and also to observe how you engage with others. There are always opportunities to make new choices. Choose wisely, Ruby. The choices you make have consequences.'

He stepped out of the car and paused a moment before he closed the door behind him. 'I hope you think I listened to you carefully and gave you my full attention?'

He smiled his usual glowing smile, pulled down the knot of his tie a little and opened the neck of his shirt. Then he was off.

Gave me his attention? That's an odd thing to say. What does he mean by that?

Somehow I managed to fill a shopping trolley by randomly taking things from shelves, trusting that whatever it was I was putting into it would suffice until the following week's shop.

It was going to be a long day.

Once home I busied myself with the laundry and cleaning downstairs. It wasn't my usual day for housework, but I didn't care, it kept me occupied. I kept hoping to catch a glimpse of Toby in one of the gardens, but there was no sign of him. In the end I had to abandon downstairs as the sweltering heat was too oppressive for anything requiring much physical exertion.

I still had my clothes to put away where I'd scooped them from the bed and dumped them on the chair the night before. As always during the day my bedroom was the coolest room in the house. The back of the house gets full sun, but the front stays in the shade until late afternoon so, with the windows open, it felt a little less oppressive. I thought I might have a shower and try Acharya's 'letting go' exercise. I sat on the bed to take off my sandals, feeling drained and overcome with tiredness. I lay down and closed my eyes for a few moments first.

I was flying, soaring like a bird into the clouds looking down on fields and trees and a river below. It was liberating and amazing. I felt held and supported and carried. It was graceful, expansive, and joyfully energising. I gloried in my power and inner strength. I was following the river as it meandered through farms and forests and woods. Here and there houses nestled together in village communities, but so tiny they looked like the model miniatures I've seen on sale in Bingham's department store. Thin lines crisscrossed the landscape between the houses and I could see the bright sunlight reflecting off the windscreens of the occasional vehicles that travelled along them.

Abruptly I was caught in an air current, propelling me faster, making me lose the euphoria and start to feel apprehensive and uneasy. The river was flowing out to sea. I tried to turn back inland, but the air current was too strong to resist. I was being pulled out to sea, losing height rapidly; almost in touching distance of the waves. In an instant, the weather turned from sunny to stormy. There was driving rain and a loud clap of thunder followed by sheet lightning flashing like floodlights across the darkened sky. The air was electric and the waves raged in response, wild and tempestuous and terrifying. At any moment I was going to be lost to the powerful crashing breakers.

I woke with a jolt. It took me a moment to get my bearings and come back to reality.

Next to me on the pillow was the handwritten envelope that came in the post. Strange; I hadn't recalled bringing it upstairs. I sat propped up with my back against the pillow and opened it.

Dear Mrs Lewis,
This is an extremely difficult letter for me to write and I guess even more difficult for you to read. I expect my name is etched into your very being as yours is into mine.

I looked down to see who it was from. It was signed Jordan Baker.

Jordan Baker is the man who killed my husband.

The blood drained from my face. The old agony and despair and fury that I'd shrunk to pea size and locked into my gut saw an opportunity to percolate back into the pores of my skin and the cells of my body. I felt both hot and cold at the same time. The fug descended with more intensity than ever before. My brain was in turmoil. I didn't know how to react, who to be. I tried to throw the letter down, but it wouldn't leave my hand.

I heard Acharya's soft Scottish brogue saying "Udgeeth pranayama, chanting breath" as he does at the start of sitting meditations. My body took over and I found myself automatically taking long deep inhalations of breath through my nose with my diaphragm and abdomen knowing exactly what to do and making long AAAAUUUUUUUUMM sounds as I exhaled slowly through my mouth. I'd not been able to get the hang of it or see the point of it at the yoga classes, but now it was instinctive and effortless.

The fug experimented with letting me return to full consciousness. It released gently until the panic rose again and then it surged back, but weaker and more distant each time. It knew what it was doing, that fug. It was like taking the stabilisers from a child's bike, but holding on until the child could balance independently. My head was clearing. I was still disorientated and reluctant, but not panicking. I returned to the letter.

I know you've recently suffered the tenth anniversary of your husband's death and, while I can't imagine how much more difficult that is for you, I too still struggle to come to terms with how it happened. I approached you at the funeral and clumsily tried to apologise. I asked you if we could meet and talk. It was the wrong time and I'm sorry. It was selfish of me. I was intruding. I let my need to try and make some kind of small reparation, if that were possible,

cloud my respect and consideration for your need to grieve and come to terms with your devastating loss. If this letter has opened old wounds still too painful to visit and you don't feel able to speak to me, I apologise. However, if you would be prepared to meet me so that I can actually express my regret to you personally, I would be extremely grateful.
My phone number is 07913 465829 or you can email me at jordanbbaker@properjob.com
Thank you for reading this,
Jordan Baker.

The heaviness and turbulence of earlier evaporated. In its place I lapsed into numbness, devoid of any feeling, completely empty, spent and exhausted.

I didn't move from my bed for several hours, falling in and out of troubled sleep. I was tempted to phone Alice and ask her to bring Ben home from school. I dismissed the idea even before it was fully formed, ashamed for allowing it into my thoughts, however fleetingly. Instead I decided to make the effort to walk across The Lawns to fetch him. I didn't care that the walk home again would make him late for karate. I needed the fresh air and the open space.

I prised myself from my bed feeling lightheaded and faint. I'd had nothing to eat or drink since breakfast and nothing at all the previous evening. I ran the kitchen tap until the water cooled and gulped down three glasses in succession. There was still no sign of Toby in the gardens. The desire to heal the damage I'd inflicted on our newfound friendship came back to stab me through the numbness.

I put on my trainers because they're more comfortable to walk in than my sandals. I didn't care that they were an odd combination to wear with my now very creased dress. There was too much going on to worry about something so inconsequential.

When I arrived at the school there was only Ben and another boy whom I recognised, but whose name I couldn't remember, still in the playground.

'Oh, darling, I'm sorry I'm late. I walked here across The Lawns.'

'No worries, Mummy, I thought you were probably translating furiously and lost track of time like you do sometimes. Anyway, it's been good to wait with Harry. He doesn't get picked up until four.'

'Oh Harry, of course. The tea boy.'

Harry laughed. 'My Aunty Emma picks me up, but she has to get my cousin from nursery first.'

'Well, we'll wait with you until she gets here today,' I said, trying to plug the void inside me. I was on the point of weakly congratulating myself that I was seizing an opportunity for a simple act of kindness when Harry's aunt drew up to the school gates and sounded her horn. Harry skipped off to meet her.

'See you,' he called.

'You missed karate last week,' I said to Ben as we set off in the direction of The Lawns, 'and now you're going to be late today. It's the last one before the summer break too.'

'Never mind. I'd rather go and see Ungrampa instead of karate anyway if that's okay?'

'Of course. Shall I come too?'

'I'm not sure.' He hesitated. 'It might be better if you let him come to you. Would you like me to ask him?'

That wasn't quite the response I'd expected. 'Erm,' was all I managed to say.

I knew Ben loves The Lawns and was relieved to see his spirits lifting as we walked in through the north gate. We left the path and made our way across the grass to the lake, stopping to watch the mallard, moorhen and coot dabbling in the water or methodically preening on the bank. His delight in their curious contortions as they stroked and nibbled in order not to miss a single feather was infectious. I suggested we might negotiate the plethora of duck poo to find a clear patch of grass and sit under the shade of a tree for a few minutes.

'What about your commission? I thought you were worried about getting it finished by tomorrow morning?'

Somewhat guiltily I explained about the email delaying the work, without being specific about when I'd received it. I had no wish to go further down the route of telling half-truths to my son, but I reasoned this one would save me yet another confession that would add to his disappointment in me. I watched him as he ran down to the water's edge to look for baby frogs. Already almost as tall as my shoulder, he was just a week off his tenth birthday, his childhood more than halfway over. With each new birthday his dependency on me was lessening, the ties starting to loosen.

He came running back, brimming with surprise. 'They've all gone already. I couldn't see any. I can't believe it. There were dozens and dozens when I came with Owen and Jake and his daddy. They were everywhere. We had to be careful not to step on them.'

I patted the ground for him to sit down beside me. On the spur of the moment, I told him about Jordan Baker's letter.

'In one way you're in the same position as Ungrampa then.' His tone was thoughtful, but simple and uncomplicated. It was an observation not an accusation. I'm used to him speaking his thoughts aloud in this way. Not that I agreed with him this time.

'I hardly think killing your father, ending his life at the age of thirty-four, ranks the same as upsetting a next door neighbour.'

'Well, yes I know what you mean, of course, but in another way it's the same. You didn't set out to hurt

Ungrampa, you were busy thinking about something else and Mr Baker didn't mean to kill my daddy, he just wasn't concentrating. Both of you did something you regret.'

'Except he was behind the wheel of a car. That has much bigger responsibility and greater consequences, doesn't it?' I found myself getting quite irate, not wishing to have a philosophical discussion with my son that might excuse the man who had ended Paul's life with a moment's carelessness.

'Sorry Mummy, I didn't mean the consequences are the same. I only meant that you and Mr Baker both feel guilty and want to be forgiven.'

Was this my on-the-threshold-of-being-ten-years-old son talking or a wise old man? When, where, how did he learn to reason like this and be so clear in his judgments and understanding?

'I'll come too,' he said matter-of-factly, leaving no room for argument about whether I would or would not go.

Ben went to see Toby as soon as we arrived home. I saw them sitting together in the Zen garden and noted that Cameron was sitting with them too. I began preparing the evening meal and then decided to confront my fear head on while the food was simmering and contact Jordan Baker before Ben came back in. I dialled his number, hesitated, then changed my mind and hung up telling myself it would probably be easier for him, and me, if I emailed first. I kept it short and to the point, finally settling on my fifth rewrite.

Thank you for your letter. I appreciate how much thought you put into writing it. I think it would be very difficult for us both to meet, but my son, Ben, wants to meet you so, for his sake, I agree.

His reply came while I was still online:

Thank you. Do you have any spare time this evening?

I ignored it. That was all a bit hurried. I had a vague notion of a meeting, if it happened at all, being at some time in the distant future.

I saw Ben outside feeding Mildred and Delilah. I started to go out to him, but sensed he was deliberately giving himself space to go over his conversation with Toby. I turned my attention to my adaptation of paella, which is an approximation of something I used to enjoy when I lived with a family in Valencia for two months as part of my degree. It's Ben's favourite. I added extra prawns because he loves them.

When Ben eventually came in, both of us were making an effort to behave normally.

'Is Ungrampa alright?'

'He says please excuse him this evening, but he isn't up to looking after me while you're at choir. He hopes that won't inconvenience you.'

'I quite understand. I've already decided not to go,' I held back on saying "again", 'this week.'

'Cameron says it's probably best if we give him some time and don't pressure him. He says Ungrampa needs to sort out how he feels and it would be good for us to respect that. I agree. Cameron's always right about this sort of thing.'

'Oh! Yes... I suppose he is.'

'Ungrampa did give me some carrot tops for Mildred and Delilah though. That's a good sign, don't you think?'

I hoped so. 'A very good sign.'

I told him about the emails while we ate the paella or "Ruby's Rubilicious Rice" as Ben christened it the first time I made it. The name has stuck.

'Today's a bit too soon though.'

'Well it's only ten to six. Why can't we meet him now before we start making excuses and change our minds? I don't mind phoning him if you don't want to. It'll be easier for me. Please may I leave the table?' But he was off to find the number before I was able to reply.

He was right of course. I was already convincing myself that it wasn't such a good idea. I didn't want to be party to the phone conversation, so I went up to re-hang my clothes in the wardrobe.

Ben came in to me and sat on the bed. 'We're meeting him in the garden of The Pie 'n' Ear at six forty-five. It's going to be all right, Mummy. We need to do this.'

'Okay, if you're sure that's what you want. I'm doing this for you.' The reality was I was dreading it.

The blistering, sticky heat of the day was giving way to a pleasantly warm balmy evening. I quickly changed into a clean dress and sandals, swept my hair into a ponytail and put on some mascara and lipstick. Ben changed from his school uniform into a pair of joggers and his "Aint I handsome?" tee shirt. My hand was visibly shaking when I put the key in the ignition and pulled off the driveway.

Jordan Baker looked equally nervous when we arrived at The Pioneer Arms. He looked strikingly older and thinner than I remembered him. I wouldn't have recognised him if we'd passed in the street. Neither of us was sure whether to shake hands; we ended up limply shaking each other's finger ends. He looked awkward. I felt awkward.

Ben came to the rescue. 'There's a table over there, look,' he said and led the way.

Jordan went inside to buy drinks. Cameron appeared sitting next to me on the other side from Ben, leaving a spare seat for Jordan. 'Well done. You'll be pleased you did this later.' I realised that Ben could neither see nor hear him.

The smell of singeing flesh wafted from the barbecue on the far side of the garden where other customers were queuing for kangaroo hotdogs and ostrich burgers. It meant we were less likely to be disturbed.

'I've rehearsed this so many times over the years,' Jordan began when he returned with three glasses of orange juice and a packet of root vegetable crisps for Ben, 'and now that it's actually happening, I don't know what to say.'

I was direct, but calm and said without being accusatory, 'I hated you for what you did and then I hated you for making me feel hatred. I don't feel like that anymore, only don't ask me to forgive you. I'll never be able to do that.'

'I hated myself too. I still do and I can't forgive myself either. I'm not expecting you to forgive me. I wouldn't ask it of you. How could you possibly, after what I did? But I do want you to know and you too, Ben, that I didn't just shrug it off and forget about it. It goes on haunting me, even after all this time. I still keep reliving it over and over. I've longed to be able to turn back the clock and… if only…'

The floodgates were opened and he poured out his anguish and suffering and his sorrow for what he had done. I listened without interrupting, his words echoing in my head and in the lump in my throat.

'I've never driven since and I never will again. I don't even like being a passenger. There's no excusing what I did, none at all. Ever since I came out of prison I've been working with the police in schools and in youth clubs, warning young people about dangerous and careless driving. I try to get the message out there so it doesn't happen to anyone else.'

Tears were trickling down his face and mine too. Ben, on the other hand, was circumspect and composed.

'When I learned that you were pregnant it made it… I don't have the words to express how that made me feel. My wife had given birth to our daughter only a few weeks before.'

'You have a daughter the same age as Ben?'

'Yes, not that I get to see her any more. My wife left me four years ago and took Liddy with her. I don't even know where they are now. We had to sell the house, quite rightly, don't get me wrong, and she had to move in with her parents. We couldn't keep up with the mortgage payments when I was in prison and I lost my job because I wouldn't drive any more. She never really got over that. I think she was more disappointed with me for that than the fact I killed someone.

'When I came out she said I'd paid my debt and it was time to put it behind me and move on for her sake and for Liddy's. How could I move on? I was alive and someone else was dead because of me, because of what I did. How do you ever put something like that behind you? She said Liddy would be better with no father than one that was a liability. I'm sorry I don't mean, you know I don't mean… I don't blame her for leaving me; I don't blame her at all. It was what I deserved.'

'No it isn't,' I found myself saying. Cameron was holding my hand; it gave me strength and resilience. 'No, that definitely isn't what Paul would have wanted. He would want you to pour your energies into being a good husband and father. He was that kind of a man. He wouldn't want your life and your family's lives wasted too. That just adds to the tragedy. I didn't know you talked to young people about the accident. That's really brave of you.'

Ben slipped his hand into my other hand.

'Jordan… may I call you Jordan? You've made me see things differently. I didn't know it had affected you so badly. I never thought about how it must feel for you. I thought of you as reckless and, oh, I don't know, heartless

I suppose. I resented you for still being alive when Paul was dead, it didn't seem fair... it's not that simple, is it?'

I was so choked with emotion it was hard to speak. My words came rushing out, taking with them much of the pain and anger I'd been clinging on to for so long.

'I've changed my mind. I do forgive you. I really do. Unreservedly.' I leaned towards him to emphasise what I was saying. 'And now you must forgive yourself and get on with being the best version of yourself that you can be. My mother used to say that to me when I was growing up. "Be the best version of yourself that you can be." It's only really now, talking to you, that I truly understand what she meant.'

'May I say something please?' said Ben in the pause that followed. We turned to him. 'I know what it's like to grow up without my daddy. I have Mummy and Granny and Ungrampa and I know they love me and I love them, but I can't ever have my daddy back. You're still alive. I think your daughter needs to know you love her. I think you should find her and tell her.'

Cameron withdrew, leaving our unlikely threesome to continue the therapy until way past Ben's bedtime. I understood why he left, he wasn't needed any more. I could handle the situation myself. When the time came to say goodbye, all three of us spontaneously hugged. An enormous burden had been lifted and the future would be somewhat easier to face for all of us.

Ben and I returned home to find half a dozen fresh tomatoes on the kitchen table and a note that said: *There are three more eggs pipping this evening. The chicks will hatch pretty soon. You're very welcome to come and see them. T*

I lay awake for a long time, but, in spite of the emotional upheaval of the previous few days, I felt relaxed and peaceful. I turned on to my back with my hands behind my damp hair, and catlike, I stretched my legs and feet. I gave a deep, releasing, comforting sigh that washed through my body and made my toes purr with pleasure in response. I'd had a shower and washed my hair and because of the heat, wasn't bothering with my nightdress or my duvet. I covered myself instead with a loose sheet because I like to sleep with something over me.

I tried to put into words this unfamiliar feeling I was experiencing. I feel... easy, I thought, testing out the word, easy and comfortable. 'I know what it is,' I smiled a warm glowing smile as I identified the feeling. 'It's contentment. I'm feeling content. So this is what contentment feels like. It's a good feeling. Is this what Jess keeps harping on about in her you've-got-to-listen-Ruby-this-is-for-your-own-good lectures?' I laughed. 'I guess it must be. Well thank you, Ms Malone, against all the odds, this time I actually agree with you. Is this how she feels all the time? Does Alice feel it too? Have I been missing out on something that everyone else takes for granted? I can't imagine Mother ever feeling like this. Or has that all changed now she's met this Andrew? Must remind Ben to phone her and thank her for the card and money tomorrow. In fact, I might even phone Jess in the morning and tell her I get this "feeling good" thing now.'

It wasn't so much a dream I had as I closed my eyes, more an impression, of an angelic chorus softly singing a restful lullaby to soothe me into sleep.

Thursday 18 July

Ben generally gets up at seven thirty on school mornings, but he was showered and dressed by half past six despite his late night.

'You're up bright and early this morning,' I said, putting the kettle on to make myself some tea. 'Only two more days at school before the summer holidays. Keen to get it over with?'

'Ungrampa's in his garden already, watering. I opened my window and said good morning to him. Come on Mummy, he says we can go and see the chicks before school.'

First Cameron, now Ben, I'm not going to be able to hide away from anything anymore. But there was pleasure and hope in my heart at the prospect, with none of the usual prowling fears or reservations.

'The chicks have hatched, but one died.'

'Oh no, is Ungrampa upset?'

'Nah. It happens all the time in nature. It's just how it is. Charlie, his cockerel, died on Monday night too. When he got up on Tuesday morning he found him keeled over. Ungrampa was upset about that; he was really fond of Charlie. He saved three of his tail feathers and then buried him under the laburnum. He's hoping one of the new chicks will be a cockerel then he'll keep him and breed from him. I said he can call him Charles II.'

I made a conscious effort to put Toby's feelings before my own and to think how difficult this meeting was going to be for him rather than be full of my own qualms and apprehension. My effort was misplaced, however; Toby was totally at ease and as enthusiastic about showing off his chicks as he had been about his plants the preceding week. This time I didn't even register surprise. Some things just don't need to be questioned or analysed. They are as they are.

Toby had separated the chicks into different free-standing runs, each with a hen. There were two with three chicks and a third, more makeshift, with the two that had hatched overnight. He was trying to catch the two new-borns, but they kept running away and the hen was pecking at him.

'He's going to spread diatom on them,' explained Ben knowledgeably. 'It protects them from red mites.'

'Oh. What's diatom?'

Toby left Ben to explain. 'You see the white powder in the soil in the runs?' I nodded. 'That's it.'

'Why are the chicks all separate?'

Toby had finished his spreading and was offering the hens dandelion leaves through the mesh. 'Go on Ben. Tell your ma what you've learned.'

'They have to be kept separate or the other chucks would attack them. None of the chucks that are mothering the chicks are the ones that laid the eggs.'

'Why's that, then?'

'They were broody and the chucks that laid the eggs aren't.'

'I can see I have a lot to learn.'

Toby handed me some dandelion leaves. 'Hold the ends between the mesh. They'll peck at them.'

I did and flinched at the ferocity of the hens pecking the whole leaves out of my fingers. The leaves dropped to the floor, where the hens ignored them.

'You have to hold the leaves a bit tighter, Mummy, so that they rip off a bit at a time. Look I'll show you.'

'We need to get ready if we're going to walk through The Lawns,' I said after I'd more or less got the hang of it. 'Thanks Toby. They're delightful. Can I come for another lesson after school? Ben doesn't have his piano lesson again this week.'

It was agreed and I was already looking forward to it. The day was going to be less fraught. I'd come such a long way in such a short space of time, but the ups and downs had been worth it.

Thank you so much, Cameron. It's been a whirlwind, but finally we're done at last. No need for any more homework now. I get it. I'm sorted. No more nightmares. From now on Ben and I will be fine. I'm truly grateful for everything.

I hesitated at first about walking to school through The Lawns because I knew Meaty Goodness would have popped into my inbox overnight and I wanted to spend the morning working on it. I had until eight am on the following Tuesday to send it off, but planned to keep as much of the weekend clear as possible to spend with Ben. Saturday was already going to be swallowed up with his swimming lesson in the morning and then in the afternoon the journey to Guildford to visit my grandfather would take a couple of hours at least each way. However, with only two days of the school year left, The Lawns was an opportunity not be missed.

We reached the south gate and made our way in. I was surprised to see how many people were around at that time in the morning. A few stray joggers on their way home, but the footfall between the four entrance gates was surprisingly heavy. We saw George with his wife and daughter taking Arnold for a walk. George stopped and raised his hat and Ben stroked Arnold, who treated him to his paw-shaking trick. I noticed how many other people smiled and said good morning to one another, obviously regulars who do this journey often. I regretted not being one of them.

By the time we were in sight of the north gate Ben and I were both hoarse from singing "Oh What A Beautiful

Morning" at the tops of our voices – yelling of a different kind from my last journey through The Lawns – inventing our own words for the lines we didn't know, too happy to care about the bemused reactions we were receiving. Some people were clearly disapproving, but more than a few joined in the fun. We even had a round of applause from two gardeners who were edging the paths. I stopped to curtsy, smiling and laughing.

Life was wonderful. Life was joyful. I determined never to let myself be pulled down by anything again.

Oh how naïve I was…

I would have loved to spend time in The Lawns for a while on the way back home, but I needed to get cracking on Meaty Goodness. I quite liked my working name, Meaty Goodness, but was hoping that it was the intention to keep the German name, Fleischige Güte Hundekuchen, when it was exported as I was already stumbling over an appropriate translation into French that didn't sound cumbersome and long-winded.

I settled in front of the laptop with a pot of coffee and one of Alice's apricot flapjacks. This, I decided, when I opened up the document, was not going to be the simple task I'd envisaged. The over-generous fee ought to have alerted me. Meaty Goodness came in four different varieties for a kick off, which increased the word count substantially.

I'm used to translating complex industrial terminology, have considerable experience of legal documents and the dry formality of directives, and constitutions I find straightforward. This assignment, however, was a different ball game. The copywriters were clearly progressive and cutting-edge. They'd adopted a humorous, casual, conversational tone using specifically German expressions and humour, making direct translation clumsy and inexact into English never mind French and Italian.

This could be challenging, but great fun, I said to Dominique in an email, checking how much licence I could have in my interpretation. I jotted down a few particular examples that would be problematic.

I can't quite see many British people hanging their endorsement of Meaty Goodness on a big bell somehow, however much they're persuaded by the dogs who own them.

I then busied myself with the English version first, my elation of the last hours creeping back as I rolled off an increasingly creative and liberal translation, sometimes laughing out loud at my inventiveness. I emailed that off to Dominique too for good measure.

A carefully worded reply came back just before I was about to leave for yoga.

We're seeing a whole new side to you here, Ruby. We're laying bets in the office as to whether it's actually you doing the translation or whether you've been drinking rather too much wine. Please delay any further work on the commission until we've checked this out with the client.

I laughed all the way to yoga.

As Cameron had assured me, there was no hint from anyone that they remembered my outburst of the previous week. I realised I'd forgotten to phone Jess about feeling contentment as I'd planned in bed the night before, but now, face-to-face, I decided it would seem silly and was better left unsaid. I couldn't find the sense of ease I'd experienced with the previous class, but nevertheless it went well and I stayed reasonably focused and relaxed.

However, the sitting meditation at the end, as always, was beyond me. My back ached and my nose itched. I spent more time wishing it was over and guessing how many more minutes might be left than I spent trying to be still and go inside. I was starting to get cramp in my left leg. I toyed with whether I dared sneak a look at the clock on the wall opposite. I would have had to turn my head and then I'd be exposed. The others would guess what I was doing. I opened one eye and tried to peer around without moving my head. The room was still and silent. Everyone else was apparently away with the fairies. Just me then that didn't get it. Typical.

Both Alice and I had to leave punctually of course because of collecting our boys from school, but we arranged to meet up with Jess as usual for a coffee at ten thirty the next day. Funny, but I wasn't looking forward to it as much as I usually did. I'm not sure why, especially as I'd felt so grateful to Jess only the night before. I wasn't in the mood for another session of Jess's coffee shop analysis. Perhaps I'd think of an excuse not to go.

Ben didn't come bounding out of school with his customary exuberance.

'Harry's got a bit of a problem, Mummy, and I'm hoping we can help him out.'

'I'm listening. Can we talk about it in the car on the way home?'

'It would be better if we could tell him now. If it's going to happen it's urgent we sort it out as soon as poss.'

'Fire away then.'

'Well, it's a bit complicated. Harry's daddy doesn't get his holidays for another two weeks, so Harry's grandma was supposed to come down from Nottingham to look after him. She always does that in the holidays when his daddy's working.'

'What about Harry's mummy?'

'Harry doesn't have a mummy, Mummy. She died. Harry just lives with his daddy.'

'I'd no idea.' *So much death, so much pain.*

'Anyway, his grandad's retiring next week and they're having a big party for him at his work so now his grandma can't come, obviously. Harry's daddy's supposed to be taking him up to stay in Nottingham instead on Saturday. It means he'll miss my birthday adventure and everything.'

'I'll stop you there.' Ben was so earnest in his appeal on behalf of his friend, how could I possibly refuse him? 'Yes, of course Harry can come and stay with us. No problem. Let's go and find him and sort it out.'

'Thanks Mummy. I knew you'd say yes, but I haven't said anything to Harry just in case. It'll only be while his daddy's at work, he won't need to stay the night.'

Harry was surprised and delighted with the offer and we arranged for his father to phone later that evening.

There was a message on the answerphone when we arrived back home, from Wendy, one of my Italian conversation ladies. Apparently Karen's granddaughter had had a baby in the early hours of the morning. It's Karen's first great grandchild so they hoped I wouldn't mind, but the three of them were going to visit the new baby that evening. Mind? I was thrilled. It had been yet another event-filled, uneven, disjointed day; not unpleasant, but nevertheless fragmented and bitty. Small pockets of this and that that didn't really hang together to make a flowing, satisfying whole. Funny, I used to enjoy the haphazard snippets jostling for position and attention, diversions that filled the hours and kept me busy. It didn't somehow have the same attraction anymore. I wanted to…? And there I was stuck. I didn't know what exactly it was I did want, but I was absolutely certain I wanted it.

With no piano lesson for Ben and no Italian conversation for me, we could take our time going to see Toby and the chicks and then have the whole evening to ourselves.

Perfect.

Ben didn't want to wait until after dinner to go and see Toby, so we compromised with a quick scrambled eggs on toast and yogurt before he dragged me across the gardens. There was no sign of Toby and no one answered when we tapped on the kitchen door, although we could hear PM just starting on the radio.

'He leaves the radio on for The Magnificent,' said Ben knowingly. 'I expect he's gone to the bottom of the garden.'

We headed in the direction of the chicken run and saw Toby concealed in a white outfit walking towards us.

'A Star Wars re-enactment?'

Ben laughed. 'It's his beekeeper's garb, silly. He must have been with his bees.'

I was just about to say, 'I didn't know Ungrampa kept bees,' but the look on Ben's face said I'd obviously been told about them. Come to think of it, it made sense of all the jars of honey I'd been given over the years. I'd thought they were a strange gift. And then there were the requests for the empty jars to be returned. It signified.

Toby came towards us, pulling off his protective gloves.

'Have you been putting on new supers?' asked Ben.

'Yes, they're getting filled up very quickly, having to check 'em every day now. You come to see the chicks again?' He unzipped his protective veil and took it off.

'Well, yes,' I said, 'but I expect you're going to be wanting to get your garb off first. Shall we come back a bit later?'

'Garb? I think you've been listening to that boy of yours. It's just called a bee keepers' suit.'

Ben and I slipped back into our garden giggling over the word garb.

'Benedict Paul Lewis, whatever will you come up with next? Where on earth did you get the word "garb" from?'

'Excuse me. Hello. Hello. Up here.'

'It's Mrs Marlow,' said Ben, pointing up to the open bedroom window next door.

'Hello, Mrs Marlow. How are you?' I called back, astonished that yet something else unpredictable was happening. My life seemed to be getting more and more haphazard every day.

'Call an ambulance. I'm trapped up here. Walter's had a fall. I think he's unconscious.'

'Oh my goodness.' I felt the familiar stirring of panic in my belly. 'I'll come over,' I said, hoping to appear confident.

'Shall I call the ambulance, Mummy?' Ben said before turning to Mrs Marlow. 'I'm a Badger, Mrs Marlow. I can come and appraise the situation if you like?'

Mrs Marlow clearly had no idea what Ben was talking about.

'He fell down the stairs and I can't get past him.'

'Hang on a moment, Mrs Marlow,' I shouted up and then said to Ben, 'Good idea. You ask Ungrampa to call an ambulance and I'll go round and see what I can do.'

'It's okay, I can call them, no worries.'

'Do you know what to say?'

'Yes, yes, we've practised this. I'm up for it, Mummy,' and he rushed inside to do the deed before I had second thoughts.

Mrs Marlow was rambling and not very coherent. 'I know the kitchen door's unlocked, it's just the side gate.'

'Try and stay calm, Mrs Marlow,' I called, crossing my fingers. 'Ben's gone to call an ambulance and I'll come and stay with you until it gets here.'

I was completely out of my depth. If the side gate was locked then the only way to get into the house was over the fence. The fence is six feet high and has Toby's carefully planted trees and bushes in front of most of it.

'You go and stay with Mr Marlow, Mrs Marlow. I'm on my way now.''

I felt impelled to take action. I couldn't allow something dreadful to happen to the Marlows while I stood by. I'd never forgive myself. I looked around the garden for something I could stand on to climb over the fence. Nothing. Uhm? The crab apple. It was well established and sturdy. I remembered Toby had climbed up to do something or other to it before it blossomed in the spring. It wasn't densely covered in leaves then of course, but if it would take Toby's weight it would take mine, wouldn't it? It was near enough to the fence to be worth considering; in fact part of it was hanging over into the Marlows' garden. I said a little prayer of thanks that I'd changed into shorts and trainers when we got in from school.

I marched over to the tree, heart thudding, repeating over and over, "I have to do this. I have to do this".

The trunk was as tall as I am. There were four main branches reaching upwards under the heavy canopy of leaves. Of the four it was the least substantial that rose imperiously towards the fence. I could see where Toby had sawn off another branch to stop the tree from growing over any further. Sod's law. The branches were adorned by a generous crop of apples and spatterings of bird droppings and were alive with a busy colony of ants.

Determined nevertheless, I reached up and took firm hold of two of the branches, ignoring the ants rushing over my fingers and down my wrists. I leaned back and tried to walk up the trunk. I started off well, but the weight of my body was too much for my arms and I couldn't pull myself up. I jumped down, trying to shake off the crawling assemblage migrating to my armpits.

'What are you doing, Mummy?' I heard an astounded Ben say from behind me.

'I'm trying to get over the fence.'

'I don't think that's going to work.'

'No.'

'Why don't we just go through the gate?'

'It's bolted.'

129

'Oh dear. The ambulance is on its way. We need to open the gate before they get here.'

'Any ideas?'

'I can climb over if you help me into the tree,' he offered.

'Definitely not.'

'Can I do anything?' It was Toby heading towards us carrying his stepladder. 'Got your ball stuck in the tree again, Ben?'

Mrs Marlow poked her head back out of the bedroom window. 'He's groaning. It's horrible. Can you hurry up?'

'An ambulance is on its way, Mrs Marlow,' Ben called up. 'Won't be long now.'

We quickly explained the dilemma to Toby.

'I still think I could jump down from the tree,' Ben said.

'I said no,' I snapped and then felt guilty that he was taken aback by my sharpness; I've never spoken to him so brusquely before. 'Sorry, Ben, but no, right? We'll put the stepladder next to the fence and then I can use the tree to steady me.'

'Up she goes,' Toby said, assembling the stepladder and trying to secure it on the uneven surface of soil and grass. 'Leave this to me.'

'I'll do it, Toby. You and Ben hold the ladder still.'

I wouldn't take no for an answer. I was determined. This was going to be my opportunity to prove to myself that I can overcome obstacles and handle emergencies. In a frenzy of nervous energy I threw myself up the ladder while Toby and Ben watched me, aghast. I could see their distress, as if they wanted to say something, but didn't dare. Once high enough to see over the fence I checked to make sure I wouldn't be jumping into a prickly bush. I was not prepared for the scene that was awaiting me. I'd never actually looked into the Marlows' garden before. My bathroom window is the only one that has full view of their garden and it has obscured glass. There was no prickly bush to break my fall, but there was a large lumpy sofa well past its use-by date pushed up against the fence. Alternatively, I could have taken my pick from a row of dilapidated assorted sofas and armchairs, similarly in role as flower beds, along the full length of the fence. In fact there was a sea of furniture and white goods spread across the wild overgrown tangle of nettles and weeds acting as a garden.

Mrs Marlow was back at the window. 'How are you getting on? Oh yes, I was forgetting. We've got too many things. Walter collects things. You have to be careful.'

'No, no problem. I'm good,' I called back, trying to clutch a swaying twig, but just ending up with a handful of leaves. I was rather hoping this was another nightmare and I'd wake up soon.

'There's a sofa up against the fence,' I said to Toby and Ben. 'I'm going to try and turn round and slide my feet down onto the back and then I can just step down.'

Six feet is far higher than it seems from the ground. I climbed onto the platform at the top of the ladder, but there really wasn't a lot of space for turning around and I wasn't happy with the gap between it and the fence. This was the moment of truth.

Crossing hands on the uprights of the ladder I turned with my back to the fence and knelt on the strip along the top. The leaves kept flapping in my face and the top of the fence was narrow and cut into my shins. I swayed alarmingly, trying to grasp a non-existent branch with my right hand. Toby stepped onto the ladder and guided my hand back to the upright and then clasped my arms to give me extra support. I lowered first my right leg down and then the left, inch by painful inch. The top of the fence was digging into my abdomen as I edged down, the leaves were completely blocking my vision and my legs were flailing as I tried to feel for the top of the sofa with my toes.

'Can I help you?' said a man's voice as someone grabbed hold of my hips to guide me down. I screamed in surprise, making Toby hold on more firmly to the tops of my arms. The stranger meanwhile continued to haul me down towards the safety of the sofa.

'You can let go now, Toby,' I called, slightly too late. I turned to see who had helped me, caught him on his temple with my elbow and knocked him over with a thud.

An alarmed Toby's head and shoulders appeared momentarily over the top of the fence and then promptly disappeared as the stepladder fell away from under him.

'Oh dear,' I heard him say.

'Mummy, Mummy,' shouted a worried Ben. 'Are you alright?'

'I've broken my nail,' I shouted back.

I tried to step backwards off the sofa, not noticing that my rescuer's legs were in the way and I somehow managed to kick him in the thigh. 'Ouch, I felt that, sorry.'

My nail was hanging off and I really needed to clip it before it tore any further, but, on the plus side, I was otherwise safely over the fence now.

'How did you get into the garden?'

'Yes, I'm fine thank you,' said the man wryly while getting up. 'Probably a bump on my head and a bruised thigh, but thankfully no nails broken.'

'Sorry, sorry. Did I hurt you? You made me jump.'

'I came in through the gate. I'm Jonty. A paramedic. Someone called an ambulance?'

'Gate's open,' I called over the fence.

'I've just remembered,' said Mrs Marlow from the window, 'Walter put the wheelie bin out to be emptied in the morning. He never remembers to bolt the gate again.'

'Where's the patient?' asked Jonty, patiently.

'At the bottom of the stairs. He won't talk to me. He just keeps groaning.'

Jonty led the way to the kitchen door.

'It doesn't open all the way,' Mrs Marlow called down, leaning further out of the window so she could still see us. 'Be careful.'

'Better not lean out of the window,' Jonty called, looking up so he could still see her. 'Be careful.'

He pushed the door, but it only opened far enough for us to edge in sideways. The stale smell of dust and dank greeted our nostrils even before we crossed the threshold. It was dark and uninviting. The kitchen was filled almost to the ceiling with plastic boxes, leaving a narrow corridor to where I knew the sink would be and another towards the hallway. The door from the kitchen to the hall was propped permanently open with a large working grandfather clock.

I gritted my teeth and pulled off what was left hanging of my nail. I didn't know what to do with it so I dropped it down the scoop neck of my T shirt into my bra whilst Jonty was surveying the stockpile in the kitchen,

'We're in, Mrs Marlow,' I called, 'This is Jonty. He's a paramedic.'

The hallway was lined with more grandfather clocks along the wall to the right. Most of them were large and heavy and ticking with deep resonant clunks. The staircase was on the left, but we weren't able see Mr Marlow because it had a solid dark oak balustrade screening him from view. We had to step carefully because of teetering piles of books that ran the whole length. The light was dim and gloomy. The front door was completely hidden by bulging cardboard boxes stacked four high with large leather suitcases wedged in front.

We turned at the foot of the stairs, to see Walter Marlow lying across the bottom three steps with his head at an awkward angle against the wall. He was covered almost entirely by National Geographic magazines. His face was grey and his breathing was laboured.

Jonty bent over to him and silently began to pass me some of the magazines. I looked around for somewhere to put them down, but there was nowhere. The pile was heavy.

'My name's Jonty. What's your husband's name?' Jonty said gently to Mrs Marlow, who was coming as far down the stairs as she could get.

'Walter. His name's Walter. Is he going to be all right?'

'Well, let's have a look, shall we?' It was easy to see why Jonty had chosen this work. He worked quickly checking Walter Marlow's blood pressure and looking for signs of injury, trying to disturb him as little as possible. 'Now then, Walter? Walter, can you hear me? Speak to me, Walter.' Mr Marlow grunted. 'Good, good, gently there, nearly done. Good man. Now can you feel that, Walter?' He felt along Mr Marlow's body and limbs where he could reach without moving him. Walter continued to answer with groans and grunts rather than words, but his eyes were open.

Mrs Marlow hovered anxiously. 'I don't think he's wearing his hearing aid.'

A woman in uniform walked into the hallway. 'This is my colleague, Lizzie,' said Jonty.

'Is there any other way out of the house?' Lizzie asked scanning the clutter in the way of the front door. Jonty acknowledged the question with a look that said the situation was serious and a gesture suggesting they were going to have to clear a path to the kitchen door.

'Where are you hurting, Walter? Sorry?' He had to put his ear close to Walter's mouth to hear him. 'Your side. Okay. On a scale of one to ten, how much does it hurt? Um? If one is hardly at all and ten is unbearable? Do you understand, Walter?'

'Eight, I think he's saying eight,' said Mrs Marlow.

'Are you the daughter?' Lizzie turned to me with a sense of urgency as she took the pile of magazines from me.

'No, next door neighbour,' I answered, moved by the kindness and compassion being shown to the Marlows.

'Would you be able to help move the books out of the way so we can get the stretcher in?'

'Of course.'

'Thanks. I'll be back in a tick, I just want to check out the best way to do this before we get started. Don't want anyone else getting injured, eh? Do you have anyone we can contact?' Lizzie asked Mrs Marlow.

Mrs Marlow shook her head. 'No, there's no family left.'

'What's your name, love?' Jonty said to Mrs Marlow.

'Barbara.'

'Right then, Barbara. Do you want to sit down, sweetheart? Good girl. Has your husband lost consciousness at all?'

'I'm not sure... I think he did for a while, but he's been groaning and groaning.'

'Well, I'm going to give you this injection, Walter, and it'll help ease the pain until we get you to hospital, okay? Does he have any medical conditions, Barbara? Diabetes? Problems with his heart?'

'He gets angina.'

'Do you know what medication he's taking?'

'I'll go and get them, they're in the bathroom.'

Ben came in to see what was happening. 'Hello,' he said, drinking in the situation. 'I'm Ben from next door. I recognise you, your name's Jonty. You came and talked to us about bites and stings at Badgers. Well, you came to talk to the Cadets really, but us senior Badgers were allowed to listen as well.'

'Hello again, mate. Yes, I remember you too; you asked lots of really good questions. This your mum then?'

'Yes,' we said together. I was grateful to be included. It felt as if I was in the way and not really helping at all.

'Ungrampa's helping Lizzie move the boxes in the kitchen,' Ben told me. 'She said she'll give you a call when they need a hand, but there's not enough space for another person right now.' He turned to Jonty. 'Jonty, I've got my Badger First Aider Award. Can I do anything to help?'

'Ah a professional. Great stuff. Tell you what I want you to do for Walter then, Ben, while I go and speak to Lizzie in a moment. I want you to sit here and talk to him and Barbara when she comes back with the medication. Okay, mate? Try not to let him drift off to sleep. I'll only be two minutes. You come and tell me straight away if he goes to sleep, yes?'

Ben changed places with Jonty and sat next to Mr Marlow just as Mrs Marlow came down with four packs of pills. Ben took them from her and handed them to Jonty.

'Thanks, Barbara,' Jonty said. 'Now, can you tell me briefly what happened?'

'He was winding his clocks, weren't you, Walter?' she said, pointing to the line of clocks fixed to the wall of the staircase. 'He keeps his National Geographics on the stairs because there's so many of them. He's been collecting them every month since 1979; still got every copy.'

'Go on,' said Jonty.

'Well, I told him the piles were getting too high, but you don't listen, do you?' Mr Marlow groaned. 'He has to stretch across them to wind the clocks and he slipped and knocked one of the piles over. He was that worried he might rip the covers, he tried to grab hold of the banister, but he missed and tumbled and it caused an avalanche to fall on top of him. He went ever so quiet and I couldn't get past him to come downstairs.' Worry and helplessness were etched into her face.

'When was this, Barbara?'

'It must have been coming up to two o'clock I think.'

'Let's get him off to the hospital as quickly as we can then. It's going to take us a little while to clear a way out. Could you go and pack his night clothes and toiletries while we get on with it?' She nodded uncertainly and made her way back upstairs. 'How's he doing, young man?'

'I'm chatting to him about his clocks,' said Ben. He turned to me, concerned. 'Are you all right, Mummy? You're being very quiet.'

'Bless you, I'm not sure how to help. I could start moving the magazines that have slipped down?'

'Well, we could do with your help clearing a pathway. No point in trying to get to the front door, it'd take far too long. We'll have to take the stuff from the hall and kitchen out into the garden for the time being I think. Call me if you need me, I need to have that word with Lizzie. Might as well make a start and take these.' He scooped up a pile of magazines.

'Not my National Geographics,' Mr Marlow suddenly exclaimed gruffly, obviously making a great effort to speak. 'They'll be ruined if they go outside.'

'We'll do our best, Walter,' said Jonty, taking the magazines anyway.

Another hour went by before Walter Marlow was carried out to the ambulance and it was over six hours since he'd fallen.

Lizzie reassured Mrs Marlow, urging her to stay at home and to phone the hospital at ten o'clock on Friday morning. 'There's nothing you can do tonight. They'll want to examine him and they'll probably give him something to help him sleep.'

Jonty, on the other hand, was more candid out of earshot of Mrs Marlow. 'The fact is, Ruby, Walter's eighty-seven, overweight and he's had a nasty fall. He's sprained his ankle and his pelvis is almost certainly fractured. It's not looking good. Barbara's going to need a lot of support over the coming weeks and you heard her say there's no family.'

'I'll do what I can of course, but we've hardly ever spoken before. We don't really know each other.'

'Better to tread carefully. Poor love, she's had enough of a shock for one day. No point in worrying her until we know for sure what's going to happen. As for you, young fella,' he said, turning to Ben, 'put it there.' He held up his fist for a fist bump.

'Smashing stuff.'

Ben met his punch glowing with pleasure.

I watched as Mrs Marlow stood on the driveway while the ambulance drove off and disappeared out of sight around the corner. The old lady made no move to come back in. I hadn't really paid much attention to Mrs Marlow before, but I could see how frail she is with arthritic fingers and swollen ankles. Her back was hunched over and she shuffled rather than walked in her Velcro slippers. There was a distinct aroma of stale urine about her.

'Come inside now, Mrs Marlow,' I coaxed gently, taking the old lady by the arm. 'Show me where I can put the books and magazines.'

'They'll have to go back where they were.' Mrs Marlow seemed taken aback that anyone would think otherwise. 'There isn't anywhere else for them to go.'

'No problem.'

When we arrived back at the kitchen, Ben and Toby were already returning the magazines and the books.

'Would it be alright if I went home now, Mummy? Only Harry's daddy was supposed to be phoning at seven.'

'I'd completely forgotten, sorry Ben.'

Toby stepped in. 'I can stay and finish taking the stuff back inside if you like, but I think Mrs Marlow might prefer you to stay with her for a little while?'

'I don't want to be any more bother. You go, dear, I'll manage the rest.' Mrs Marlow wandered off inside the house, obviously in a daze.

'As I thought,' said Toby. 'I'll pop Ben home and mind him while you sort things out here. Think this situation calls for a woman's touch. We left your side gate unbolted so we can get back in.'

It was a solution that I had to settle for and one that Ben was happy with. 'Harry's number will be on the caller display. If you explain what's happened, I'll phone his daddy when I get back. I'm going to try to persuade Mrs Marlow to stay with us tonight.'

I followed Mrs Marlow into the kitchen, but there was no sign of her. All the houses on the cul-de-sac were built to the same 1930s design. I made extensive alterations when I reorganised my downstairs rooms, but nevertheless I am, of course, familiar with the layout of the Marlows' house.

I stepped back into the hallway. The under stairs cupboard, which in my house was extended sideways into the new utility room to create a cloakroom, was completely blocked by the tower of books; the doors to the lounge and dining room were behind the row of grandfather clocks and the cardboard boxes and suitcases obstructed access to the front door. Both rooms and the front door were completely inaccessible. That and the gloom created an eerie silence as if the sheer volume of clutter sucked dry all sound from the outside world.

'Mrs Marlow?' I called upstairs.

There was no answer, just a heaving emptiness. I made myself climb to where the stairs turn to the left.

'It's Ruby, Mrs Marlow, from next door.' Still no reply. 'Can I come up?'.

I noticed there were yet more grandfather clocks on the landing walls right across the doors leading to the two bedrooms at the front of the house and more piles of books on the floor. A single dim light bulb hung from the ceiling, dismal and depressing. I heard the toilet flush and Mrs Marlow came out of the bathroom.

'Oh, I thought you had to go back home.'

'It's alright, Mrs Marlow. My son, Ben, has to make a phone call so Toby's gone back with him. I'll stay and bring the things back inside. Can I get you anything first?'

'Will you make sure it goes back like it was before? Walter won't like it if it's not all in the same place. His books were all sorted and his magazines were in date order.'

'I think perhaps we can sort them later. How about if I just bring them in for now? Do you have anywhere to sit?'

'We sit on the bed.'

'Oh Mrs Marlow, I don't know what to say.'

'I gave up trying to get him to stop collecting things years ago. It makes him happy, you see.'

I didn't see, not really and I wasn't sure whether I was being invited to laugh or commiserate. I smiled weakly instead.

'Do you want to have a little rest then? Toby and Ben have already brought in the magazines and most of the books. I'll make a start on bringing the boxes back into the kitchen.'

I struggled to pile the heavy plastic boxes. They seemed to be full of china. It was hard to tell because the contents were carefully wrapped in tissue paper. I edged further into the kitchen, planning to make Mrs Marlow a hot drink. There was almost no space and no sign of a cooker, just a greasy, grimy microwave. There didn't seem to be a fridge or a washing machine either. Most of the worktop space was covered with half full tins of soup, packets of food and yet more boxes. The sink was piled high with dirty mugs and plates. I rescued a mug and rinsed it, but decided instead I was going to insist Mrs Marlow came home with me. I went back upstairs and tapped on the bedroom door. There was no answer so I crept in. Mrs Marlow was asleep on top of the bed, snoring softly.

This room was clearer than the kitchen. The only furniture was a double bed, a specimen human skeleton dangling from a stand, a standard lamp without a shade and a row of maybe thirty chairs stacked five and six high along the outside wall. I recognised them as the same kind of red plastic chairs used at the Academy. Assorted clothes were heaped on to them, suggesting they were doubling as a wardrobe. Although the window Mrs Marlow had called out from was still open, the pungent smell of stale urine was stronger in there.

The Marlows' bedroom is the equivalent room to Ben's. I couldn't help thinking how lovely Ben's room is, with his more or less tidy shelves housing his favourite toys and books and his desk with a blue and purple lava lamp he'd chosen himself. His bed and his maple wardrobe and chest of drawers and stripy blue curtains that match the bedding and the rug on the floor make his room warm and inviting and comfortable.

Mrs Marlow looked withered and old and troubled in her sleep. She didn't look restful and peaceful, but exhausted and anxious. I wasn't sure whether to wake her or let her sleep. I didn't have the means to lock the kitchen door behind me or bolt the side gate and I was concerned that my neighbour would wake up and find herself alone. I knelt on the dusty faded carpet next to the bed and reached out to her hesitantly.

'Mrs Marlow?'

Mrs Marlow woke up instantly. 'I was just dozing,' she said as if she was expecting to be reprimanded.

'That's good. I'm sorry to disturb you. I've brought the rest of the things in. I'd really like it if you came and stayed with me tonight. I don't like the thought of you being here alone.'

'Oh no, I can't do that. Walter wouldn't like it if I wasn't here to look after his collections. I never go out. He likes me to be here all the time.'

'You'd only be next door, Mrs Marlow. We can make sure everything's locked and safe.'

'No, but thank you. You've been very kind. I don't know what we'd have done if you hadn't helped.'

'Can I get you a drink and something to eat then? Let me do that for you at least.'

'Do you have a telephone?'

'Yes, I do.'

'Well, in the morning I have to phone the hospital at ten o'clock. Would you help me to do that? We don't have a telephone.'

I promised I would.

With great reluctance I resigned myself to the fact that Mrs Marlow was doggedly determined to stay put. In fact I had the distinct impression that the old lady just wanted to be left in peace. I allowed myself to be escorted downstairs and heard the side gate being bolted after me.

I crossed from the Marlows' drive to my own feeling flat and hung over. I'd set out doggedly to do all I could to help. It hadn't turned out quite like that though. I relived my efforts to climb over the wall and squirmed. At the time I thought I was being single-minded and practical, but, with the benefit of hindsight, I could see I was being gung ho and ridiculous. In the end it was other people, not me, who'd been proactive and resourceful. Ben had helped far more than I had and it was Toby who'd cleared a path through the kitchen without being asked. He just saw that it needed to be done and had quietly got on with it. It had also been his idea to put the magazines and books on the plastic boxes while they were outside so they wouldn't be spoiled. Even when I'd tried to take care of Mrs Marlow and be the person to ensure she was comfortable and put her mind at rest, she wasn't interested.

Maybe I do still need more help after all, Cameron. I thought this morning I could cope with anything. I was kidding myself; I'm just as useless as I've always been.

Toby had put my bin out for me ready to be emptied the following morning. I remembered that just the previous Sunday he'd turned up without a word and he and Ben washed my car because he knew I was busy. I only found out because Ben told me. My guilt over how I'd neglected him on Tuesday throbbed in my throat once more. How could I have been so unaware and indifferent?

When I went to go through the side gate, it was bolted, but the front door had been left on the latch so I could let myself in. Ben was on the turn in the stairs, just going up to bed. He was bathed in a mellow golden glow from the evening sun that spilled through the stained glass window.

'Is Mrs Marlow coming?'

'No, I couldn't persuade her. Did you catch Harry's daddy?'

'Yes, he'd like to come and discuss next week with you on his way home from work tomorrow. He'll be here about six. He says will you phone back if that's not convenient.'

'That's good then. Thank you for doing that. I was proud of you this evening, Ben. You did really well. I'm sorry I snapped at you, I just didn't want you to get hurt. Night, darling. No reading tonight, alright? Sleep well. Last day in Year 5 tomorrow. Big day.'

'Oh and I phoned Granny and thanked her for the money too. Night, Mum Plum,' he said and blew me a kiss. 'Love you dots and spots.'

'Love you oodles and spoodles.'

Toby was in the kitchen washing up the dishes from the scrambled eggs on toast earlier. 'I put the kettle on when I heard you come in. Can I invite myself for a cuppa?'

'Thank you.'

'Not looking good for the old fella, is it? The ambulance driver, Lizzie, is she called, said he might not make it given how long he lay there and his age and health.'

I busied myself making the tea. 'Poor Mrs Marlow. I'll run her to the hospital in the morning. Shall we go through to the lounge?'

Toby held the door open then followed me into the lounge. I switched on the lamps and drew the curtains even though it wasn't yet dark. It felt more comforting.

'I don't want you to feel put on the spot,' I began, 'but I want to ask you a difficult question.'

'Oh yes?'

'It's about me, really... The other day, Tuesday, when I upset you, when I was thoughtless, I can't tell you how much I regret that.' He nodded. 'I'm not always very easy to talk to, am I?'

He cleared his throat. 'I sometimes find you... difficult. You don't always listen and you don't seem to notice you haven't.'

My immediate reaction was to be defensive, but I caught myself in time. I'd asked for feedback and I was getting it. This was no time to run away.

'And sometimes, sometimes you get yourself into such a stressful state, it frightens me.'

'Frightens you?'

'You seem to be out of control. I worry about how Ben copes with it.' I drank his words in, but didn't say anything. 'Like tonight when you were trying to get over the fence, you were... I'll tell it like it was, fanatical. Makes me feel... awkward.'

'You've been very honest. Thank you.'

'Ben was just trying to help and you bit his head off.'

'I was worried he'd fall and break his neck. I'd never have forgiven myself if... I just apologised to him.' I lapsed into thought for a moment, hesitating, summoning the courage to speak openly. 'These past few days... I'm beginning to realise how I've been behaving and I want to make changes.'

I watched Toby come into his stride now. While normally a taciturn man, he was seizing this opportunity to explain the effect I have on him.

'You used to give me the impression you didn't like me much, found me boring.'

He hit a nerve. I couldn't deny what he was saying; he was spot on.

'I did you a disservice, Toby. You've been a loyal and reliable friend. I owe you a great deal.'

We lapsed into silence and drank our tea.

'Can I share something with you?' I asked eventually, nursing my empty mug. He nodded. 'I'm not trying to excuse the way I behave, but to explain.'

He took his pipe from his pocket and held it up as a way of asking permission to use it.

'Of course.' I smiled in spite of myself.

'Helps me concentrate.'

'Sorry. I'm being a bit serious and heavy, aren't I?'

I got up and drew the curtains back again. The sky was a mixture of deep red and rose pink hues with orange tinges.

'Look, it's beautiful. It's going to be another lovely day tomorrow I think.'

He crossed over to the window to join me. 'Let's enjoy it outside, shall we? Shame to miss such a glorious evening.'

I grabbed my woolly jacket from the cloakroom and threw it round my shoulders and we went and sat on the rather twee wrought iron chairs with matching table – a present from Mother – on the decking outside the conservatory. I closed my eyes and took a deep breath, letting the tension drain from my jaw and my shoulders. The air was still and calm after all the exertion of earlier in the evening.

'Everything seems better when you're outside,' Toby said simply. 'Now, I'm listening. What is it you want to say?'

I was grateful he'd had the wisdom to go out into the garden. I wasn't coming from a place of emotional angst now. I could quite simply detach myself and recall the details I wanted to share without reliving them.

'My friend Jess, she's a counsellor, she says when we have an issue that troubles us, if it's something very deep, we keep reliving it over and over again. Different people, different places, even different situations, but the same old issue.'

'Mm, I heard a programme on the radio about that sort of thing,' Toby said, holding his pipe to his lips and taking a puff.

'Well, Jess reckons that the issue won't get sorted until we recognise the pattern and actively try to change it.'

'Makes sense.'

'The thing is with me, my father walked out on us when I was four and Jess thinks I've never properly come to terms with it.'

'Is that what you think too?'

'I don't know what to think.' I fell silent for a while and Toby held the silence. 'I still remember the morning Dad left really clearly.'

I looked at Toby and saw that I had his full attention. It made me feel confident to carry on, safe to explore painful memories.

'It was a Saturday morning. He hadn't been at home at the weekends for ages, Mother always said he was working, so I was really excited when I woke up and he was still there. I thought at first he was making a special effort to spend the day with us, then I heard him arguing with Mother in the kitchen. They'd shut the door so I wouldn't hear them, but I sat on the stairs listening. I remember thinking how different the hallway looked with the door shut. I didn't remember ever seeing it shut before. Funny the details you remember.'

'Yes.'

'My dad was shouting and I could tell Mother was crying. He came out into the hallway, snatched his car keys from the table and slammed the front door behind him. I remember feeling the slam, it felt so final. He didn't notice me on the stairs. He never said goodbye. After he'd gone, Mother made me some toast and told me he was moving in with her friend Rebecca and they were going to have a baby. Simple as that. She's rarely mentioned him again, even now.'

'Not surprised you still remember that. It was a big deal.'

'Yes, it was. It changed our lives forever. I used to think, when I was older, I used to think it was all my fault, I should have stopped him going. I could have spoken to him or run out after him and he might have changed his mind about leaving.'

'But you know that can't be true?' Toby puffed sagely.

'Yes, that's what Jess says. She says we know it's irrational, but we still punish ourselves. And now if something dreadful is happening, something inside me takes over, subconsciously you understand, and I have to try to put it right.

If I can stop whatever it is, like with the Marlows, then it will somehow turn back the clock and stop my dad from leaving too. It's a bit weird, isn't it?'

'You're never going to be able to right every wrong. You're doomed to fail before you start.' Toby was proving more perceptive than I'd given him credit for.

'I know. I do know. Jess says that too. She says I either set myself up for failure or I run and hide and pretend something's not happening so I don't have to sort it out. She says I sometimes mentally switch off when other people have problems.'

'I've noticed.'

I stared at him for a moment, shocked by his sardonic quip, then found myself laughing.

'You're such a good friend, Toby. I'm sorry I waited so long to appreciate you.' He smiled, a little embarrassed. 'It's funny,' I went back to my story, 'I remember when Mother used to get cross with me when I was a child, I used to put my hands over my ears and shout "lah, lah, lah" pretending I couldn't hear her. Jess says I'm still doing that metaphorically. It's a way of protecting myself, yes, but it's misguided because I'm not facing up to things, not dealing with them, so they keep happening again over and over.'

'And now you are?'

'Facing up to things?' I shrugged. 'I'm trying. I didn't know it would be so bloody hard.' We both laughed. 'The first step, apparently, is to recognise how I'm reacting to a situation. I've not managed to jump that hurdle yet.'

'You're very tough on yourself. Maybe if you treated yourself more kindly?'

I felt suddenly self-conscious as I realised we'd been making eye contact during the whole exchange.

'Thanks for letting me ramble on. You're really good to talk to.'

'Perhaps I recognise myself in some of the things you're saying,' he replied, puffing on the briarwood. 'I fill me time with me garden. Gardens don't have emotional outbursts, they don't judge or criticise or tell you what you should or shouldn't do.'

'You're changing too though. I've noticed. You seem happier.'

'Funny you should say that. Ben's noticed too. Think it's since the woman's been visiting me.'

'A woman's been visiting you? Who is she?'

'Haven't the slightest. Just turns up every now and then and we chat things over.'

'Is she Neighbourhood Watch?'

'Doubt it. Keep meaning to ask her, matter of fact, but then I forget. Not really important, I s'pose. She reminds me a bit of me ma. Got the same smile. Always smiling, just like Ma. Talked a bit about you, as it happens.'

'Really?'

'She was asking me about the other evening, all the carrying on. She said you were struggling to come to terms with things and you needed me support. How about that?'

'I don't know what to say.'

'Ben knows her. Seen her chatting to him too.'

Could it be? It must be. Who else could it be?

'Got something to tell you before I say goodnight.' Toby grew serious now. 'I've an appointment to see a solicitor tomorrow afternoon. Time I made a new will. Not that I'm planning to pop me clogs for another decade at least, two or pushing three if Him up there is kind to me, but I want things sorted. Do you remember, I told you me only relative's me cousin in South Africa?'

'Yes I do,' I said, thinking that Toby was going to ask for help to trace her.

'Well, she's got pots of money. Her husband's some kind of business howdy-doody. She's older'n me, anyway. She's in no need of my bit of property. So, I'm leaving everything to Ben. Best you know, saves complications when the time comes.'

Friday 19 July

I wasn't able to go into town as planned to get a birthday present for Ben and then meet up with Alice and Jess for our usual coffee and natter because of lending my phone to Mrs Marlow. I left it until the last minute to go around to her house as it wasn't something I was relishing. I'd never noticed before, but both the upstairs and downstairs bay windows and the window above the front door have their curtains drawn. Mrs Marlow was obviously up and about because the bin had been taken back in, but the side gate was bolted. Now what was I to do? One thing was for certain, I was not going to climb over the fence again.

I knocked loudly on the gate and waited, but there was no reply. I tried the doorbell on the front door and heard the dulled reverberation inside. I waited again, but still no response. I pressed the bell once more in a series of long sharp bursts. Nothing. I decided Mrs Marlow must be hard of hearing. I was about to go home when I heard the gate being unbolted.

'Oh, it's you,' said Mrs Marlow, opening the gate a few inches and peering out. 'I thought we said ten o'clock?'

'Yes, that's right.'

'Well, it's still only eight minutes to, dear. Would you be so kind as to come back at ten?' She disappeared behind the gate and bolted it.

'Mrs Marlow?' I called, but my neighbour had clearly gone inside again. I sat on the front doorstep and waited. I didn't know what else to do.

A few minutes later Mrs Marlow unbolted the gate and came out. 'Ah, there you are. Good morning. Did you bring your phone? Here's the number.' She handed over the card Lizzie had given her.

'You want me to make the call?'

'If you wouldn't mind, dear.'

'Shall we go inside?'

'No, it's perfectly fine here, thank you. If you'd just make the call. The young lady did say ten o'clock, remember?'

I dialled and got through almost immediately. I turned to Mrs Marlow when the call was over to find the old lady had escaped back through the gate and bolted it behind her. Not again, I thought and repeated the doorbell ringing ritual.

Eventually Mrs Marlow opened the gate enough to peer out. 'Yes? Did you want me?'

'I got through to the hospital. Your husband is comfortable and he's resting. He's in Sir Percival Southwell ward. Visiting isn't until two thirty, but I have to pick up Ben from school and we wouldn't be back in time. They said if we go now, they'll let you see him for a few minutes.'

'I can't. I can't leave the house. Could you go?'

'No, Mrs Marlow, they won't let me see him, it has to be you. He'll want to see you, I'm sure. I'm happy to take you.'

'I'd better not.' Mrs Marlow was obviously a force to be reckoned with.

'I'm sure he'd be happier if you went and reassured him that his books and magazines haven't been damaged?'

'Will it take us very long to get there?'

'Half an hour at the most. I'll pop home and look at the map of the hospital on my computer to see where Sir Percival Southwell ward is first so we don't waste time when we get there.'

'Aren't you clever?'

'Can you be ready in about ten minutes then and we'll get straight off?'

I wasn't sure how to feel about taking Mrs Marlow to the hospital. It's where Paul died, but it's also where Ben was born; one of those sad ironies that life sometimes throws up. I was thankful to see Sir Percival Southwell is in a separate wing from the main entrance so we would be well away from both A&E and Maternity.

I resigned myself to the fact that Mrs Marlow would have gone into hiding again, but found her already standing by the car waiting. She'd tied her wispy grey hair into bunches sticking out at right angles to her head directly above her ears, exposing the bald patches on her scalp. She'd also pencilled dark brown eyebrows too arched and too long then finished off the creation with a circle of rouge in the middle of each of her cheeks and a profusion of face powder. She had on a thick moth-eaten knitted red poncho over her clothes despite it being another hot day and was still wearing her slippers.

'Did you want to change into some shoes, Mrs Marlow?' I suggested, wondering if I might also broach the subject of toning down the makeup.

'I can't get my slippers off any more, not since my ankles swelled up in this hot weather. I always have this problem when it's hot. They'll go down again when we have a cold snap.'

No, better not mention the makeup then.

I tried to make conversation on the journey, but Mrs Marlow chose not to join in. The undeniable tang of urine was making my eyes smart and jabbing at my nostrils. I made a mental note to disinfect the car seat when I arrived back home.

'Won't be long now, Mrs Marlow,' I said as we drove through the hospital entrance. 'We have to look out for Car park C on the left. I expect it'll be signposted.'

It was easy to locate, but was practically full despite it being outside visiting hours and it took a while to find a suitable parking space. I knew from the online map that Sir Percival Southwell was somewhere in the building ahead, but there was no signpost. I hope it's not going to be far, I thought when I saw how slowly my neighbour was shuffling. Mrs Marlow has a way of throwing her weight from foot to foot so as she shuffles she sways, reminding me of the Weeble characters I played with when I was a toddler.

I led the way through a side door and we found ourselves in a long corridor. Just ahead was a lift. I'd understood the ward was on the ground floor and chastised myself for not thinking to bring a printout of the map. There were no signs giving directions, but Mother taught me to give the appearance of being confident even when I wasn't feeling it, so I said, 'This way,' and summoned the lift.

There was a notice next to the lift that identified the mortuary as being on the lower floor and audiology on the floor above. I remembered seeing something about audiology when I'd looked online so I decided that would be a good start. Unfortunately, we ended up in a corridor exactly the same as the one on the floor below.

'Will you stay here a moment, Mrs Marlow, while I investigate the best way to go?'

I spotted double doors further along the corridor and headed towards them. I heard the ping of the lift and turned as Mrs Marlow wandered into it.

'No, wait,' I called, but was too late.

By the time I'd rushed back to the lift it had gone to the next floor. I watched it go up to the fourth floor, crossed my fingers and hoped that Mrs Marlow wouldn't have strayed too far by the time I caught up with her. It seemed to take forever for the lift to come back down again. The doors opened to reveal a man and a woman dressed in white coats.

'Did you see an old lady wandering about by herself?' I asked as they were about to step out.

'Yes,' the man said, 'she seemed a bit confused. She was mumbling, but we couldn't tell what she was saying. We were going to call security. Is she with you?'

'Yes. Thanks,' I said getting into the lift as the doors were closing again. I sighed with relief when they opened on the fourth floor and I saw Mrs Marlow further along the corridor still waddling and shuffling painfully slowly in the direction of a turning to the left whilst chatting away to a bearded man carrying a clipboard.

I chased after them.

'Oh, there you are dear,' said Mrs Marlow. 'This nice young man is taking me to see Walter.'

'Turn left, then right,' said clipboard-man. 'Can I leave you to take over now? I was supposed to be going in the other direction.'

'Thank you,' I replied, relieved that good fortune had intervened to take us to the right place and ignoring the niggle trying to remind me that Sir Percival Southwell was supposed to be on the ground floor.

We turned the corner and headed for an opening on the right. Above it was a sign announcing that we'd reached The Walter Clifton Clinical Neurophysiology Unit.

'Aren't we going in?' said Mrs Marlow.

'It's the wrong Walter, I'm afraid.'

'Are you sure, dear? That nice young man seemed to know.'

'Yes, look at the sign. It says Neurophysiology. We want Percival Southwell ward.'

'I can't really see very well without my glasses.'

That explains the makeup then, I thought. 'Come on, there's another lift over there, look. We need to go back down again.'

The lift took us down past the Eye Outpatients Clinic – seeing that would have Ben roaring with laughter – to the main entrance, which I had particularly wanted to avoid, but at least there'd be a reception desk. In contrast to the quiet corridors, the main entrance was a hive of bustling activity. There were long queues at the reception desk. My heart fell until I saw out of the corner of my eye, directly across from the glass-fronted entrance doors, a taxi rank.

'Come on, plan B.'

The taxi driver was leaning against a cushion on the passenger door of his car reading a newspaper. He looked up and smiled. 'No problem,' he said opening the car door for Mrs Marlow. 'Hop in, love. I'll have you there in a jiffy.'

He was as good as his word and moments later we were back in the original car park.

'Ignore that door,' he said, pointing to the one we'd gone through previously. 'See the turning over there? The entrance is just on the right.'

'I'm so grateful, thank you. We could have been wandering around all morning. There should be a notice.'

'You mean like that one?' The taxi driver grinned and gestured towards the large sign next to the ticket machine.

I laughed. 'Yes, like that one. How much do I owe you?'

'No, get away with you. It's a pleasure to help out two such gorgeous young ladies.' He papped his horn and drove off.

'What a nice man, so kind,' I said, smiling.

'I've never spoken to a darkie before,' said Mrs Marlow.

My eyes widened and I was about to challenge her, but bit my tongue when I saw Mrs Marlow's vacant expression. Some battles are doomed before they begin, but it left me feeling uncomfortable.

'Hmm,' was my pathetic response and, 'He was very helpful and thanks to him we know which way to go now,' my miserable attempt at making amends.

Luckily we found Sir Percival Southwell ward easily and buzzed to be let in. A nurse took us to the relatives' room as the consultant was doing her ward rounds.

'She'll be a few minutes, then she'll come in and chat with you and you'll be able to see your husband,' the nurse said holding the door open for us to go in. 'There's a drinks machine in the corridor.'

We had the room to ourselves. It was small, but bright and airy with comfortable seats. There was a noticeboard with a poster about the correct way to lift heavy objects, a list of visiting times and warnings not to smoke or use mobile phones inside the hospital.

'Are you okay, Mrs Marlow?' I could see the whole experience was something of an ordeal for her. Mrs Marlow chose not to reply yet again and we sat in a strained silence as I read and re-read the notices.

Eventually the door opened. A surprisingly young woman came bustling in. She looked harassed and in a hurry. 'How do you do? I'm Rachael Sutton, Orthopaedic Consultant. I'll come straight to the point.'

She sat on a seat opposite and leaned forward, enunciating slowly and raising her voice as if she expected Mrs Marlow to be hard of hearing. 'Now Mrs Barlow, I need to warn you, it's not what you're going to want to hear. Your husband's had a nasty fall and it's shaken him up quite a lot. We've taken x-rays and he's going to need an OIRF because he has an unstable fracture to his pelvis… his pelvis? Yes? We've given him medication to help with the pain so he might seem a bit groggy.'

Mrs Marlow stared at her blankly, but the consultant seemed not to notice. 'The problem is he isn't strong enough for us to operate right now. We're keeping him in, obviously, and we'll look at the situation again after the weekend. You need to be prepared for him to be with us for quite a while, I'm afraid. Nurse will give you a list of visiting times and what you'll need to bring in for him.'

'Oh,' said Mrs Marlow.

'I understand you're having some "difficulties" at home? There'll be someone coming to see you from Social Services to assess the situation, but I'm guessing your husband will probably need to recuperate in a nursing home. We can organise all that for you. No need to worry. Now are there any questions?'

Mrs Marlow looked bemused.

'Well, if you do think of anything, Mrs Barlow, be sure to ask Sister, won't you? I'm sorry to be in such a rush, but I was due in theatre 15 minutes ago.'

She took hold of Mrs Marlow's limp hand and shook it and then left as hurriedly as she'd arrived.

I could see Mrs Marlow hadn't really understood. I was surprised by the doctor's brusque manner and apparent lack of empathy. The contrast between her attitude and the paramedics' the previous evening was stark.

The nurse came back and held the door open.

'We're ready for you now, Mrs Marlow. This way,' he said. 'I warn you, your husband's a bit sleepy.'

Left on my own after the old lady had shuffled off with the nurse, I picked up a leaflet about spotting the warning signs of a stroke and looked at it without reading, except I noticed that the man in the photos looked a bit like Reg who services my car.

The nurse returned. 'I understand you're a neighbour? Would you be willing for us to use your phone number if we need to get in touch?'

'Of course.' I nodded. 'But I'm going away for the whole of August.'

'Oh dear. Is there anyone else?'

'Maybe; I'll check it out and get back to you.' I was reluctant to offer Toby's number without first making sure he was agreeable. 'I don't think Mrs Marlow took in what the consultant was saying,' I began. 'She didn't... she was...'

'Abrupt?' replied the nurse, half-smiling. 'Yes, we've all been on the receiving end of that. She's an amazing surgeon and the patients are in good hands medically, but her bedside manner...,' he was clearly choosing his words carefully, '...has, shall we say, a little to be desired. Thanks for the warning. I'll have a word with Mrs Marlow myself.'

I wanted to say more about my concerns for the Marlows, but Mrs Marlow came back into the room.

'He's asleep, I tried to wake him up, but he's fast off. I want to go back home now, dear.'

'Would you mind just sitting down a moment first, my love? There's a couple of things we need to go through,' the nurse explained.

Mrs Marlow passed wind, loudly, as she obediently sat down. 'Will it take long? Only I've got things to do.'

'Not long. We want to make sure you understand what's going to happen to your husband now, alright? Did the doctor– '

'Oh! We haven't seen the doctor yet, silly me. I was forgetting. Will he be long?'

'Mrs Sutton? She came in to speak to you? She's the consultant, the surgeon who'll perform the operation. Your husband has fractured his hip and his bones will have to be held in place with pins or a plate. We'll explain it all properly to you both when the time comes and answer any questions so don't worry about that now. But we can't say when it will be because he's too poorly to have the operation just yet.'

'Yes, that's right, dear.'

'And then when it's time for him to leave hospital we're going to arrange for him to go into a nursing home.'

'No, he wouldn't like that. He likes to be at home you see, but thank you.'

'It's not quite as simple as that, Mrs Marlow,' the nurse continued patiently. 'The paramedics don't think it would be safe for him to go home. Someone from Social Services will come and talk to you about the help he's going to need.'

'No thank you.' She stood up. 'Can we go now?'

'I did my best, Mrs Lewis,' the nurse said as we made our way to the exit. I indicated I understood with a tilt of my head and I shrugged.

I was quite pleased not to speak on the way home; I had some thinking to do. I wondered what could have been the determining moment that the Marlows had decided to let their acquisitions accrue to the point where they'd taken over. Was it gradual? Was it conscious? Had they always meant to sort them out at some future date, but never actually got around to doing it? What had prompted keeping all that stuff in the first place? Was it a reaction to some trauma in the distant past? What had been their hopes and dreams and expectations when they first moved into the house? Surely not what they'd ended up with? Surely? How had they drifted away from their aspirations to settle for what they'd now created? Were they "settling for", or did it make them happy? Was I making a judgment based on what I'm comfortable with?

I glanced over to Mrs Marlow, dozing beside me with her mouth wide open. Perhaps people think the same thing about me. Perhaps they think I'm wasting all of Ben's childhood by working so much. Is that what Alice and Jess think? Is that what Toby thinks? Why do I work so hard? Why have I put myself in a situation where I'm working full time in my translation business and part time teaching as well? My mortgage is paid, I'm able to pay the bills, we have a comfortable lifestyle, so what am I doing it for? Especially when it makes me worry about spending enough time with Ben? What kind of future am I drifting into?

Those were sobering thoughts. The Marlows' clutter seemed to represent a clinging on to an unhealthy compulsion for possessions to the point where there were so many it had become dysfunctional and dangerous. I could see that clearly. It was obvious. But was that really so different from the busyness that was cluttering my own life? And Ben's? Was my busyness just a clinging on so I wouldn't have to let myself feel the grief of losing my father and then Paul and my worries about something awful happening to Ben that I force below the surface?

My childhood was compromised by Mother's obsession with work and I'd suffered because of it, we both did, not financially or in terms of lost opportunities, but in our relationship. I was closer to my grandparents than I was to Mother. They were the ones I turned to when I needed emotional support.

'I'm sorry, Ben, I didn't realise... I didn't understand,' I said out loud. 'I'm going to do everything I can to put you first from now on. I promise.'

'What?' said Mrs Marlow. 'What did you say?'

'We're just about home,' I replied shaken out of my thoughts.

I pulled up outside the Marlows' home and helped my neighbour as far as the gate.

'Can I get you any shopping?'

'No, that's fine, dear. Walter does all the shopping. I'll wait until he gets back home,' and she was off through the gate, bolting it behind her.

I tried to put the old lady out of my mind when I got back home. I was mentally exhausted; worried and exhausted, but I had work to do. If I was going to keep my promise to Ben then I had to let go of my concerns for Mrs Marlow and focus instead on Meaty Goodness while he was at school.

I turned on the computer to check my emails. Dominique had good news. Allerbestes Tierfutter were delighted with my creative translation. So much so they were going to use 'Delicious Bites of Doggy Delights' as a strapline on their British packaging and hoped I would come up with something comparable in French, Italian and, incredibly, in German. They also added that whilst it captured the spirit of what they were wanting to say, they weren't quite sure exactly how I'd arrived at that particular phrase. Actually, neither was I. I checked. "Hunden schmecken die zarten Fleisch-Häppchen", yes, they had a point I suppose, but it was near enough considering the mood I'd been in.

I dashed off a reply asking if Tuesday's deadline could be extended. That was a first. I had never in almost nine years of working for the agency asked for extra time before. I decided not to mention the reduction in the amount of work I'm prepared to take on in the future until an appropriate opportunity presented itself.

I worked uninterrupted for just over two hours and was partway through the Italian beef and liver variety when I switched off the computer. I left ten minutes to practise a few yoga stretches before setting off across The Lawns to meet Ben. Ideally we're encouraged to practise an hour a day every day. 'Well, ten minutes of downward and upward dog is a start,' I told myself and smiled at the idea of swapping one doggie-related activity for another.

The mood was high in the school playground. Staff and children mingled with parents and carers, wishing each other a good summer and exchanging goodbyes until September. Alice came over with an excitable Jake and an ever-playful Ben.

'How's your neighbour? Is he going to be alright?'

'Yes and no. It's his wife I'm more worried about. I'll tell you all about it in the car on Wednesday. I'll phone you to make arrangements, but I think we should probably leave at half nine. I haven't heard from Jess, is she still coming with Esme?'

'Yes, only they're going to make their own way there in case Esme has one of her moods and they need to make a quick getaway.'

Goodbyes over, Ben and I headed back home through The Lawns.

'Fancy a Knickerbocker Glory?'

'Scrummee,' said Ben with the emphasis on the 'ee'.

I expected the café to be full of other mothers and children with the same idea, but we had a choice of seats.

'Inside or outside? You choose a seat and I'll get the ice cream.'

The Sunny Days Café is expertly staffed by adults with learning difficulties. It's especially popular for its lunchtime menus and a growing following of local pensioners are said to make, in some cases, daily pilgrimages to enjoy them. The ice cream bar is a relatively new summer venture, exceeding even the most optimistic expectations. They specialise in favourites long forgotten by most other establishments: Peach Melba, Banana Split, Chocolate Pear, Fruit Sundae and, for those with big appetites, the giant Knickerbocker Glory.

I placed the order for Ben and an Earl Grey and carrot cake for myself then joined him outside in the sunshine. He was watching the youngsters in the adjacent play area with its imaginative wooden structures where children can climb, jump, swing, tunnel and crawl.

'You used to love the play area. Are you too grown up for it now?'

'Sort of. We have a brill time when I come with Jake and Owen, but not anymore when it's just me. It didn't matter when I was little, I was happy to make up my own games. Only some things just aren't as enjoyable on my own now.'

He'd obviously been giving the matter careful thought. I nodded in agreement. I could identify with that.

'What's been your favourite memory of Year 5 then?' I asked changing the subject.

'Oh goodness, so many to choose from. I loved doing the show at Christmas and when we made soap and building the totem pole in the playground; that was awesome. I've loved all of it really. I think what I'll miss most is Mr Gupta. I expect Mrs Meadows will be good too, but Mr Gupta makes lessons fun. He tells us stupid jokes and makes us laugh. We all sang "For He's A Jolly Good Fellow" at home time. He didn't know we were going to sing it, we kept it secret. Bunny and Kimberley cried of course. Like they usually do.' He rolled his eyes in mock condemnation.

I took before, during and after photos when the Knickerbocker Glory arrived and applauded when he managed to demolish it.

He groaned, holding his tummy. 'I can't move, Mummy. You'll have to give me a piggyback. I can't walk home.'

'That's a shame,' I said impishly, getting up and moving off. 'See you around sometime then.'

'Mummy!' he yelled and chased after me.

We ended up playing 'tag, you're it' all the way through The Lawns. I staggered to the south gate out of breath. 'It's no good. It's too hot to run any more, I'm puffed. You'll have to give me a piggyback.'

'Thanks, Mummy,' Ben said grinning happily when we arrived back home. 'That was a perfect way to end year 5.'

He disappeared to do his own thing, giving me time to have a quick tidy up before Harry's father arrived. The doorbell rang. Right on time I thought as I went to answer it, preparing my best caring-mother smile.

'Hello again.' It was PC Gabrielli.

'Is something wrong? Oh, not Mel again, surely?' I thought that episode was well and truly put to bed.

'Er… No, I understood you were expecting me? I spoke to Ben on the phone? I'm here about my son, Harry.'

I realised I was standing with my mouth open. 'Ohhh! No. Yes. Sorry. Of course. Come in, come in. I hadn't realised you…'

He was laughing. 'I thought you would've guessed from the name. There aren't any other Gabriellis round here.'

'As you say.' I could feel myself blushing.

I closed the door with a little too much enthusiasm and danced, overly brightly, to the kitchen. Stop it, stop it, just relax for goodness' sake. You're making yourself look like an idiot. I smiled, hoping he hadn't noticed. I saw from the twinkle in his eyes that he had.

I blushed again and cleared my throat. 'I… erm… it's, I didn't know Harry's surname that's all, so I was a bit surprised.'

'I've embarrassed you, sorry. It is an incredible coincidence, isn't it?'

I laughed, worrying that it sounded forced. 'I thought so too,' he continued, 'but because you made the generous offer I assumed you were okay with it.' He held out his hand. 'I'm Matthew. Can I call you Ruby?'

I relaxed; he'd understood. 'Please do,' I said, shaking his hand. 'Sorry for making such a fuss. It was just such a surprise, I was a bit flustered. Weird things like this keep happening to me lately. I should be getting used to them by now. Can I get you a tea, coffee?'

'Actually I'd prefer something cold please. It was so hot in the car.'

We could hear Ben playing the piano as we went into the lounge. He was bashing out The Entertainer at twice the speed it's supposed to be played.

'Hi,' he said and then sheepishly, 'Sorry Mummy, I got bored.'

'So Ben, I get to meet you at last. Harry talks about you a lot. You're a good friend to him. Thank you.'

'And Jake and Owen. We're all good mates. Shall I go and see to Mildred and Delilah, Mummy, while you do the grown-up stuff then?'

'He's a top lad, your boy,' Matthew said when Ben had gone. 'I'm glad to be able to speak to you about what he did for Harry. I was really worried about him before Ben stepped in and fixed it.'

'I'm not really sure what you mean?'

'The bullying?'

'I thought it was Mr Gupta who sorted that out?'

'No, it was Ben,' Matthew was emphatic. His tone was measured and serious. 'It was all thanks to Ben. You should ask him about it, really. It's not often I use moral imperatives, but I think in this case, you really should.'

'I will. Thank you.'

Later that evening when I heard a tap on the conservatory French window, I thought it must be Toby, but it turned out to be Cameron.

'Might I come in?'

'Yes, please do,' I said holding the door open, 'it's really good to see you.'

'I thought it timely to chat.'

'Oh okay. Do you want to come through to the lounge? Can I get you a drink?'

'I'm fine thank you. The lounge is an excellent idea.'

We went through in silence. I indicated the armchair and sat on the sofa. He looked into my eyes and held my gaze for what seemed like an eternity. I felt myself zone out and then back in again.

'There's been much for you to process these last few days.'

I felt the floodgates open and my words spilled out in a torrent. I hadn't realised I'd been holding in so much emotion.

'I felt fidgety after Ben went to bed tonight. I decided not to mention the bullying for the time being, not on the first evening of his summer holiday. Neither of us wanted to watch a film so we chatted instead about going to France as usual for the summer. I think he was feeling as restless as I was. A mixture of the anti-climax of finishing school for the summer, the break in and the upset with Toby, Jordan Baker, the events with the Marlows I guess... so much for him, for both of us, to deal with and all in three days. And on top of that, for my part, my reaction to the meeting with Matthew took me completely by surprise.'

I looked to Cameron for a response, but he was simply giving me his full attention without interrupting.

'I'd forgotten what it feels like to be attracted to a man again and, after all, he was only here to make arrangements for Harry... I don't know whether he feels the same way as I do or not... or even whether he'd be interested in getting to know each other. What a trite phrase. He might be in a relationship already. Do I want a relationship?'

I lapsed into silence waiting for a reply, but Cameron said nothing.

'I'm not making any sense, am I?'

'On the contrary. You're remarkably coherent.'

'Jess says I overthink.'

'Uhuh.'

'I should be working really.'

'I sense a "but".'

'I switched my computer on and off again. I'm not in the mood for translating dog food into Italian. Do you think Matthew will take up my offer to teach him Italian...?'

My question wasn't intended to be rhetorical, but Cameron left it hanging.

'I was playing the piano when you knocked. It's years since I've played more than carols at Christmas. I used to know Grieg's Piano Concerto off by heart. I played it in a concert we put on to raise funds for Children in Need when I was at uni. I was making a lackadaisical attempt to play it again with the hotchpotch of phrases I could remember.'

'Is this what you'd like to talk about?'

He was right, of course. Anything to divert the chaos in my head. 'I do that a lot.'

'Uhuh.'

'Avoid talking about the elephant.'

'Uhuh.'

'It's what Ben and I were doing this evening.'

'Which elephant is it in particular you're avoiding?'

'My life whizzes around me, never giving me time to touch down, never giving me time to reflect on what I've lost, never giving me time to be miserable. I make myself indispensable to the smooth running of other people's lives, always busy, busy... Actually, I like it that way.'

'You like the busyness?'

'Sadly, yes I do.' I was being honest. 'I guess it stops me being aware of how lonely I sometimes feel. If I fill my time then everything must be fine, only...' I struggled to put these feelings into words. They consumed me, yet the words to describe them were elusive. I tried a different approach. 'Alice and Jess are really close friends, but they can't begin to understand how hard it is for me, you know as a single parent.'

Cameron nodded. I wondered if he was judging me. We neither of us spoke for a while.

'Toby says you've been talking to him?'

'We talk to people all the time.'

'He didn't seem to know you're a guardian angel.'

'We have many guises. We come in many forms. Guardian angel is your description. Our mission is to support, to protect and to guide.'

I let that wash over me. Something else I didn't understand.

'He says you were talking about me?'

'The subject came up. We've also been speaking with your friend Alice. Her life isn't as cosy as you seem to think.'

'Alice? Alice has everything. Pete. Money. A big house. A loving family.' And then I remembered. 'Oh, you mean the baby. Of course. I forgot about the baby.'

'Her baby. Yes. Her daughter. She and Pete still grieve, I guess they always will, just as you will. You have more in common than you think.'

'She never talks about it anymore. I tried to comfort her at the time, but I said all the wrong things... It was a few years ago and very close to the anniversary of Paul's accident.'

'Don't say "yes" to this without thinking carefully.' He studied me.

'That sounds ominous.'

'Remember I said to pay attention to your dreams? Tonight, if you choose, Alice will come to you and tell her story. Neither of you will remember anything about it in the morning, but the details are not important. It would be therapeutic for her and you'd be left with more understanding of your friend and the opportunity to be more compassionate towards her.'

'How can it be therapeutic if we don't remember?'

'As I said, it's not always the details that are important. Sometimes they can get in the way of the truth. You feel the truth of something with your heart, not with your head.'

'The truth?'

'The meaning, the significance.'

'I'm not sure I really understand, but I want to be a better friend to Alice, as she is to me. If a dream will help with that, then I don't need to think about it,' I said. 'So, thank you, yes.'

I thought I'd fall asleep quickly after agreeing to the dream, but as usual my mind was reliving the events of the day so I was feeling wide awake and restless again...

...Alice is sitting on the armchair in the lounge where Cameron sat earlier in the evening, except... it isn't the lounge. I'm not really sure where it was, it seems to be floating surrounded by candles lighting up a dark void. I can see myself from behind sitting on the sofa, a dim, shadowy figure.

Alice addresses me directly, 'You and Jess freak me out sometimes. We're an odd combo to be friends, really different, you know? Don't get me wrong, I'm ever so fond of both of you, but sometimes you exhaust me. No kidding. You're mega driven and Jess psychoanalyses everyone. Between buzz,

buzz, buzz and "Would you like to talk about it?" it's hard work trying to keep up with you both.'

I feel no emotion, completely open and ready to receive her candid thoughts.

'Yes, course the three of us are good friends, but I would say it's Jenny who's my best friend.' She laughs. 'Do you still say 'best friend' when you're thirty-three? Um, I suppose I just find Jenny easier to get on with. We have a lot more in common, want the same things. I can think of lots of little examples...' She goes quiet for a moment and becomes more subdued, 'but the big one was when my beautiful Eloise was stillborn. I thought of all people you would be the one that understood best because of what happened to your husband. Do you remember? You said you knew it was difficult, but what you can't change you have to put behind you and move on? You hoped that helped. Ruby, Ruby, I was so not in a place to hear that...

'Jess was no better, for all her psychology. She held my hand and told me to let it all out, she was listening. Like I knew what to say! I was so overwhelmed, I had no words. Come on!

'But Jenny? Well, Jenny cried with me...

'I've never told you the full story, because you've never asked. In fact, you talk a heck of a lot about you, but you don't ever ask how I am. You give the impression that you have this idealised picture of me in your head when, in fact, you don't bother to properly get me at all.

'Did you know they had to take my womb away? Did you ever wonder why me and Pete have never had another child?

'I can't make babies any more so I make cakes instead. It's a bit of an obsession. I'm good at making cakes. People love to eat my cakes. It makes them happy. Making cakes makes me happy. I take comfort in the bottom of a mixing bowl, Pete takes comfort in the bottom of a glass. He drinks too much. He knows he does. But he won't admit it.

'I've turned it into a proper business. Birthday cakes, anniversary cakes, Christmas cakes and cupcakes. I haven't started to advertise yet, but I'm always busy. Word of mouth. It's the best recommendation. As you know, I've been making birthday cakes and Christmas cakes for friends and friends of friends for years. I went from making a cake every now and then to making them regularly every week. That's the thing with cakes; there's always another birthday or another anniversary.

'You said it was a blessing I had Jake. Reassuring me that time heals. You, of all people. I suppose you were trying to be kind or you didn't know what else to say.

'Eloise Joy was born six years ago today at three forty-two in the afternoon. She weighed six pounds, thirteen. They took us to a special bereavement room at the hospital so we could say goodbye in private. We washed her and dressed her in the clothes we would have taken her home in. And then we cuddled her. She looked perfect, just like any sleeping new-born, except she was so, so still and cold and she wasn't breathing. Pete said he kept expecting her to wake up. We didn't cry, neither of us, not then, we wanted to remember every moment.

'We never saw her alive. I felt her alive inside me for all those months, but then she died. The cruellest thing was they couldn't give us a reason. The placenta had become unattached, but they didn't know why. She never took a breath. It had been a normal labour, but she didn't survive her birth into the world. I knew there was something wrong, I could tell by the look on the midwife's face. Stephanie, her name was, Stephanie. She wheeled in a monitor and turned the screen away from us, then she sent for the obstetrician. She didn't put Eloise on my belly, like they'd done with Jake. I didn't hear my baby cry. "You have a daughter" she said, and put her in a cot the other side of the room where we couldn't see her.

'The obstetrician looked tired and haggard, as if she hadn't slept for days. She didn't make eye contact. She examined

Eloise and said there were complications. Then she took Pete to one side and told him. She hurried out and left Pete to break the news to me. Pete was amazing. He was my rock. Even now when I look back to that time, I'm astonished by his strength.

'When people ask me, I say I have two children, but only one of them is still with us. Pete tells people she was born sleeping – he read the expression on someone's blog. We have footprints and prints of her hands, that's all. We could have taken photos, but I said no. I might have felt differently if her eyes had been open. I wish I'd seen her with her eyes open. Pete would have liked photos, I knew he would, but he didn't make a fuss. We sang Gentle Jesus at her funeral. I can't bear to hear it now.

'Jake was really excited about having a new brother or sister. We'd prepared him in all the ways they tell you to, made sure he knew what to expect. My Mum came over to stay with him when I went into labour so Pete could be at the hospital with me. She told him it was time for Mummy and Daddy to bring the new baby home. He drew her a picture to say welcome to the family. Mum didn't know what to do with it. She kept it and gave it to me on the first anniversary.

'How do you tell a four year old…? How do you explain?'

I'd had no idea of how awful it had been for her. How could I have been that unaware and insensitive? I must have been so preoccupied with my own problems that I paid no attention to what she was going through. Just as I hadn't thought of Toby after the burglary.

'Pete says wedding cakes are more lucrative, fetch a better price than birthday cakes. I'd love to have a go at making wedding cakes so I've enrolled on a two-year course in Sugar Craft and Royal Icing at your Academy starting in September. It's only one day a week, but I get a diploma at the end of it.

'Jake said to me, 'Where does all your love go when somebody dies?' It doesn't go anywhere, Jake. It stays stuck in your throat, in your longing to cradle your baby in your arms. It was my job to protect her, to keep her safe. They tell you it's not your fault. They say you mustn't feel guilty, it was nothing you did wrong; there was nothing you could have done that would have made a difference. But I do blame myself. If only I'd eaten more healthily or if only I'd rested more or if only I hadn't insisted on vacuuming the day before she was born or a hundred other if onlys. Why didn't I know? Why didn't I know something was wrong?

'Pete sometimes goes to her grave even after all this time, takes flowers and sits and talks to her, tells her what we've been doing. He says it helps him keep her alive in his memory, lets her know she'll always be remembered.

'I don't go with him.

'I can't.

'Funny, I was the one who couldn't hold it together in those first eighteen months and Pete was the one who was strong – now it's the other way round. I've learned to live with it, mostly, to make it more bearable, just like people said I would, but Pete's still broken-hearted. He should talk to Jess, but he won't.

'I've called the business Celebration Cakes. Pete's had cards printed for me. I've passed my health and hygiene certification. I've notified HMRC. I'm registered with Hegley small business support group...

'...I have a devoted husband. I have a wonderful son. And I make cakes.

'Thank you for listening. It means a lot.'

I am feeling so much love for Alice. I want to hold out my arms to her and cry with her as Jenny had done, but the candles flicker and the image of her fades and I am left in darkness.

Saturday 20 July

I woke up having had the weirdest dream. Goodness only knows what I was supposed to make of it. I couldn't properly recall the details except it was something about Cameron sitting in the armchair in the living room listening to me playing Grieg's Piano Concerto. Only that didn't seem quite right. I had a hazy notion that there was something else, something more important, but I couldn't remember. So what happened to telling me to pay attention to my dreams and that all will become clear in good time…? Er… when? I had a busy day ahead so I had to put my questions on hold until later. I resolved to ask Cameron to explain the next time I saw him.

The plan was to drive straight from Ben's swimming lesson, his last until the new term in September, to my grandfather's nursing home in Guildford. I wanted to check all was well with Mrs Marlow first, but the old lady had reverted to ignoring the front door bell again. I tried to quell my anxieties about her suffering a stroke or a coronary or some other such fate. I left some bread, milk and eggs in a shopping bag below the large post box fixed to the wall next to the side gate, with a note to say I'd be home by about eight o'clock.

Swimming lesson over and car fuelled, we set off. I was tempted when Ben asked if he could travel in the front with me, it would make talking so much easier, but common sense prevailed. We agreed he would play a game on his iPad until we reached the A303 and then I would turn the sound off the satnav until we were approaching Hook.

'I'll need to concentrate then. I'm not all that sure of the way, but it gives us plenty of time to chat before we get there.'

It isn't very often that anything to do with arrangements fazes Ben and he happily settled down with his game.

'Alright,' I said as I took the slip road onto the 303 half an hour later, 'this next bit's going to be straightforward; we just need to look out for the M3, that's all. I have all sorts of things I want to ask you.' I looked at him through the rear view mirror to see how he reacted. 'I was going to ask you about Harry being bullied.'

I changed lanes to pass a huddle of slow-moving lorries. Considering it was Saturday morning there was surprisingly little traffic.

'That was ages ago. It was Max and Luke and Sam, especially Sam. They didn't realise how much they upset Harry. They thought it was only a bit of fun and they enjoyed making him cross. They hid his books and pencils and kept calling him Harriet. Once they put a live worm in his lunch box.'

'Ugh, that's disgusting.'

'Then, when Year 5 went to visit the gurdwara – d'you remember? – we had to leave our shoes on racks outside and they hid his shoes. They didn't own up to it and Harry had to go back to school on the bus with no shoes on and then he had to go home in his plimsolls. He told me he was going to pretend to his daddy that he'd lost them so his daddy wouldn't come into school and make things worse.'

'What would you have done if they'd done that to you, Ben?'

'That's a good question. I'll have to think about that. Anyway, everyone on the bus was laughing as if it was really funny, only I think there were a lot of us who didn't think it was funny at all, but didn't dare say so. We all knew who'd done it, including Harry. We had to sit in the hall at lunchtime until someone owned up, but no one did.'

'So then what happened?'

He shrugged and said simply, 'I stood up and said to Mr Gupta and Miss Hucknall, "We all know who hid the shoes, but no one wants to tell you because no one wants to be a snitch". I said, "I think the people responsible don't deserve our loyalty because Harry doesn't have his shoes now and it isn't fair that the rest of us have to miss playtime." I asked the teachers if we could all be given a piece of paper and have a secret ballot and we could put a tick if we wanted the culprits to own up or a cross if we thought it was okay for them to get away with it because it was just a bit of fun.'

'Good idea, Ben. Well done for thinking of it. Did it work?'

'Mr Gupta asked everyone to put their hands up if they thought it was a good idea, but only a few people did because the rest were all too scared. Mr Gupta could see that too. He said, "Well, we'll try it anyway and see what happens", but Max stood up and said, "It was me and two others. I'm really sorry. It was meant to be a joke". Everyone clapped and cheered, so Luke and Sam stood up too. Mr Gupta asked them where the shoes were now, but they'd thrown them on the back of a pick-up truck that was parked outside the gurdwara and then when we came out it had driven off. They thought they were going to get into real trouble so they didn't say anything.'

'Was it Cameron who gave you the idea to speak up like that?'

'Cameron? No. Cameron wasn't there. It just seemed the best thing to do.'

'I'm proud of you.'

'Well, in a way, it was Cameron who taught me to stand back and just watch. It helps you because you don't get upset or cross, you just look at what the options are.'

'I was wondering, what do you make of Cameron? You know, the way he just pops up every now and then?'

'I know what you mean.' Ben smiled as he switched off his iPad. 'He always seems to turn up at the right moment and he knows what to say. I like him.'

'Yes, so do I,' I agreed although I wasn't sure "like" was the exact description I would choose. 'He makes me think.'

'He makes you step outside of yourself and makes you watch what's happening, you know, look what's going on.'

'Makes you analyse the situation?'

'I'm not sure what "analyse" means.'

'Sorry, it means… er… work out why it's happening, make sense of it.'

'No, no, the opposite; just watching, seeing, like looking at what's going on as if you're not part of it.'

'That's what you did when we met Jordan Baker? Yes?'

The traffic slowed while several vehicles joined from a slip road. I couldn't safely change lanes because there were already other cars in the outside lane.

'I guess.'

Ben had done it again, pulled the rug from under me. I was seeing him through different eyes and beginning to understand why I was getting so much feedback about his uniqueness. What concerned me was why Cameron had chosen to spend time with Ben. What was it about Ben that had led Cameron to single him out? Was he protecting Ben because something terrible was going to happen to him? Was it something I ought to be worried about? I felt the familiar sickening dread creeping through my veins and throbbing in my temples.

Thinking back now to that misguided, muddled thinking reinforces just how much I've achieved in the last two weeks; how much my attitude, and so my behaviour, has changed. Remarkable.

The entrance to The Sycamores could easily have gone unnoticed. It was opposite a builders' merchants along a side road on the outskirts of the town and tucked in behind an imposing stone wall to the right and a high gorse hedge to the left. The driveway curved sharply and led to a long narrow tree-lined car park down one side of the large, impressive nursing home. Apparently, according to Mother, it had originally been built in 1840 as a grand country home for one Major General Theodore Beechdale and his family and the generations of the Beechdale clan that followed. Mother had informed me it had been converted to a boarding school in the 1970s then reinvented for a second time into the present nursing home for the elderly at the turn of the millennium.

'We're a bit too early,' I said as I parked. 'There's hardly any other cars here yet. Do you mind if we sit for ten minutes before we go in? It might be a bit embarrassing if they're not expecting us yet.'

The truth was I was feeling apprehensive about the visit. It's three years now since my grandfather moved to The Sycamores. How had I let so much time elapse without visiting him? I'd always intended to. Mother visits fortnightly and has suggested we might go together many times. I said I would, and meant it when I said it, but then I let some deadline or commitment take priority. We wouldn't have been there then if Mother hadn't been going away. And yet I owe this man so much. My grandparents had been my soft place to fall for all of my childhood after my father walked out.

'Do you remember your great-grandad?' I said to Ben as he climbed into the front with me.

'I remember him being at Granny's bungalow a long time ago. I remember he used to sit in the armchair by the fireplace and he liked Murray Mints, but that's all. I don't really know much about him.'

'He used to be a teacher like Granny. My grandmother was a teacher too. She taught the piano similar to Jacqui - only her pupils came to her house. My grandfather taught Latin in a boys' grammar school.'

'I've heard of Latin. Isn't that what the ancient Romans used to speak? Why did boys have to learn it? What's a grammar school?'

I laughed. 'Schools have changed a lot since Grandad started teaching. Girls and boys often went to different kinds of secondary schools. Schools weren't grouped together as academies in those days. Granny says The Sycamores used to be a girls' boarding school. Latin wasn't taught at the school I went to, but there's a few schools that still teach it now.'

'It's no good, Mummy, you've lost me.' He rolled his eyes and waved his hand back over his head.

'Another time,' I said, laughing.

'Tell me about your grandad and you.'

'Do you know, he was always such good fun. I bet he was a brilliant teacher. It was him that taught me to drive and, when I went to university, he and my grandma bought me my first car. It was a pale green Volvo V40. I can't tell you how much I loved that little car. It gave me freedom, you see? It made me very popular too, I got lots of invitations.'

'I get it, you mean so you could give people lifts.'

'Exactly. I sometimes used to be the only one who came home sober. Grandad said there was a condition to being given the car: I had to promise not to drink and drive.'

'You don't often drink alcohol anyway, do you?'

'No, I suppose I never got into the habit.'

'Jake's daddy drinks a lot.'

This was a revelation. 'Really?'

'He was a bit "merry" at the barbecue; that's what Jake's Mummy called it anyway. They had an argument because she didn't want him to open another bottle of wine after Owen and his family went home, but he still opened one and they'd already had loads.'

'Possibly it was because he'd had such an enjoyable evening. Some adults do that sometimes.'

'Maybe, but Jake told me his daddy gets "merry" every night.'

I wasn't expecting that. It certainly wasn't something Alice had ever mentioned.

It had turned two o'clock and there were still no other cars arriving. 'I suppose we'd better go in. There's a door open over there; shall we see if it's a way in?'

The door led straight into a large kitchen. I ought to have guessed from the several large roll topped bins outside.

'Can I help you?' asked a man in a chef's black and white check outfit. He was wiping away spills from the shiny stainless steel surface of the central island.

'Sorry, we thought this might be a shortcut. Where's the main entrance?'

'No problem, you can get in this way. I'll show you. You must have parked in the staff car park. It doesn't matter, but the visitors' car park is at the front. You drove in through the tradesman's entrance.' He laughed. 'Not quite as grand as the front.'

He took us through a door that led straight into a dining room and through an archway into a sitting room and then through into reception.

'This is Philip, our General Manager. I'll leave you in his capable hands.'

'How do you do?' Philip shook my hand. 'I see you've met David, our chef? You'll get the chance to sample some of his delicious pastries a little later. I don't think we've met before? Do you have a relative living with us already or are you wanting to see what we have to offer?'

'We're here to see my grandfather, Lionel Gadsby? I'm Ruby Lewis and this is my son, Ben.'

'Oh yes, you must be Josephine's daughter. She said to expect you. I've had apologies from her and her brother, your Uncle Kenneth? I gather they're both away on holiday this week.'

He gave us a tour of the music room and another smaller TV lounge and spoke about the facilities and various activities that were available. We returned to the sitting room David had brought us through when we arrived.

'My grandfather doesn't seem to be here.'

'I'll get my wife to take you to him. He likes to have a nap in his room in the afternoons. Would you excuse me?'

A woman came and introduced herself as Clare and took us in a lift up to the next floor. We walked along a wide sweeping corridor. There was grey patterned carpet on the floor, photographs of famous gardens on the walls between the doors and a table with a huge display of asters in front of a window at the end. Clare tapped on the door bearing a nameplate saying Lionel D Gadsby. There was no reply, so she popped her head around the door and stepped into the room.

'One moment,' she said.

'What's the D stand for?' whispered Ben.

'Daybrook. It was his mother's maiden name,' I whispered back wondering why we were whispering. The surroundings seemed to demand that of us.

Clare opened the door wider for us. 'He's awake. Come on in.'

My grandfather was sitting in an armchair by an open window, looking much frailer than I remembered him. He was wearing headphones and seemed not to notice us go in.

'Afternoon, Lionel,' said Clare, taking off his headphones. 'It's your granddaughter and great-grandson come to see you.'

He turned and beamed a smile of happy recognition. My first impulse was to smile back as I was flooded with his familiar warmth, until I realised that his pleasure came from seeing Clare, not me.

'Are you going to go out into the sunshine and talk to them?' Clare asked encouragingly.

He looked at Ben and I as if seeing strangers. 'How do you do? It's very nice to meet you, but would you mind? I'm listening to Afternoon Drama on the wireless. It's an Agatha Christie.' He took the headphones from Clare and replaced them on his head.

'Sorry. He has good days and bad days with his memory. Why don't you come with me, young man? I'll take you to see our new fish pond and we can give your Mum a few minutes to sit with your great-grandad. Are you interested in fish?'

'As a matter of fact, I am,' said Ben with the knowledgeable air of someone given access to privileged information. 'Our neighbour's an expert and he's been teaching me about them. I saw the pool outside when we went through the dining room. It's brilliant.'

'Don't wander off,' I said.

'I'll keep my eye on him Mrs Lewis, don't worry,' Clare reassured me.

Grandad seemed not to notice I was still there. I looked around his room and recognised some of the furnishings from my grandparents' home. There was a photograph of their wedding on the dresser. It had been taken in black and white, but had been colourised, which gave it an incongruous, unnatural quality. I remember it hanging in their hallway. It represented some of my most treasured memories, days spent in the sanctuary of my grandparents' care.

I thought back to when I used to sit at the table in their dayroom, polishing their silver tea service. I was transported back to a time when I felt safe and loved. I could almost smell the petrol-like aroma of the polish and feel again the satisfaction of buffing until the silver was gleaming. It was a chore regarded as mine whenever I went to stay. That and popping the peas that I'd helped to pick from the garden, from their shells. Or holding skeins of knitting wool wrapped around my outstretched hands, dipping and lifting my arms, allowing the yarn to be pulled free by my grandmother as she wound it into balls. Or helping my grandfather clear snow from the pathway. Or raking the grass cuttings after he'd mowed the lawn. They were jobs I loved doing, satisfying, innocent and familiar.

I lived with my grandparents for several months after my father left and stayed with them often when Mother was away on one of her many courses or studying for her doctorate. I was well into my teens before she was home more often and even then she would be away giving lecture tours. It was only with the hindsight of adulthood that I realised Mother had been depressed and unable to cope in those first months of readjusting. Why do we not discuss it, even now?

'What's that you've got there?' said my grandfather, putting the headphones around his neck and holding out his hands towards the photo. I always loved his hands with his long elegant fingers when I was a child. He used them with the grace of an artist. I'd especially liked to watch him as he held a pen or a fork or turned the pages of a book. They were old hands now, with loose skin, age spots and prominent veins, but I saw they were still deft and capable as he took the photograph from me.

'It was on your dresser, Grandad.'

He studied the picture, his hands trembling a little. He traced the outline of the couple with his finger and smiled fondly. 'Who are they? Do I know them?' It was upsetting that for me he was so instantly recognisable and familiar, while for him I was locked away in some hidden compartment of his brain.

Mother and Uncle Kenneth take it in turns to come and see him every week, I thought as I stepped out onto the terrace in search of Ben. What do they say to him? Has he forgotten them too?

Ben spotted me first and came running over.

'Guess what? Robert and Nancy are here. We're sitting over there, look.' He pointed to a group of tables by the pool outside in the sunshine where visitors and residents had gathered to tuck into the refreshments. I smiled politely, suppressing the groan that begged to surface. My cousin Robert stood and waved me over, then greeted me with a perfunctory kiss on the cheek. His new wife, Nancy, made no move to acknowledge me; she was hiding behind dark sunglasses so it was difficult to read what she was thinking.

'What a lovely surprise,' I said in an effort to hide my ambivalence. 'How was St Tropez? I trust the weather was as gorgeous in the South of France as it's been here.'

'The less said about the honeymoon the better,' Robert snapped, glancing at Nancy and taking her hand. 'We came back early.' Nancy said nothing. 'There's food inside. You two go and grab something and then join us.'

'I waited for you Mummy, but I've seen what's on offer. It's smakkeruby yumminess.'

We went inside to the table of sandwiches and nibbles. David, the chef we'd met earlier, was serving.

'Help yourselves,' he said, handing us plates with paper napkins. 'It's taken three of us all morning to prepare this spread, it needs eating. Don't let me down.' He winked at Ben. 'I'm relying on you to polish it all off.' He pointed to the next table with desserts. 'I recommend the chocolate mousse. It's my speciality and a favourite with the residents.'

Robert had his arm around Nancy when we went back outside, but the friction between them was palpable. We resorted to polite conversation about the food. I had the distinct impression that Nancy didn't like me. We'd only met once before at the wedding, and even then it had been a fairly brief introduction. Nancy is Robert's third wife. He is forty-eight and she's twenty; younger than all three of his daughters from his previous marriages. Robert already has two grandchildren.

Is Ben just observing, I wondered, or is he feeling uncomfortable too? How do I do the detachment thing without making a judgement?

Ben was enjoying the chocolate mousse with strawberries, making sure that each spoonful held a portion of mousse and a single slice of strawberry. Oh dear, does he get that from me? Have I already programmed him to be ordered and methodical? Am I inadvertently stunting his creativity? I felt awkward and anxious and self-conscious. Not again. Not now. Remember to breathe. I was much happier simply avoiding fraught situations like that.

'It's really nice here,' I offered, trying to break the tension. 'I'd no idea it would be so pleasant. It's more like a four star hotel than a nursing home.'

'So it should be,' retorted Robert, 'the amount it's costing. It's almost £4000 a month for the old guy to live here.' I was stunned as much by my cousin's attitude as by the cost. 'Yeah, that shocked you, didn't it? Kenneth has power of attorney so he gets to sort out all the finances. You won't be getting the large inheritance you're expecting, that's for sure.'

I felt as if I'd been slapped. Whatever I replied it would sound as if I was grasping when an inheritance was something I neither cared about nor had ever considered.

Ben put his spoon down and said softly, 'This is a lovely place to be and Great-Grandad's happy here.'

Robert opened his mouth as if to reply, but then seemed to change his mind.

'Please excuse me,' said Nancy, speaking for the first time. 'I need to go to the loo.'

She got up to leave. Robert looked concerned.

'Go with her, Ruby.'

'But I don't need to…'

'Please.' It was an order, not a request.

I did as I was commanded, feeling as if I was leaving my son in the lion's den.

Nancy had taken off her sunglasses and was standing by the washbasins looking into the mirror. She'd clearly been crying and was visibly shaky. She replaced the sunglasses as soon as she heard me come in and started to wash her hands, but it was too late, she'd already been discovered.

'What happened, Nancy? Are you alright?'

'Oh, I saw a big spider and it scared me,' Nancy replied, not very convincingly.

I realised that what I'd taken for indifference and judgement in Nancy was actually insecurity. I didn't want to probe, so decided I would do what Jess does: create a space for Nancy to open up if she wished to.

'It's a shame about your honeymoon.'

It worked; Nancy seemed to crumple.

'Did he send you to check up on me? I expect you think I'm stupid. I know what it must seem like.'

What would Jess do now? She wouldn't say anything. She'd just wait and ooze empathy, I thought and remained silent.

'He gets so jealous. He thinks other men are eyeing me up all the time and he thinks I'm encouraging them. The men on the beach and in the hotel. Just now, in the dining hall, I smiled at the man who gave me a plate and Robert thought I was chatting him up. I was just saying thank you, that's all.'

'Have you talked to him about how it makes you feel?'

Nancy shook her head. 'He thinks other men won't be able to resist me so I shouldn't look at them. It's a compliment really; it's because he thinks I'm beautiful.'

'It's not okay to treat you like that though. What about respect and trust?'

There was a thump on the outer door. 'Are you still in there, girls? You've been ages, what on earth are you doing?'

'Just coming,' Nancy called. 'Please don't say anything,' she whispered. 'You'll only make things worse.'

We stepped out to an impatient Robert. 'We're going. Have you got everything, darling?'

Nancy nodded and went back to not speaking. I noted the controlling way my cousin grasped his new wife's hand. I wanted to object on Nancy's behalf, but instead just said, 'Where's Ben?'.

'That's a turn up, your old mater getting married again, what?'

'Oh, you know about that?'

'Sure, she introduced us to the poor sod at our wedding, didn't she, Nance? Better be off then.' He delivered another insincere kiss on my cheek and waved a twenty pound note in my face. 'Here, give this to the boy for his birthday.'

What I really wanted to say was, 'Stuff it,' what I actually said for the sake of politeness was, 'Thank you'. *Politeness! That's how people like him get away with intimidating others. Doesn't he realise how difficult he makes it for people to like him?*

'Bye,' said Nancy. 'Nice meeting you again.'

'Aren't you going to see Grandad before you go?'

'No point. He doesn't even know what day it is anymore. We only came to please Kenneth so he wouldn't keep droning on at me for not visiting. Well, honour's satisfied now. Make sure you tell your mother I was here.'

'Oh, but... '

'Payback time.'

'I don't understand. Why are you so cross?' His sudden anger came from nowhere. What was the point of being there if he wasn't going to see Grandad?

'It's obvious. I never wanted to come here in the first place, then when I get here you're dominating Lionel as usual and the sodding cook's chatting up my wife.'

'What do you mean, "dominating"?'

'Don't pretend you don't know what I'm talking about. Tell me when either of the grandparents ever bothered to squeeze time for me into their poor-helpless-little-Ruby-her-daddy's-gone-and-left-her crusade.'

I flinched from the bitter sting of his words.

'They ignored the fact that they had a grandson as well as their precious Golden Girl so why should I make an effort now? Got a problem with that? Shattered your cosy fantasies of the idyllic loving grandparents, has it?'

He was visibly shaking as the venom poured from his mouth. Nancy moved closer to him, putting a supportive hand on his chest. I felt the ice of her accusatory scowl.

'Poor Little Princess, mustn't upset her. Find her a sticking plaster, someone.'

He stared at me with contempt and I returned his stare, determined not to be the first to look away.

'Mary doted on me. Let me have anything I wanted, always buying me treats and spending time with me, giving me hugs. Sometimes I used to stay over and go night fishing with Lionel. We were really close.'

'Robert, I–'

'Don't interrupt, I've not finished. It was nice. I was happy. I was special. That was until Alec upped and left and your fucking mother went to pieces. Suddenly it was all Ruby this, Ruby that and I stopped existing.'

'You're exaggerating. It wasn't like that–'

'You think? My thirteenth birthday was on the Sunday and we were all supposed to be going out for lunch, me, Kenneth, Carmel, Lionel and Mary, to celebrate. I was looking forward to it, you do at that age, it's important, a landmark. Instead of that, Mary phones up at the last minute and announces they can't come because Alec's walked out and Josephine turned up on their doorstep in a state and dumped you on them.'

I wanted to remind him it was thirty five years ago, but thought better of it.

'Get it now? Penny beginning to drop? Then when Mary got ill it was me who was sent to boarding school. Should have been you.'

'I'd no idea you felt like this–'

'Don't give me that crap. You knew exactly what you were doing. It was deliberate, like you were sticking two fingers up to me and saying "She's my grandma now, she doesn't care about you anymore".'

'I was four when my father left.'

'What does being four have to do with it? You've always been a manipulative little bitch. Well, I've said it now. If you'd have kept your mouth shut instead of telling me what to do... I expect you'll go crawling to Josephine and I'll get it in the neck from Kenneth. What's new?'

I tried to make sense of what he was saying. It made no sense. Our grandparents loved both of us.

'Come on Nance,' he said eventually. 'I'm done here.'

They turned and strode away hand in hand. I watched their straight backs as they rounded the corner out of sight.

I didn't move. My breath came in gulps. My temples throbbed. I wanted to run up to my grandfather and protect him. I wanted to grab Ben and go home. I wanted to stop the hurt tearing at my throat and lungs. I wanted not to have gone to that place.

A young couple threw me a courteous smile of acknowledgement as they went to pass by. The woman looked concerned and came over.

'Is anything the matter?'

'No, um, yes, it's nothing... I was just told something that gave me a bit of a shock, that's all.'

'Shall I get someone?'

'No, really I'm fine. I'll be fine. Thank you. Honestly. Thank you, really.'

'Well, if you're sure? Maybe you should sit down for a few minutes, get your breath. It doesn't feel right, leaving you like this.'

'That's really kind of you. I just need a few moments on my own.'

The couple nodded, but seemed reluctant to go. I wanted to scream at them to leave me alone. I smiled feebly. They returned my smile and tentatively continued on their way.

I couldn't decide what to do. I made my way back into the Ladies and looked at my reflection in the mirror over the washbasin just as Nancy had done what by then seemed like a lifetime ago. The shock of Robert's attack was made worse by the off-handedness of Nancy's complicity. It felt like a betrayal from this woman I barely knew.

I'd trusted Robert to stay with Ben. I was concerned about where he might be. I looked into my eyes glaring back at me. I heard Mother's often repeated mantra after Paul died: "What you can't change you have to put behind you and move forward. It's the only way." For Ben's sake I needed to get a grip on myself. The familiar shutters came down. I smoothed my eyebrows with my fingertip, ran my tongue over my lips, took a deep breath and then went in search of Ben.

The sun had gone in and the sky was overcast. Wind was flapping the canvas parasols over the tables. I went into the sitting room that David, the chef, had taken us through when we arrived, but there was no sign of him. I found him sitting at a table in the dining room, playing cards with an elderly woman in a wheelchair.

'Hi, Mummy,' he called. 'Iris, this is my mum; you can call her Ruby. Mummy this is my new friend, Iris. She knows Great-Grandad.'

'Lionel's granddaughter,' said the warm, smiley Iris. She had years of laughter and happiness etched into the wrinkles on her face. 'He told me about you. You speak lots of languages.'

'But he didn't recognise me.'

'It's only his meds, he'll remember you next time. You'll have to organise it so that you come before he takes them, like your mam and your uncle do. I've met your mam's young man too, by the way. Very nice. Good job for her I'm not twenty years younger.'

'Iris's been teaching me how to play poker.'

'Poker!'

'Absolutely, he's a natural.' Iris grew more serious. 'He's a very special boy, your son. I mean very special. You mark my words. He's a gift.'

I shivered. 'Thank you,' I replied, unsure of what else to say.

I felt as if my body had been drained of blood, my legs trembled, my mouth was dry and I felt dizzy and light-headed. Iris's words felt like some sort of threat. I didn't want Ben to be marked out as "very special". I didn't want him to be a gift. It sounded menacing, like some sort of omen that something catastrophic was about to unfold.

It was another hot sticky night despite the cloud cover. I dipped uncomfortably in and out of sleep. I thought I heard a sound outside, but it became part of the dream I was having where I was presented to Jess, only I thought she was the Queen. I heard a pulsing buzz. Jess, the Queen, was standing in front of a weather map and pressing the remote control to change the graphics once, twice, three times in short loud bursts.

It wasn't Jess, it was the doorbell. I sat bolt upright, suddenly wide awake. I turned the clock towards me – I liked to keep it facing away from me at night so I wouldn't spend sleepless hours constantly checking it – it said two forty-four.

I felt my heart thumping in my throat. Something must have happened to Mrs Marlow. Or Mother; her plane's crashed and there are no survivors. Scenarios rattled in my mind as I scrambled in the dark to pull the curtains back at the same time as I grabbed my cotton dressing gown. The doorbell buzzed again.

I flung open the window and looked down. It had started to rain. Mel stepped out of the shadowy porch into the steady drizzle and looked up at me, clearly distressed.

'Sorry to wake you, Rubes. You've got to help me. I've not got nowhere else to go.'

'Well you can't come here, Mel, not after what you did. It's the middle of the night, for goodness sake.'

'I know, I know. I said I'm sorry, right? I've been chucked out the squat. I need somewhere to stay. Just till the morning?'

'Oh sugar lumps, I must be crazy, I'll come down. Be patient and keep quiet. I'm going to check on Ben first.'

I closed the window. Now what was I supposed to do? I couldn't just leave the wretched girl standing at the front door in the rain, who knows what she'd do next? I tiptoed into Ben's room. Unbelievably, he was still fast asleep. I closed his door again quietly, braced myself, went downstairs and opened the front door, determined not to be taken in by a hard luck story. Mel was holding a much-blooded rag to her nose and her right eye was puffy and almost closed, an indication of the bruising on its way.

'Shush,' I said sharply, pointing upstairs where Ben was asleep. I led the girl into the kitchen. 'You look a mess. Sit down and tell me what happened.'

'There was a fight.'

'I can see that. Did Ed do this to you?'

'No, not Ed. It was Cat.'

'Who's Cat?'

'Ed's girlfriend.'

'Hang on. I thought you were Ed's girlfriend?'

'I'm his... other girlfriend. Cat was in Brighton seeing her mates. We weren't expecting her back till next week, but Bitch Fliss, the bitch, phoned her and told her me and Ed'd got it together so she came back and went ballistic.'

I thought for a moment, weighing up my options. 'This is what we're going to do, Mel. We're going to phone your mother. Right now. Don't argue or you'll be out on the street.'

I was expecting excuses, prevarication, histrionics. Instead Mel started to cry, real tears of misery. 'Okay then,' she said, 'first thing in the morning, I promise, but I've not got no credit left on my phone.'

'No. Now. I'll phone. I don't trust you not to pretend to call.' I fetched a pen and notepad and pushed them across to where Mel was sitting. 'Give me the number. Remind me of your surname again? Catch something?'

'Kaczmarek.'

The phone rang out, I suppressed my nerves, wanting to stay in charge, but I could feel my heart thumping. After a handful of rings someone picked up the receiver.

'Mela? Mela, is that you?' said an anxious woman's voice.

'No, Mrs Kaczmarek, but she's here with me and she's safe. My name is Ruby Lewis. Mela's going to stay with me tonight, but she'd like you to fetch her in the morning.'

'Oh thank God, thank God. Thank you so much. You've no idea how worried we've been. Can I speak to her?'

I passed the phone to Mel and put some milk in a saucepan to make us both a hot drink.

It was another hour before we turned in for the night and all I wanted to do was sleep. My dream life showed no mercy, however, when my chattering mind eventually succumbed to sleep. In contrast to my usual all-consuming dreams, I was both an observer yet peculiarly still aware of my reactions.

I saw myself on a soft white sandy beach with rhythmic waves chasing playfully onto the shoreline from a vast sparkling blue ocean. I thought I'd died or that I was being shown my death. The sun was warm and wholesome. Somewhere in the distance Acker Bilk was playing Stranger on the Shore on his clarinet. I hadn't heard it for years, but I remembered how much my grandmother had loved it when I was growing up. There was a figure walking towards me, at first just a speck in the distance, in no particular hurry, letting the waves lap over her feet. As the observer, I knew it was Mel. As the participant, I felt no surprise.

'Are we going to torment her?' Mel called out to someone out of sight as she drew closer.

I turned to see who she was addressing. Sitting nonchalantly on a rock was a demon. Waxy red skin, black rimmed eyes, horns and a long sweeping tail with an inverted suit-of-cards spade at the tip. It was sitting cross-legged and looked frankly bored. It finished the apple it was eating and threw the core into the air, watching it explode in a ball of fire.

'She's been doing a perfectly good job of tormenting herself.' Steam was trailing from its lips. Its voice was Robert's.

I looked closer and the demon's face kept blurring alarmingly into Robert's morphing back again in a continuous loop.

'Maybe we should have a little fun though. What do you think?'

'Yeah. What shall we do?' Mel rubbed her hands together in expectation.

'She used to like collecting shells for her grandad. Perhaps she'd like to collect some for him now? Give her a bucket'.

Mel was instantly holding a metal bucket, which she thrust into my hand. 'Only whole shells though, no broken ones,' she demanded.

'Why of course,' said Robert/the demon.

'There's a hole in the bucket,' I protested. I could hear "Many Voices" somewhere in the distance singing "There's a hole in my bucket" as if it were an oratorio.

'Get on with it,' said Robert/the demon impatiently. 'It's already a quarter to.'

I looked around. 'There aren't any shells.'

'Oh, there aren't any shells, poor Rubes,' Mel mimicked.

'Well, I'm always one to oblige a princess.' Robert/the demon, beckoned Mel to join him on the rock. The rock transformed into Mother's garden swing with its gaudy floral awning, then raised itself onto stilts high above the sand. Meanwhile, the sand sucked in the sea with a rumbling slurp and what had been beach and sea shore was now a boggy quagmire with stranded flapping fish and a scurry of agitated crabs.

'Get digging,' Mel yelled and Robert/the demon's laughter rang out like a blast from a furnace.

I watched as the quagmire begin to swallow me and I sank deeper and deeper into the slime and mud. It was already up to my chest.

'Help me. Please, help me,' I called out, but Robert/the demon and Mel were sipping green cocktails with cherries on sticks and little paper umbrellas.

'Cheers,' they said, raising their glasses.

Once the mud reached my chin, I had no struggle left in me. I didn't want to fight any more. It was as it was. I didn't care what happened next. It was just another story unfolding. My moment of surrender coincided with the flutter of a candyfloss cloud as it wafted gracefully from the sky and parked beside me. Toby was sitting on the cloud plucking a harp. He was dressed in a long white robe and was sporting a huge pair of wings, the white feathers tipped with gold. He had a golden halo above his head and his smile revealed a set of gold teeth that sparkled in the sunlight.

'Can I be of assistance?' he asked amicably as if passing the time of day. He reached for my hand and pulled me effortlessly from the quagmire on to the cloud with a satisfying shhlopp. The quagmire gurgled its disgust.

Robert/the demon, his face still constantly switching from one to the other, rose onto his cloven hoofs and spat fire at the cloud as it began to glide upwards to the sky. The flames engulfed the cloud, which lost its balance for a moment, until the flames gathered themselves and headed back to their source. A game of ping pong ensued with the fire travelling back and forth from cloud to Robert/the demon again, but with each journey it lost more and more of its blaze until it became no more than a wisp of smoke. Robert/the demon was furious and pushed the hapless Mel into the quagmire.

Meanwhile, the cloud was gathering momentum and floating higher and higher. I couldn't see myself anymore, just Robert/the demon, who reached for a bow and shot a flurry of arrows into the cloud. With each arrow that pierced it, the cloud began to deflate.

Suddenly I saw myself on the cloud. It felt springy and bubbly, not at all as I imagine a cloud ought to feel.

'Sit tight,' said Toby. 'Nothing to worry about; like hair and nails, it'll grow back again.'

And it did.

Just as the cloud drifted to safety out of reach of the arrows, a giant Robert/demon's face appeared from nowhere. 'This isn't the end, I'm not finished yet.'

The face grew larger, much larger than the cloud. It switched from Robert to demon and then to my own face at increasing speed. I felt a rising panic, but Toby was more jovial than I'd ever seen him.

'Blow. If you don't want it, blow it away.'

Why are you hesitating? I thought, exasperated by my dream-self's reluctance. Blow, for goodness' sake.

I began to blow, uncertainly at first, but with more and more conviction as the face drifted languorously away, carried on an air current until it was no more than a dot. I waited for it to disappear. Toby was watching me.

'It's not going to disappear completely. It will probably always be there, unless you decide to call it back and challenge it, but it's where it's manageable. See? It can't affect you from over there.'

'Thank you.'

'You're very welcome. So now you've learned how to surrender and let go. Another homework completed. Well done. Time to get some restful sleep now.'

My lids grew heavy and at last I succumbed.

Sunday 21 July

Mrs Kaczmarek arrived just before midday. She was a tall, dark-haired, striking woman, probably mid-fifties, who introduced herself as Lena. Mel was still asleep in the spare room.

'I'll wake her in a few moments,' I said, 'but can we just chat first? I've something I want to tell you. It's awkward.'

'Is she in trouble again?' Lena clearly expected the answer to be yes.

'There was a bit of bother, but never mind that right now. No, it's not that.' I took a deep breath, 'It's the reason she gave me for why she ran away. It's just that she told me she couldn't talk to you about it… nevertheless I think you ought to know.' I had practised what I was going to say and was grateful that neither Ben nor Mel was around while I said it. It was trickier than I'd envisaged with Mel's mother actually sitting there in my kitchen.

'And what was the reason?'

'She said…look I'll just say it, alright? She gave me the impression that your… boyfriend… was sexually abusing her while you were at school.' It came out in much more of a rush than I'd intended.

Lena nodded. 'It doesn't surprise me, I thought it would be something like that.'

'You mean you already knew?'

'I knew she would have spun you a sob story. She's good at that. Did she also tell you she has two older brothers and a sister?'

'No, she never mentioned siblings. I assumed she was an only child.'

'It's not a good idea to assume anything with Mela. Her dad and I have been married for thirty-two years. There is no question of any abuse, trust me. There is no boyfriend.'

What could I say? I felt more than a little naïve.

'Oh don't worry, you're not the first to be taken in by her and I don't expect you'll be the last. I don't know where she dragged the school teacher story up from in that muddled brain of hers. Don't get me wrong, I'm her mother so it's my job to love her, but sometimes I wonder what it was we did so badly wrong in a previous life that we ended up having a daughter like her. She's been more trouble than all three of the others put together. Her dad and I are publicans. We run a pub in Cromer.'

'Cromer?'

'Yes, it's on the east coast, in Norfolk. We used to run The Hearty Goodfellow here in Hegley until a couple or three years ago. Mela grew up here, you see. We should have known this is where she'd be. She was supposed to be going to stay with her sister in St Albans; needless to say she never arrived. The thing is she sent Kristina, that's her sister, a text from my phone to say she wasn't going. Krissy thought the text was from me and Mela was still at home. Meanwhile, we thought she was at Krissy's – she'd deleted the message and Krissy's reply, of course. What with one thing and another, we're so busy right now, it wasn't until last weekend that any of us realised she'd gone missing again.'

'Again? She's done something like this before then?'

'You could say. It was London last time. Even the police aren't interested anymore now she's turned eighteen and she's done it so often. It doesn't stop us worrying though. I'm sorry you've been put to all this trouble. I think it's time to wake her up. She has some explaining to do.'

The next hour or so was pretty uncomfortable, with tears and recriminations, apologies and promises, not really conducive to my spending several hours being creative with German dog biscuits. Mel's right eye was now completely closed and the swelling was augmented by impressive deep red and purple bruising so Lena decided they would have to visit A&E before they could begin their eight hour journey back to Norfolk.

'Let's just hope they don't keep us waiting all afternoon or we'll end up having to stay with Krissy in St Albans overnight. I warn you now, your dad is not going to be best pleased.'

Lena had already made clear how inconvenient it was taking the busiest day of the week away from the pub, particularly as it was the holiday season and they also had six sets of B&B guests to cater for on top of their usual Sunday carvery.

After they'd left, I didn't like to think of the conversation mother and daughter would be having in private or the promised reception that Mel would have from her father when she arrived back home.

I went up to strip the spare bed so the sheets could wash while Ben and I had a late lunch, a way of symbolically drawing a line under my encounters with Mel. I wanted to cleanse myself of the whole saga first then I could at least attempt to settle down to my work for the rest of the day and probably the early hours of Monday morning. As I was about to leave the spare room with the bedding under my arm, I noticed the digital clock from the bedside table was missing.

I had yet another disturbed night, unable to sleep in spite of working on the translation until gone three, because of the thoughts going round and around in my head. I was finding it difficult to cope with so many experiences in such a short time;

as if I was on red alert waiting for the next explosion. If this was Cameron's doing, which I rather suspected at the time it must have been, then he was bombarding me with too much too soon. How was it helping me to sleep when it was keeping me awake?

I tried to sort my head out.

I thought wistfully of my grandfather and how protective he and my grandmother had been as I was growing up. I felt again the aching sadness of seeing such a change in him and the gnawing guilt of putting off visiting for so long. And Robert and his bellicose outburst about my relationship with them? I shuddered. I had no idea what that was about or where it came from. What did he mean, they had no time for him? It wasn't true. I remembered how much he upset our grandmother with his rudeness and his behaviour sometimes. Mother said it was because he was a teenage boy and his parents were too soft.

And what of his relationship with Nancy? In spite of Nancy's sudden cold shoulder – fear of Robert probably – I felt a lot of sympathy for her. I despair about their future happiness together. Was this typical of him, but I'd not noticed before? What a pig-headed monster he's become. I'd always felt uncomfortable around him; let's face it he was a bully, but I'd put it down to my self-doubts and his self-confidence. Actually self-confident people often made me feel that way, even Jess a bit.

Another thing I did, I recognised, was to assume that Nancy was being aloof towards me because she didn't think I was worth bothering with, when all the time it was Nancy's own insecurity that made her give that impression. Quite ironic really, my own insecurity made me misinterpret Nancy's insecurity. Come to think of it, I probably gave other people the impression that I was being aloof, when actually I was feeling insecure.

My head was screaming, I was driving myself slowly crazy. You're not helping me, Cameron, with your bloody homeworks. I almost prefer the nightmares to this.

Had I finally said goodbye to Mel and her unpredictable behaviour? What a toll that must be having on her family and it wasn't likely to be something that would change very much any time soon. Was there someone abusing Mel? Mel's parents were clearly run off their feet with their workload. Had Mel actually been telling the truth and was being abused? I remembered I'd believed that part of Mel's story, that hadn't felt like a lie. Even if her mother doesn't have a boyfriend; that bit of her story had seemed authentic. Perhaps someone who worked at the pub, or one of the regulars? Perhaps the running away really was a cry for help? Lena seemed to be too busy to notice when Mel had gone missing for several days. Was she too busy to spend time with her daughter and find out if there was an underlying worry making her keep running off? I flinched at the idea. Was there a lesson in there for me, too? Did I spend enough time with Ben?

The Mel thing happened because I'd been overambitious about the small act of kindness, so it couldn't have been something that Cameron had engineered for me to experience. What then? I was reminded about what Ben had said when he differentiated between an action and the consequences: I'd hurt Toby through thoughtlessness and Jordan Baker had caused Paul's accident through thoughtlessness. Ben wasn't saying that the consequences, the outcomes, were the same, only that they had both been caused by lack of attention. I was beginning to sound like Jess; that's the sort of observation she makes.

The threads of the last days' hotchpotch of experiences were starting to make some kind of weird sense. Cameron wasn't engineering the situations because it didn't actually matter what the situation was, there was always something to be learned. Oddly, I was beginning to understand what the homeworks were about. Maybe I had to wake up to how I was choosing to behave first, before I could sleep without nightmares?

I gave a long sigh of release and decided I'd resolved what was keeping me awake. In an effort to invite sleep, I turned off the lamp and tried to get comfortable.

I'd hardly shut my eyes when my tangle of thoughts began thundering again. How had I not grasped that the man I now vaguely recollect Mother introducing me to at the wedding, was someone significant? How come everyone else seemed to know? Hmm. I remembered I'd seen Cameron among the guests and I thought he was stalking me; that may well explain it. I'd been preoccupied by Cameron's motives. Yes, that did indeed explain it. It was Cameron's fault.

Let me sleep now. Please let me sleep. I'll be tired tomorrow. I don't want to do this now. I don't want to have these thoughts. Just let me sleep.

I closed my eyes again.

And what about Alice and Pete? Does Pete have a drink problem? I'd never even considered that. All this time I've spent envying Alice her charmed life. Why hadn't Alice shared it with me? Did Jess know? Should I mention something? Ask her outright?

Errrgh! I sat up and put the lamp back on. I drew up my knees and wrapped my arms round them.

And then there was Mrs Marlow. What on earth was I going to do about poor Mrs Marlow?

It was all too much. I got up, made myself some hot milk and took it into the conservatory. I would have liked to have gone out into the garden, but it was raining quite heavily so I sat instead in the shadows looking out, listening to the steady pitter-patter as it fell on to the glass roof.

An idea took shape as I sipped the milk, an idea which would make such a difference to the next few weeks. Usually I looked forward to spending August in France with Ben. I hadn't even begun to make preparations yet this year. Ever since Ben was a toddler we'd camped at a site in the Dordogne owned by my friends, Felice and Luc. It had been an ideal arrangement because I was able to continue working part time, but still keep an eye on Ben playing safely with my friends' three children. Felice and Luc in turn were grateful that they didn't have to worry about juggling childcare while they were busy with the campsite. It's a site used in the main by French holidaymakers who return every year, so for a few short weeks we were part of a community of friends. It also meant, of course, that Ben had to learn to get by in French before he even started school, but that was hardly a disadvantage.

However, this year I was not sure I wanted to spend so long away. I particularly wanted to be around for Mrs Marlow for one thing. Maybe we could just go to France for a fortnight, or… alternatively… Felice's children could come over and stay with us. We might be a bit cramped, but I'd make room somehow. Now that was something to think about. And maybe… what if?… how about if I also told Dominique I can't take on any more work before September?

I felt a surge of energy; the kind that comes when something falls into place and feels right. Nursing a long-forgotten sense of adventurous joie de vivre, I was able to return to bed and finally escape into slumber.

Monday 22 July

Yet again Mrs Marlow didn't respond when I rang the doorbell. The bags of food I'd left out had both been collected, presumably by Mrs Marlow, but there was no acknowledgement. I phoned the hospital straight after breakfast and was, as before, assured that Mr Marlow was comfortable, but they could only discuss the details with Mrs Marlow. Patiently I explained, once more, the situation with Mrs Marlow and my concerns about her not answering the door, but was told, equally patiently and for the third time, that Social Services had been informed. I guessed the hospital staff were now seeing me as a nuisance. Quite how Social Services were going to persuade Mrs Marlow to respond to their visit wasn't clear. I toyed with fantasies about offering them my garden fence to jump over and left another bag with more milk and bread, some cheese, a banana, a slice of apple pie and a further request to get in touch.

I tried to put it out of my mind and broached the subject of cancelling the holiday with Ben as he poured milk onto his Shreddies.

He was enthusiastic. 'Does that mean that instead of going to Nottingham next week Harry can come here again? Hey, we'll have to teach him French so's he can talk to Nicolas, Enzo and Camille. Can we put the tent up in the garden and sleep out in it?'

I laughed. 'Yes, if you're the one to break the news to Ungrampa that his perfect lawn's going to get wrecked.'

It had to be a working day, so I was thankful that Ben had Harry to play with. The rain continued relentlessly, putting paid to the boys' hopes of building a den in the garden and by lunchtime they were already bored. Left to his own devices Ben is happy to read or draw or do puzzles when he's stuck indoors, probably Harry is too, but none of those pastimes appealed when there was a friend to share with.

I took some readymade puff pastry out of the freezer. 'Ever made palmiers?' I said to Harry.

'No, I don't know what they are.'

'They're yummy scrummy Rubyliciousness,' said Ben by way of explanation. 'Shall we make them with cinnamon or with parmesan?'

'How about,' I paused for dramatic effect, then drumming my hands on the table, 'best of both worlds? Some of each.' I was delighted by my light-heartedness and the boys' response.

Ben busied himself showing his friend how to make the pastry treats, but I stayed in the kitchen with them anyway, basking in the pleasure and satisfaction of a day of treasured ordinariness, free of incidents and challenges. The way Ben leans his head to one side whenever he's concentrating on something practical reminds me of Paul. It made me smile. What an odd behaviour for his son to have inherited. The palmiers turned out rather too thick because the boys were too impatient to let the pastry completely defrost making it difficult to roll out, but they didn't care. They were more than happy with their creations and asked to take photos of the finished delicacies before they sampled them.

'Here's a thought,' I suggested. 'Why don't you keep a holiday scrapbook with pictures and photos of all the things you do? You can use PowerPoint now you're the experts at it after all that work with Mr Gupta on your Egypt projects. Actually you could send a copy of it to Granny, Ben, instead of writing her that letter if you want to.'

It was decided.

'Will you take photos of my birthday adventure then?'

'Of course.'

Ben, Jake and Owen had been to the Winnersley Forest Experience with the Cubs during the May half term. They'd had an "amazing", "wonderful" time, which they'd talked about endlessly for days. Ben had persuaded me that his tenth birthday should be celebrated with an Adventure Day spent there with his closest friends. Harry was invited too, of course, but isn't a Cub and hadn't been there before.

'Show Harry the website while I sort the washing out,' I said, 'so he knows what to expect.'

When Matthew arrived to collect his son he was bombarded with stories of the day. I could see his enthusiasm was disguising how he was really feeling though.

'Boys, boys. I give in. You can play on the Xbox while Matthew takes five and has a cup of tea. Yes, Ben, it's extra.'

Ben was thrilled. His time on the Xbox is normally rationed and he'd already spent two hours on it the previous day whilst I talked with Lena Kaczmarek and Mel.

'Is something worrying you?' I said once the boys were settled in the lounge. 'You look troubled.'

'That's very perceptive of you. I was trying to hide it. I try to keep work separate from being a dad, but I've just spent all afternoon attending an RTC on the Winnersley bypass. The south bound road's completely blocked and will be for a couple more hours yet.'

'Was anyone hurt?'

'Two people badly injured and three fatalities. It'll be on the local TV news I expect. A toddler and his grandparents. A caravan jack-knifed across the carriageway and hit the Peugeot with the three of them in it, then they were hit again by the car behind them. They didn't have a chance.' He put his head in his hands. 'You never get used to accidents like that. You put on a professional front for those involved, of course, but it gets to you. Laura, the officer who was with me when we came to your BIP– sorry, burglary in progress, had to tell the driver of the caravan about the deaths.'

'That's how my husband, Paul, was killed.' I spoke quietly, almost to myself, remembering how I was told of Paul's accident. Matthew looked at me, but didn't speak. 'In a road accident. He was knocked off his bike and thrown across the windscreen of the car that pulled out in front of him.' I shuddered with the startling realisation of the horror of that for Jordan Baker; no wonder he was haunted by the memory of it.

'I'm sorry.'

'I met the man who killed him. Only last Wednesday, actually. He wrote to me and asked if we could meet. Ben came too.'

'Did it help?'

'Yes, I think it did. He wanted to meet before, after it first… but I couldn't face… Ben never knew his dad. The accident happened before he was born.'

'It never goes away, something like that, does it?'

'Ben said you lost your wife too?'

'Nineteen months ago, yes.'

'So you understand what it's like.'

'Yvonne wasn't in an accident. She died when she had an epileptic fit.'

'How awful.'

'I got a phone call at work from Harry's school to say she hadn't turned up to collect him and she wasn't answering the phone. I knew straightaway. I knew. She'd been having fits since she was a child and they were mostly under control, but she was at home by herself. If I'd have been there, do you know what I'm saying, if someone had been there…. '

'I didn't know people could die of epilepsy.'

'It's unusual, but it happens. Like cot deaths. Rare and no one really knows why. She was on the waiting list for a seizure alert dog. It could have, might have, saved her.' He paused. 'It must have been the same for you? Starts off like a normal day, nothing special, you get up, go to work and then out of the blue your whole world collapses and it's never going to be the same again.'

'Yes. It was the suddenness of it that got to me when Paul died. You don't think anything like that will ever happen to you. No one else really understood; their lives still carried on as normal. They tried to be kind, but that made it worse. They tiptoed round me and I didn't want that.'

'Me too.'

'I was lost, I didn't want to believe it had happened. It made me feel as if I could never trust anyone or anything again.'

'I know what you mean, it seemed impossible that I could ever rebuild my life. I had to make myself for Harry.'

We fell silent for a moment.

'At least Harry had known his mother, but he took it very badly,' Matthew said thoughtfully. 'Well, of course he did. It changed him completely. He'd never been particularly outgoing before, but after she died he just withdrew into a shell.'

'Is that why he was bullied, do you think?'

'Oh I'm sure of it. I had to get special permission from the Force to work only Monday to Friday day shifts so I could be there for him, but keep working. Emma, Yvonne's sister, offered to take him to school and pick him up. It meant him moving schools though. Emma lives this side of Hegley you see; we live out on the Manor Farm Estate. The kids at Manor Farm were his friends and they supported him. It was a shock when he moved to Hegley Lawns and found he was target practice.' He paused to reflect. 'Mr Gupta rang me about the shoe incident. Harry never actually told anyone about what had been happening before then. It's heart breaking. He was trying to spare me.'

'We have a lot in common, and so do our boys. It's good they're friends.'

'Thanks for that. It helps talking about it. And thanks for today too.' He smiled. 'Hopefully I won't arrive here such a nervous wreck tomorrow.'

'Nessun problema. Mi ha aiutato anche.'

Tuesday 23 July

The rain had more or less cleared by breakfast on Tuesday morning and there was another warm start to the day, although the sky was still overcast.

'Let's hope we get spells and not patches for my birthday,' said Ben.

'Oh absolutely, I couldn't agree more. And it's good to know that at least one of us knows what we're talking about.'

'It said on the radio sunny spells with patchy rain.' He giggled.

I grinned. 'I could do with a spell to make Mrs Marlow answer the doorbell,' I said, searching in the fridge for something to tempt the woman in question. 'I'm just going to pop round with these bits and bobs before Harry gets here. Will you be okay by yourself for a few minutes?'

As I approached my neighbour's drive I saw with apprehension that the bag from Monday was still there. On closer inspection, however, I discovered that it was empty apart from the banana loitering at the bottom.

Mental note then, Mrs Marlow doesn't like bananas. After another abortive attempt to persuade the recalcitrant old lady to respond to the doorbell, I decided to take matters into my own hands and contact Social Services directly. I was asked to hold the line while the switchboard operator tried to establish who best to put me through to. He did his best, but after several frustrating minutes I still wasn't able to speak to the person appointed to explore the Marlows' situation. I had to be content with leaving my details and settle for someone contacting me later in the afternoon.

When Harry arrived, our first task was to set off for the supermarket to shop for the weekly groceries. It was good to have the boys helping me for a change although it took twice as long and cost almost twice as much. We joked about the car tipping backwards and having to drive home using only the back wheels with the bonnet pointing to the sky because of the weight of the shopping we piled into the boot.

'Your mummy's really nice,' I overheard Harry say to Ben as they clambered into the back of the car.

'I know,' Ben replied, 'she's the best.'

'Right boys,' I announced when we arrived back home and finished putting everything away. 'The more I get done today, the more time I'll get to spend with you the rest of the week. So?'

'So,' said Ben taking up the baton, 'our job is to occupy ourselves and let you get on?'

'You goddit, dude. A woman's godda do what a woman's godda do.'

The boys groaned. 'See what I have to put up with?' Ben said to Harry.

'You're as bad as my daddy. He's always putting on funny voices.'

'There is an alternative of course. We can sit around bantering all day, cancel tomorrow's birthday bash and I can catch up with my work then instead.'

I sliced two cantaloupes in half and left them to scrape out the flesh and make smoothies while I set to work in the office. I could hear them chattering and giggling. It was lovely to hear, lovely to have Ben home every day. I smiled to myself at how much my priorities had changed in just a few days. The school holiday with Ben is far too precious to fill the days with working when I don't need to. Usually, even when we're away on holiday, I don't give myself a break. Madness. I counted my blessings that we can afford for me to take the time off.

An hour later I'd cancelled Ben's piano lessons, my Zumba classes, choir and my Italian group until further notice. I decided to carry on with yoga, because it was helping me when I felt anxious. I phoned Felice and invited her children over for August. Felice was delighted to accept. They would put their children on a plane at Bergerac airport (they are sixteen, fifteen and twelve) and we would meet them at Heathrow. I then phoned Dominique to explain that as soon as Meaty Goodness was complete I'd be taking a break until September. I had to leave the message with Sylvie. Dominique was away on holiday for three weeks.

I felt a weight drop from my shoulders. A weight I hadn't realised had been lodging there. A weight that was not welcome to take up residence again.

Just one more task before I could turn my attention to Meaty Goodness. I finalised the arrangements for Ben's Adventure Day at the Winnersley Forest Experience. Alice and Jake were going to travel with Ben and me. Alice offered to drive over and leave her car here so they wouldn't have to be picked up, allowing Ben longer to open his cards and presents. It occurred to me that Alice often makes thoughtful gestures like that and I rarely thank her or appreciate the thought. Owen's mother, Jenny, was going to travel separately and give Harry a lift because he lives nearer to them than to us. Jess was coming too with her youngest daughter, Esme. Jess's older daughters, Ava and Ursula, are sixteen and seventeen respectively and sufficiently responsible to be left to their own devices for a day. Esme, however, is thirteen and a whole different undertaking. She's been diagnosed as having ADHD and her behaviour can be as demanding as it is unpredictable.

'She can go from being the sweetest, most lovable child in the world one minute to a raging torrent of volatility the next with no warning,' Jess had confided. Consequently, the otherwise bright, articulate Esme was kept on a tight rein. Jess allows herself a get-out clause by having her own means of removing her daughter from a situation if circumstances demand.

The boys tapped on the office door. 'Close your eyes,' Ben said and I was presented with a tall glass of delicious smoothie and a chocolate biscuit. 'Elevenses.' The boys grinned happily.

I thanked them graciously. 'Come and tell me when it's half twelve and I'll make us some lunch. What do you have planned until then?'

And, of course, Ben being my son, it was all planned. They were going in the garden to try to find enough wind to fly his kite. They'd already photographed the stages of making the smoothies in readiness for their holiday scrapbook. I was denied the privilege of a sneak preview, but requested to take photos of the kite flying.

The translation work was a joy. I loved the freedom I'd been given to be creative and spontaneous. 'It's almost worth getting a dog,' I congratulated myself, 'just so I can buy the biscuits.'

After lunch, Ben hunted out his skittles from a cupboard in the utility room where they'd been relegated the previous summer, and the boys made the most of the afternoon sun. My translation work continued to flow, but I had to stop to answer the phone. It was someone introducing themselves as Helen Eastwood, returning my call from Social Services.

'I called on Mrs Marlow yesterday morning,' Ms Eastwood said, 'but she was out. I've put a letter in the post to her today asking her to phone so we can arrange a mutually convenient time for me to visit.'

I sighed and explained that Mrs Marlow would not have been out, she just doesn't answer the door and she doesn't have a phone. I described again, as I had already stressed many times to the hospital staff, the seriousness of the situation. Ms Eastwood had been told of the clutter and she knew the age of the Marlows, but she did not realise that she was dealing with a recluse who seemed not to be taking good care of herself.

'Thank you for your concern. It looks as if I'm going to have to lie in wait until she comes out to collect one of your food parcels.'

'Otherwise there's always my adjoining fence.'

Many a true word…

Wednesday 23 July

Ben's tenth birthday. He was up before seven excited that the day he'd been waiting for so eagerly had finally arrived. He wasn't to know that I'd had less than four hours sleep for the fourth night in a row. I wasn't going to spoil his moment by asking for another half hour, but I wished I'd been less obsessive about finally finishing the translation. My eyes were scratchy and my body sluggish. I promised myself an early night. He sat on my bed to open his cards and presents. I bought him the turbo radio controlled car he'd been lusting after ever since the anticipation of and then the enjoyment of the ones at school summer fair.

'I saw it in the window of Sherwood's at the Lakeside Centre, so I sneaked in and got it while you were at your swimming class. It was hidden in the boot of the car when we went to Guildford.'

He skipped round the room holding it up like a trophy and shouting 'Oh wow!' over and over. I laughed. 'I chose the right thing then, eh?'

'Oh wow!' he said again, giving me a hug.

'Come on, let's see what Granny got for you.'

'Don't you know already?'

'I've no idea.'

'Oh dear,' he said with a wide grin and eyes sparkling. 'Should I be taking a deep breath?'

His grandmother's presents are invariably something educational and we shared the expectation of this being yet another earnest attempt at providing him with opportunities to broaden his knowledge.

'Bless her,' I said, 'she means well.'

'I know.'

It was a heavy parcel. He picked it up and shook it. 'It feels like something in a box.' He carefully prised the sticky tape away, unfolded the shiny wrapping paper without tearing it, then opened the box. 'It's the Harry Potter books.'

'You'll enjoy those.'

'Guess what? They're all in French!'

I thought he was joking. He wasn't. We laughed.

There was a rat-a-tat on the conservatory window while we were sitting down to breakfast. It was Toby, of course, waving a card. Ben ran to let him in through the conservatory.

'Happy Birthday, Ben. Hope I'm not too early?'

'Perfect timing,' I said pouring him a cup of freshly ground coffee as he sat at the table with a carefully wrapped parcel.

'This is the first part of your present.'

Ben felt through the purple paper. 'It feels like something to wear, except there's some sort of bendy strip. Whatever can it be?'

Toby was beaming while my son eagerly tore open the wrapping. Toby was as excited as Ben.

'Oh Ungrampa,' Ben said, holding up a white suit. 'Mummy, it's bee keeper's garb. Is this really for me? It's perfect, it's perfect. Thank you. Thank you. Thank you. This is going to be my best birthday ever.' He put the helmet on his head and pulled the netting down then pulled on the white gloves, jumping up and down.

'Toby you must have spent a fortune,' I said, somewhat embarrassed, while Ben ran off to look at himself in the cloakroom mirror.

'Not really. Got it off eBay.' He turned to Ben as he came back into the room. 'Want to know what the rest of your present is?'

'There's more?'

'Not till next spring. How about we start you up with your own colony? You'll have to learn how to look after it properly, mind. I'll build you your own hive next to mine. What d'you think about that then?' He was chuckling to himself. I could see the joy that had gone into planning the gift and I was delighted that Ben's reaction did not disappoint him.

Alice took one look at me and offered to do the driving. Such kindness again. I accepted graciously and within minutes of setting off, I'd fallen asleep. Alice woke me just as we were about to pull into the Winnersley Forest.

'Oooh, sorry about that. I didn't get chance to work on Saturday or most of Sunday,' I explained, stretching, 'so I ended up staying up until the small hours on Sunday and Monday night and again last night to get it done. I can relax for the next few weeks now though.' I yawned. 'It's all sent off and I'm not taking on any more work until September.'

'Gordon Bennett, Ruby, what's come over you? No, seriously, I don't remember you ever having a break from working since I've known you. You've been driving yourself into the ground.'

'Am I really that bad?'

'Trust me, you're a breakdown waiting to happen.'

The words echoed in my head. *I'm a breakdown waiting to happen.*

As arranged, everyone met up in the car park so Ben had time to open his cards and presents before the adventure began. He was skipping around with jubilant anticipation. Jake gave him a Nerf gun, Owen a cricket bat, Harry an Xbox Lego game and Jess a Ben 10 baseball cap and rucksack. After photographs and a few more 'Wows!' around the car park from Ben, a few practice shots of the Nerf gun by all, mothers included, and a forceful extraction of the baseball cap from Esme's head by Jess, the goodies were safely stowed in the boot of Alice's Subaru estate and the excited enthusiasts headed eagerly towards the reception area, where the instructor, Rhodri, was waiting to greet them.

Rhodri was clearly well practised in his safety briefing and practical demonstration, stressing to the would-be adventurers the importance of following his instructions, without dampening their fervour with weighty words. Before he let them loose on the "nursery runs" as he called them, he threw questions at them, checking that everyone was clear what was expected of them and what they could expect. Even so, Jess took Esme to one side to make her own checks. Judging by the stories I've been told, she knows from experience that her daughter is expert in looking as if she's absorbing vital information while her mind is busy dancing to a different tune. I'm rather good at doing that myself.

'We use a double clip system from Germany,' Rhodri explained to us anxious mothers staring up at the zip wire. 'It means the youngsters have more freedom to experience the taste of danger without it actually being dangerous. They don't need to be supervised in the trees anymore because it's impossible to undo both safety clips at the same time.'

'Three of the boys have been before with the Hegley Lawns Cubs,' said Alice, 'so we've heard all about how much they enjoyed it, but I must admit I hadn't realised it would be quite so high.'

Rhodri laughed and moved on to a group of teenage girls that had just arrived.

'Can't I go with them instead of the little boys?' demanded Esme, pouting.

'No,' said Jess flashing her "end of, don't push it" stare. The message was clearly received and understood.

We mothers gathered at the foot of the imposing pines while the children queued for their turn to climb the steps to the platform.

'Don't look so worried, Mummy,' said Ben with excited expectation. 'You heard what Rhodri said. We've got the harnesses to stop us from falling.'

I smiled half-heartedly. Rhodri's hardly more than a boy himself.

Harry was at the back of the queue. 'Sorry your grandmother couldn't be here,' I said to him. 'I'll take lots of photos and you can send them to her.'

'She gets hayfever, so she'd probably have spent the whole time sneezing anyway. But she'll love to see the photos.'

There were three practice runs, each progressively a little higher and longer. A noticeable quietness descended on all four of us parents as we watched the children glide across.

Esme went first, totally fearless as she zoomed along the zip wire with her arms and legs stretched into a star shape while screaming with delight. The four boys began a little more hesitantly, clinging on to their harnesses at first, but gaining in confidence with each run until they too attempted the star shape. Screaming appeared to be the order of the day.

Rhodri joined them again. 'Right, practice over. Ready for the Cresta Run? It's the big one. Thirteen metres high and a hundred and seventy metres long. Are we ready?'

The children nodded. None of them had been on the Cresta Run before.

'I said, "Are we ready"?'

'Ready,' they shrieked together and rushed to where he was pointing.

Rhodri walked over with us women. 'This one's going to take mental strength for you to watch ladies, I warn you. It's perfectly safe, but it's a lot more extreme. It's deliberately designed to push them beyond their comfort zone.'

'Must admit I'm a bit concerned about Esme,' confessed Jess. 'She throws herself into everything with no fear of the consequences. She can't help it.'

'They've all got the hang of it now and remember it's impossible for them to fall,' Rhodri reiterated.

He led us through the majestic pines to a clearing below the midpoint of the Cresta Run. I remembered how high the fence had felt when I'd climbed over into the Marlows' garden. The zip wire towered more than six times higher. I could feel my pulse throbbing in my neck and the blood drained from my face. From where we were standing we could see neither the start nor the end of the run because of the steep slope of the land. I looked at my friends laughing and joking to manage their apprehension. They were in a different universe. How could they laugh and joke when their children were exposed to the certainty of terrible disaster?

The air was pierced by a blood-curdling yell as Esme came hurtling through the trees. 'Hi you lot,' she bawled, 'you look like ants down there. This is amazing,' she sang out, making the 'zing' zing as she disappeared out of sight again.

Owen then Jake followed and Harry was next, more tentative, but nevertheless, squealing with joy. I saw Cameron, still in a suit and tie, with arms and legs akimbo, was right behind him, squealing too. What was he doing here? Why now? I had an overwhelming premonition of looming danger.

I knew by his scream that Ben was on the wire. It didn't sound like a scream of delight, it sounded more like a scream of sheer terror. Why was Cameron with Harry? Why wasn't he with Ben? My breath came in wild gulps.

'Help him, someone, help him.' I screeched, running towards the trees.

Jess ran after me and spun me round, holding me firmly by the shoulders. 'There's nothing to worry over,' she said calmly and firmly. 'He's having fun.'

'No, no. You don't understand. Something's wrong. I can tell. I'm his mother. The zip wire's going to snap.'

'Stop it,' Jess instructed, forcefully shaking me. 'It's no more than another one of your panic attacks. Let it go, Ruby.'

Just at that moment, Ben came soaring into view bellowing, 'I'm flyyyyying'.

I was conscious of feeling more and more lightheaded and distant. There were yellow spots dancing in front of my eyes blurring my vision, my mouth was dry, my lips and my fingers were tingling. The trees and the ground became a pulsating swirl of green and brown. I could feel myself swaying.

'I need to sit down,' I managed to say.

I felt arms guiding me to the ground. Someone handed me an opened bottle of water and said, 'Sip this'. It was Jess's voice. I opened my eyes and Jess was crouching next to me, Alice was standing at my feet.

'It's okay, Ruby, you fainted, but you're fine. Sit still for a few moments and keep sipping the water,' said Jess gently rubbing my back.

'It's lack of sleep,' said Alice anxiously. 'She hasn't been getting enough sleep for days.'

I had the sensation of rising, as if I'd been underwater and now was floating up and bursting through the surface. I remembered doing that as a child when my grandfather took me swimming and threw a coin into the pool for me to recover. I'd take a deep breath, swim down under the water and then push off the bottom to rise triumphantly, waving the coin. This was a similar experience, as if I'd been holding my breath for a very long time, but now I could gasp victoriously for air. I looked at the concern on my friends' faces. They'd been joined by Jenny, who'd come over to see why we'd been delayed.

'Where's Ben?' I said.

'The kids are having a great time, don't worry,' Jenny reassured me. 'They're just about to head for the rope bridge.'

We heard Jake calling before he came charging through the trees towards us. Owen and Harry were not far behind.

'Quick.' He was gasping for air. 'It's Ben. You need to hurry. He's stuck.' He bent over putting his hands on his knees trying to get his breath back. 'I've got… stitch.'

A surge of electricity propelled me to my feet. I rounded on Jess and struck her hard across the face. 'I told you. I told you. You wouldn't listen.'

Jess reeled backwards with her hand to her cheek. I felt the forest start to spin. It was like I was caught in the eye of a tornado and the surroundings were rotating around me, giving me flashes and glimpses of what was happening. I saw Alice talking to the boys. I felt the sting in my hand where I'd slapped Jess. Jake's face zoomed in on me. Harry was saying something, but his words were floating and disjointed. 'Missed the net… Rolled… Hanging.' 'Hanging' boomed and clanged as a physical force punching my belly. And all the time the trees, my friends, the children were spinning and spinning out of control while I was rooted to the spot.

'For God's sake someone, get Rhodri,' I heard Alice shout and then I felt Jenny pushing me.

'What are you doing? Get off me. I have to go to Ben. I have to save my son. He's going to die. He's going to die.' I struggled to shake Jenny off, but Jenny's grip tightened.

'I'm taking you to him. That's where we're going.' I heard the panic in Jenny's voice.

We stumbled through the trees following the zip wire high above us until we came to another clearing. Ben was dangling from the wire just out of reach of the platform where he should have landed. He was crying.

'Mummy. I'm stuck. I need help.'

He was still alive. Alive. The forest stopped spinning, but now I was spinning instead, whirling and swirling in a vortex.

'I don't know what to do. Please, I don't know what to do. Help me. Get him down. Please get him down.' I was desperate. It was my fault for bringing him to this dangerous place. It was madness. I should never have agreed to this.

'It'll be alright, Ruby. Jess's gone to find Rhodri. Rhodri will know what to do. Ben's stuck, but he's not hurt.' Even in my frantic state, I could feel the tenderness in Alice's response.

Jenny put an arm round me. 'Try to calm down Ruby, for Ben's sake. Ben's calm, look.' Her voice sounded reassuring. 'How you doing, Ben?' she called up.

'How am I going to get down?' Ben called back. 'I can't reach the platform. Is someone coming to get me down? I feel sick.'

'I'm sorry, Ben. I'm so sorry,' I wailed.

'Hold on, Ben. Rhodri's on his way to get you down.' Jake yelled, not very confidently.

'Okay.' Ben sounded vulnerable and anxious. 'Only the zip wire keeps tugging. I think there's someone coming down the wire. They'll crash into me.'

At the briefing Rhodri had been most insistent that only one person was allowed on the wire at a time.

'I'm coming to get you,' I shouted up to him, kicking off my sandals and running to the steps leading down from the platform. My agitation made me miss the first tread and stumble. Jenny grabbed me to steady me, but we both realised we were too late when we heard the ratcheting of someone zooming into view.

I stepped away from the ladder, forcing myself to watch. Convinced I was going to see my son die.

It was Esme. 'Lift your legs up, Ben, I'm going to grab you,' she hollered.

Within seconds she was behind him and caught him round his waist with her left hand as she reached for the rope net with her right, and swung them both onto the platform out of sight.

I saw Alice instinctively pull Jake to her. Harry slipped his hand into mine. I squeezed it.

The next few moments felt like an hour. No one moved. No one spoke.

Eventually Esme leaned over the edge waving. 'We're okay,' she called down.

'Ben?' I managed to call, 'Ben?'

His ashen face appeared over the platform. 'Esme rescued me. We're coming down.'

'I'm coming first,' Esme yelled, taking charge, 'so I can watch him coming down. He's just thrown up and he feels a bit shaky.'

Jess and Rhodri pulled up on the pathway to our right in a motorised buggy. They came rushing over to the relieved group who were all talking at once as Esme and Ben stepped safely on the ground. I didn't join in. I bent down, scooped Ben close to me and held him tight.

'I'm fine, Mummy. Can you let go of me now?' I didn't move. 'Please?' I realised he was embarrassed because I was clinging on to him as if he was a toddler. I reluctantly let him go and settled for resting my hand on his back.

'We saw what happened as we were driving along,' Rhodri said. 'That was a very brave thing to do young lady, but foolish and dangerous. You could have both been badly hurt.'

Esme smiled as if it was inconsequential. Jess put her arm round her daughter and shook her head resignedly. Ben's knee was bleeding. I gasped.

'It's just a cut. I bashed it when we landed.'

'Don't worry darling, we'll soon have it patched up. I've brought a first aid kit.' I hoped I was giving the impression of more composure than I was feeling. 'Thank you so, so much Esme.'

'Can I give you a hug?' Esme asked. 'You look as if you need one.'

I let the teenager, tall like her mother, take me in her arms and I wept silent tears of relief.

Ben was adamant he was absolutely fine after his ordeal and wanted to join his friends on the rope bridge.

'How did it happen?' I asked while I cleaned his knee with an antiseptic wipe. I was relieved to see that despite the blood, it was just a graze.

'I went to grab the net to pull myself on to the platform, but I missed it. My arm went through one of the spaces and I couldn't catch the rope in time because I rolled back on the zip wire.'

'How can you roll back? I don't understand.'

'Your body weight makes a slight dip in the wire and it made me roll back.' He shrugged his shoulders as if he wasn't really sure himself how he'd missed the net. 'Everyone said to try and swing myself and they'd grab me, but swinging made me go further and further back. They all rushed off to get help and I was on my own for ages. It was a bit scary.'

'My poor darling.'

'Where were you? I thought you were coming to the end to meet us.'

'Yes, sorry darling. We were on our way,' I lied.

I should have been there. It really was my fault. I'd let him down. And I couldn't even have the decency to own up to it. *Did I really slap Jess? Oh God. I slapped Jess across the face.*

'It's alright, Mummy. Don't worry. It was an adventure. I'm fine now. Can I go and play with the others please?'

He scampered off wearing a sticking plaster on his knee like a badge of honour. I joined the other women who had spread out rugs and were busy setting up an al fresco lunch. The rope bridge and the barrel walk were in full view so we could keep an eye on the children. They were talking about where to place the food. No one mentioned what had just happened. It seemed deliberate. I felt detached as if I was a distant observer. As if I wasn't actually there.

Alice had lovingly prepared the usual picnic goodies, but the centre was dominated by the cake she'd baked. Although I'd commissioned her to make it, she'd kept the design of it secret. Even Jake hadn't had a sneak preview before the grand unveiling. There were gasps and a round of appreciative applause when Ben was invited to take off the cover. She'd recreated the scene around us, with chocolate icing and green fondant trees covering the base. Two trees on the top had a wire strung between them stretching across the middle of the cake and below were five children made of fondant icing. Here and there she'd dotted realistic stones made of chocolate and little tufts of fondant grass. She'd fixed a sign with a real stick that said Happy 10th Birthday Ben in tiny lettering.

'I bought the stones,' she said modestly, 'I didn't make those myself.'

I thought it remarkable that I seemed to be the only one who was still upset about Ben's "adventure". Spirits were high as the ensemble piled into the goodies. Meanwhile, it was all I could do to toy with a cheese roll and stop myself from running away.

'It feels really free. You're travelling through mid-air,' said Owen. 'Can we come again, Mummy?'

'We'll see what Daddy says,' Jenny replied. Owen is the eldest of four children.

I couldn't imagine ever agreeing to Ben coming again.

'Nobody tells you what to do, that's the best bit,' offered Esme, looking pointedly at Jess and sticking her tongue out. Jess said nothing. She just leaned over and took a strawberry off Esme's plate and ate it. Everyone laughed.

'It's so scary looking down,' said Harry. 'You think you're going to fall, but the harness is there to hold you. I had to keep reminding myself.'

'Yes, well you know you'll be safe if you do fall, but your body just doesn't want to test it as you fly round the forest,' said Ben, elongating the word 'fly' and using his hand to demonstrate. 'You don't...hang about... when you're actually doing the flying.' he added, cracking up at his own joke and inviting everyone else to laugh with him.

'Don't hang about, very funny. We all wondered what you were... waiting around for. Get it, waiting around?' Jake joined in the fun.

'He was waiting for Esme to give him a lift.' Owen could hardly get the words out he was laughing so much.

'Did anyone take a photo?' Esme asked.

'No, you'll have to do it all again,' Jake replied.

Alice threw a glance towards me. 'Okay now,' she said to the children, signalling that the joking should stop. 'I want to know what you thought of the ride, Jake.'

'The worst bit was jumping off the platform, then it was brill. You feel as if you're stepping off into thin air, like you're flying, then you get this massive adrenalin rush as you whoosh down the zip wire,'

'Ooooh, get you,' piped up Esme. 'Adrenalin rush.'

Jake leaned across to try to take another strawberry off her plate, but she wasn't going to get caught like that a second time and she hurriedly snatched the plate out of the way, tossing the contents into the air. Suddenly it was raining fruit. Jess tensed as if she half anticipated an outburst, but she needn't have worried: like everyone else, Esme found it hilarious as she scrambled to retrieve the scattered strawberries. Grateful to Alice for changing the way the conversation was going, I fixed a smile on my face so it looked as if I was enjoying the horseplay too.

Happy birthday was sung, the cake cut and eaten, saving a slice for Matthew and another for Toby, and there was still plenty of time left to have a go on the climbing wall.

'How about I stay and help you clear up, Ruby, and then Alice and Jenny, you can be on photo duty?' suggested Jess.

'I'm sorry I slapped you,' I said after Alice and Jenny had gone.

'Thank you,' replied Jess as she began picking up the paper plates and putting them into a black plastic bin liner. 'You've hardly said a word all lunchtime. How are you feeling?'

'Oh, you know.' I shrugged. 'I'm feeling a bit silly now, I'll make sure I get an early night tonight.' I concentrated on putting the leftovers back into the cool boxes.

'Is that all it was then? Lack of sleep?'

'Don't, Jess. Not today. I'm just tired, that's all.'

'You're shutting everyone out again.'

'What do you mean?' Jess didn't reply, but continued to put the empty drink cartons and other rubbish into the refuse bag. 'Jess?'

'How is running away helping you? Look at me, Ruby, I'm not the enemy, I'm your friend and I can't bear to see what's happening to you. None of us can.'

'None of you? You've been talking about me behind my back then? Is that what friends do?'

'What, we should just watch you go under?' If she was waiting for a reaction, I didn't oblige. 'I'm sorry, I don't mean to upset you. I'll shut up if that's what you want.'

'I don't know what I want. These last few days, there's been so much happening, one minute I'm on a high, the next I plummet. I try to hold it all together and mostly I do, it's just that...'

'I know, but the way you deal with things sometimes is self-defeating. It isn't what happens on the outside that causes the panic attacks. It's what you're suppressing inside. Just let it all go. Relax a bit more.'

'I can't. I don't know how to. I don't even where to start. I feel that if I dare to let go, I'll fall apart. What Jake was saying about jumping off the platform and being on the zip wire, that's what my whole life feels like, except I don't have a harness to save me from falling.'

Jess gave me a hug. 'Come on, let's go and watch them on the climbing wall. Perhaps you could have a go on it and see how it feels?' she said leaving me in no doubt that she was only half joking. 'Maybe I've overstepped the boundaries already, but I just want to leave you with another way of looking at things?'

'Go on.'

'Instead of focusing on what you're running away from Ruby, focus on what it is you want to run to.'

For the rest of the afternoon I continued to feel totally disconnected from myself. I was aware that I was apparently joining in the fun, for all the world giving the appearance I'd put the earlier episode behind me and was a happy relaxed mother enjoying her son's birthday celebrations. Inside I was completely numb. I knew Jess was trying to help, but she'd left me stripped bare, totally exposed and vulnerable. With no refuge. With nowhere to hide. Swallowed by my deepest fears.

I was amazed at myself for being able to seem so normal and yet I also recognised that's what I'd been doing for years. The only difference was, and it was a huge chasm of a difference, I could no longer deceive myself; fool myself into believing I was coping. I could no longer split myself and operate as two discrete beings: the person on the outside who was competent and capable and the person on the inside who was living on a knife-edge.

A breakdown waiting to happen.

The Ben and Jake that got into the car to go home were not the excitable and eager boys of the morning. They still felt the exhilaration and euphoria of their experiences, but they were pleasantly weary and happily tired. Within minutes they were curled up on the back seat and fast asleep.

Alice saw them through her rear view mirror. 'Just look at them,' she said, startling me away from my thoughts. 'Absolutely zonked. I always think Jake looks so much younger when he's asleep, like butter wouldn't melt. You think you'll never get cross with them again when you see them like that, don't you?'

'I don't get cross with Ben anyway.'

'Oh come on. This is me you're talking to. I've got a son as well, don't forget. There are times when Jake drives me up the wall and I'm inches away from slapping him.'

'No really, Alice. I'm not making it up, Ben doesn't ever misbehave. He never has.'

I don't think she believed me. We sat in silence for the next few minutes.

'Jake had a lovely time today, thank you,' she said eventually.

'Do you worry sometimes that something awful might happen to him?'

'Of course. Doesn't every parent? But you can't wrap them up in cotton wool. I feel so sorry for Joseph Greasley. His parents don't let him out of their sight. They live a few doors away from us so I suggested to Fiona, his Mum, we should share the school run; it made sense, to give us both a bit of extra time. She absolutely wouldn't hear of it. The poor kid isn't allowed to go anywhere without one of his parents. They never go out together in the evening, because they won't even leave him with a babysitter.'

'I'd never do that. I want Ben to be strong and independent, I want him to be resourceful and know how to look out for himself. But… that isn't really what I'm getting at.'

'What then?'

'Sometimes, I wonder if… do you know that saying, "what will be, will be"? Perhaps some things are already decided and there's nothing we can do to change them?'

'Don't go there, Ruby. It's been a fabulous day for everyone and even though Ben got stuck for a while, nobody's been hurt. He's bounced back and he's fine. Kids are surprisingly resilient. You heard them all joking about it. Leave it at that. Don't spoil it.'

'Yes, you're right. I'm sorry.' I wished I'd never raised the subject; better not to share those fears with anyone else. I felt a flash of my old adversary, embarrassment.

'It's weird them being such good friends, don't you think?' Alice offered. 'With Ben being the youngest in the year and Jake being the oldest boy?'

'I didn't know Jake was the eldest.'

'Yes, Millie Radcliffe's two days older than him, otherwise he's the oldest in the year.'

'I've never really thought of Ben being the youngest before, but I suppose he must be.'

Oh dear, did that mean I expect too much of him? Did I over estimate what he was capable of doing? Was this something else I'd got horribly wrong? Was it a mistake to encourage him to be autonomous? Should I be more protective?

I didn't want to spend the evening alone. I went with Ben to give Toby his slice of birthday cake as an excuse to ask him if he would spend the evening with me. He's turned out to be someone I can open up to and share with comfortably. I was confident he could help me sort out this knot of uncertainty and anguish exploding inside me. Catharsis.

We expected him to be in his garden, but there was no sign of him. Ben knocked on the kitchen window with the air of someone conducting a familiar procedure. Toby was a while opening the door. He was dressed too smartly for working in the garden.

'I was just showering and changing. I'm off out on a jaunt this evening since you're not going to be choiring. Saw an advert for a talk about permaculture at the library so I bought meself a ticket. Still got time for a bit of cake with the birthday boy first though.'

'Have a lovely time,' I said sincerely in spite of my disappointment.

I suggested to Ben he might want to stay up and watch a film in honour of his birthday, but barely ten minutes into The Big Noise he was struggling to keep awake and I shooed him off to bed. I toyed with the idea of phoning Mother in Turkey, but what would I say? I searched the TV for something, anything, to watch, but couldn't concentrate. I ran a bath and poured in six drops of the lavender oil Jess gave me weeks ago. I'm supposed to relax in it for twenty minutes to feel the full benefit. I managed five, give or take, and was anything but relaxed.

It was still only just after nine. I decided to have an early night, but wasn't hopeful of falling asleep and was more than a little anxious about what I might dream. I sat up in bed with a notebook and pen and opened a double page. I wrote "What am I running from?" on the left hand page and "Where do I want to run to?" on the right. After much careful thought and consideration I wrote "me" under the first heading and "don't know" under the second, and then ran out of ideas. Impasse. I hunched down in bed and stared up at the ceiling. There's a crack in the plaster I hadn't noticed before. Just a fine hairline crack. I noted that I'd better get it fixed. Or perhaps I'd just ignore it, wait and see if it grew any bigger. I didn't want to think any more. My head hurt. I didn't want to feel any more. At least not painful, disturbing, unsettling feelings. I sighed, closed my eyes and melted into a dreamless sleep. My body's own wisdom kicked in at last and found a perfect solution.

I woke again in the small hours hardly aware I'd been sleeping. I'd left the curtains drawn back and my room was bathed with ghostly silvery moonlight. There was a full moon. I slipped out of bed and went over to the window. The street below was hushed and still. The moon and the streetlamps cast shadows here and there, picking out rooftops and cars and shimmering on the hedges and bushes of my neighbours across the road. I breathed the serenity into my core and held it there, then tiptoed back to bed carrying the stillness and quiet with me.

So often I dreaded waking in the early hours in the morning with my mind in overdrive as it had been so many times these last two weeks; but I was feeling something akin to peace, as if I'd woken from an operation, but was still woozy from the effects of the anaesthetic. I had no fight or struggle left in me. I surrendered again to a welcome deep healing sleep.

Thursday 24 July

Ben presented me with four pieces of buttered toast, a couple of bananas and two glasses of milk (he isn't yet allowed to make a hot drink unsupervised) in bed. I'd slept through until almost eight o'clock.

'I thought I'd better wake you, Mummy. Harry will be here soon.'

'Then we should make a start on this feast,' I replied, pulling the duvet back for him. He obligingly snuggled in next to me and we feasted together.

I was showered and dressed by the time Matthew dropped Harry off, but only just. I left the boys loading the photos taken over the last few days onto the computer while I popped next door on my now daily duty to take Mrs Marlow fresh supplies. Hopefully, Helen whatever-her-name-is would be sorting out something more permanent sooner rather than later.

Once again Mrs Marlow had left the bag from the previous day.

I looked with some trepidation for what it was she didn't like this time. On Ben's birthday it had been a tin of tuna. There was no food in the bag, just a list printed with a pencil in capital letters on the back of the note I left on Saturday morning: *"TEA BAGS, SHUGGER, TAMATOE SOOP, TOLIET ROLS"*. No "please". No explanation. And no reply. If the situation wasn't so hopeless, it would be funny. Perhaps she thought the shopping fairies were helping her?

I phoned the hospital for an update on Mr Marlow. They were very sorry, but confidentiality regulations meant they could only give information to Mrs Marlow. Please would I urge her to get in touch, Mr Marlow is worried about her. I suggested they might phone Helen thingy at Social Services. Dammit I still couldn't remember her surname. I asked to speak to the male nurse I saw when I took Mrs Marlow to visit last week. He'd seemed approachable and had some understanding of the difficulties with my neighbour. Apparently he was on his honeymoon. Dammit again.

I was determined to remain upbeat for the boys' sake and not let myself slide into the confusion of the previous afternoon that was still bubbling in my jaw and in the pit of my stomach.

The boys had a delightful morning sorting through the photographs of the last few days, contacting Jake and Owen and Jess to add their Winnersley photos too and choosing which to use in their holiday scrapbook. Then they showed me how to use PowerPoint. I was impressed by their motivation, their expertise and confidence. At eleven o'clock I had to forcibly evict them from the computer and thrust them into the garden to get some fresh air and exercise. Having promised Ben unlimited access to the computer since I won't be needing it for work, I reneged and imposed a two hour a day ration while the weather lends itself to more active pursuits outdoors. I'd totally underestimated the boys' ability to concentrate on a single project for a substantial period of time. I thought the generally agreed consensus is that children are supposed to get bored after a few minutes unless they're playing hours of computer games. So how have those commonly heard phrases, "children have no staying power these days" and "children expect instant gratification" developed?

It was Toby's day to work on our garden, but I rescued him with coffee from a barrage attack from the Nerf gun.

'How was last night's talk?' I asked him.

'Yes. Interesting. Got to chat with the man giving it after and he's going to come and see me garden and suggest what more I can do. He's a bee keeper too. How about that?'

'Sounds good.'

I sat back in my seat and felt my whole body relax. Just talking to Toby seems to help me unwind.

'Thank you for Ben's gift. It was such a surprise. I think it's his favourite.' I said. 'He loves spending time with you, you know. And you've taught him so much.'

'He's a happy little soul, bundle of energy, bright as a button. I'm very fond of him, difficult not be. Has such a lively sense of humour, loves playing around with words, makes me laugh. Completely different from me when I was a nipper.'

'Why what were you like as a child, Toby?'

'You wouldn't have had much time for me then, don't s'pose. Didn't mix much with other people. Was quiet and shy, kept meself to meself. Ben's not like that. Got a completely different personality. In another way, though, he's just like me. I see it in him. He understands growing things and they understand him. Got an affinity with the natural world. Not something you can be taught, that. You either have it or you don't.'

'Yes, he's always loved Nature. I don't know where he gets that from. I thought it must be because he spends so much time with you.'

'Oh, it's much more'n that. He's always wanting me to explain things to him, wants to learn about the seasons and how things grow. You should see the joy on his face when something he's planted starts to sprout. Wouldn't be surprised if he didn't grow up to be a scientist.'

'I don't know the first thing about gardens, I'm so grateful he has you to encourage him.'

'Do you remember when you first asked me to look after him?'

'Gosh it was years ago. It must have been when my translation work really started to take off.'

'Just every now and then you said.' He laughed. 'Little did I know.'

'How embarrassing. I've a lot to answer for haven't I?'

'Turned out well though, eh? Must admit I was reluctant at first. Never had any children of me own, 'course. It was unheard of in those days for... unheard of for people like me and Paul back then. Felt a bit nervous. Didn't know the first thing about looking after kiddies. Needn't have worried, took to him straight away.'

'I seem to be apologising to you a lot lately. I'm not the same person now that I was then, Toby.'

'You did me a favour. He's a pleasure to be around. Couldn't love the little lad more if he really was me grandson. He's such a great kid, the grandson I never had.'

'His Ungrampa.' I felt so completely happy in that moment, all the troubles forgotten. 'Perhaps I can be your Undaughter?'

He laughed and he looked completely happy too.

'Do you know how that started?' he asked.

'Um no actually, I don't.'

'You know how he's always making up names for things? Garb?' We laughed. 'He asked me one day – oh years back now, he must have been four, going on for five maybe – he said he didn't have a grandad, would I be his grandad. I said that might be a bit awkward, because I'd have to be your pa to be his grandad. A few days later he said he'd had a little think about it and would I be his ungrandad then. Said I'd be honoured. He wanted to know if I had a grandad. I told him I'd been lucky when I was a lad because I had two grandads. He asked me what I called them, so I told him, one was Gramps and the other was Grandpa, so he said he'd call me Ungrampa if I was happy with that. I said I'd be delighted.'

He went back to dead-heading roses and I vacuumed upstairs before getting lunch. I think we were both in a rosy glow of knowing we had cemented our friendship.

The doorbell rang just as the boys and I were finishing lunch on the decking outside the conservatory. A smartly dressed woman with deep set eyes and hair screwed into a tight bun on top of her head, was standing in the porch.

'Mrs Lewis?' She had a trace of shiny amber lipstick on her front tooth.

'Erm, yes?'

'I'm Helen Eastwood, Mrs Lewis.' She waved some sort of identity card with her photo on it. 'We spoke on the phone on Tuesday about your neighbour, Barbara Marlow?'

Eastwood, of course. That's it.

'Yes, I remember. Have you managed to persuade her to talk to you?' I was fascinated by the lipstick smudge. I found myself running my tongue along my own tooth.

'Perhaps I could come in a moment? You may want to sit down.'

'Of course.' I led the way into the lounge. 'Sorry, it's a bit messy in here. It was my son's birthday yesterday; these are his presents,' I said trying to ease the awkwardness between us. I cleared a space on the sofa and we both sat.

'I'm sorry to have to tell you this, I have some bad news. I'm afraid Walter Marlow passed away shortly after ten thirty this morning.'

'Oh no, but he can't have, I phoned the hospital... they didn't say anything was wrong, only that he was worried about his wife. If they'd warned me, I would have somehow found a way of getting her to the hospital.'

'It was very sudden. His heart just gave up. There was nothing they could do.'

'Poor Mrs Marlow. How's she going to cope?'

'My colleague's with her now. We had to force the gate in the end, she gave us no alternative, she wouldn't respond to the doorbell. We're moving her to Aspley Grange in Winnersley for the time being so we can make an assessment of her needs. It's very sad, very sad, but she'll be well looked after. They'll be happy for you to visit her.'

I didn't know how to react; whether to go and tell Toby and the boys. I looked at Helen Eastwood, but couldn't read her expression.

'Mrs Lewis? Are you OK? Would you like to speak to her before we set off?'

'Set off?'

'To the care home. Aspley Grange. We're taking her there right now.'

I followed the social worker to the Marlows' house. There was a dark red Vauxhall estate parked outside. A man I recognised from choir held a door open for Mrs Marlow to get in.

'Richard?'

'Hello Ruby, I didn't realise you were Barbara's neighbour. Would you like a few minutes?'

'Yes, please.'

My eyes were drawn to Mrs Marlow, still in her slippers and wearing the moth-eaten red poncho. I felt a huge well of affection for her. 'I'm so, so sorry about your husband.'

'Oh, don't you go worrying, my dear,' replied Mrs Marlow cheerfully as she climbed into the car.

'I think she's in shock,' explained Richard. He seemed to need to apologise for the old lady's failure to realise she was being invited to stop and talk.

I squatted down to the car to make eye contact. 'They'll take good care of you at Aspley Grange I'm sure, Mrs Marlow. I could come and see you at the weekend if you like?'

'Yes dear. Did you get the toilet rolls? Only Walter's going to need them when he gets home. We've run out.'

'Oh, but...'

Richard led me away from the car. 'Don't worry. Don't worry. You can see why she can't stay here? She's been very lucky to have you to look out for her, but leave it to us now. She's in good hands, I promise you. We'll sort everything out.'

I stood and watched them drive away, raised my hand to wave, but the old lady wasn't looking. The raw numbness that had swamped me when I first learned of Paul's death coursed once more through my veins. The pain of it took me by surprise. I tried to dismiss the feeling, but it wouldn't go away.

I turned to go back home, avoiding looking back at the Marlows' house, and prepared myself to break the news to Toby and the boys.

Despite the sadness of the Marlows' news, I set off for yoga at the normal time, leaving Ben and Harry in the garden with the obliging Toby. I was a little uncertain about seeing Jess and Alice again. They've been party to one of my panic attacks on numerous occasions and I was always left feeling rather self-conscious and inferior. Their efforts to put me at ease only made it worse and I was still delicate under the forced cheerful surface. However, there was a new woman joining the class, Shirley, who'd been a regular yogini (her description) in Wimbledon for years by all accounts, but had recently relocated to the area. Thankfully I was able to retreat humbly to the shadows and let Shirley step willingly into the limelight. I didn't mention to my friends what had happened to the Marlows. Maybe I would tell them the following morning when we met for coffee.

The class began as usual, but I wasn't troubled by any of my customary insecurities where I convinced myself that other people were watching me and judging; instead I felt withdrawn, invisible, on the fringes. I recoiled into myself and followed Acharya's softly spoken brogue as he invited us to ease into the movements. Downward dog was no longer my bête noir, in fact it had become my favourite. I flowed gracefully into the posture, keeping my focus and enjoying the wonderful stretching sensation.

As I began the descent and followed through into the upward counterpose with the positive energy still flowing unhindered through my mind and body, I slowly raised my head, remembering to keep my gaze focused forward as my eye line went from the carpet to the windowsill to the grass outside and to a pair of brown suede loafers standing on the grass. The loafers contained a pair of feet that were attached to a pair of legs. It was Cameron, smiling of course and making a thumbs-up gesture.

I returned his smile.

Alice and Jess stayed for a cup of tea after the yoga class because they had no need to rush home now it was the school holidays. Esme was spending the afternoon playing volleyball and then ice skating with her elder sisters and a friend so wouldn't be finishing for another hour. Jake was at the cinema with Pete. I made my excuses on account of Ben and Harry.

'Jess can't make it for coffee tomorrow,' said Alice. 'How about you bring the boys over to mine for lunch instead? They can play outside, we've got the pool out, and we can have a natter about what you wanted to talk about in the car yesterday.'

'You mean…about fate?'

'Yes fate. It wasn't the time for that conversation then, not after such a lovely day, but actually I have the same worries as you. It would be good for us to share our thoughts. About twelve suit you?'

'That would be great, thanks,' I replied.

As I'd anticipated, Cameron was waiting for me in the car park. I instinctively hugged him to hide my tears of relief that he was there. Once again I sensed the strength of his inner stillness and serenity.

'I've been on such a roller coaster these last days. It's all been too much, I'm not coping.'

'You've had an emotional tsunami, but it's just the process you've needed to go through to heal years of negativity. Shall we walk?'

'Yes, I'd like that, but I mustn't be long, I've left the boys with Toby.'

He set off towards a footpath through the trees, leading to the boating lake.

'I didn't know this path was here,' I said following him, 'I thought you had to walk round.'

He smiled.

We went through an opening to the lakeside. There was a rowing boat moored to a wooden platform.

'This is for us,' he said and stepped in.

'Are you sure it's safe?'

'Of course, my dear. Here, give me your hand.' He chuckled.

'I meant safe for you.'

There was a mist hanging over the water as if it were early morning just as dawn was breaking. The mist held the soft tranquillity of the lake and surrounding trees as Cameron rowed skilfully, with only the sound of the gentle repetitive splash as the oars dipped and rose through the water, pulling us rhythmically towards the centre.

'Where is everybody? It's usually packed here at this time of year.'

Cameron didn't reply. There was a distinct shift in him as he settled the oars into the boat with just the paddles hanging over the sides; a shift to a place that was deeper and more intense. I saw behind his jovial exterior a wisdom and clarity I hadn't perceived before, although I recognised that it had always been there, just below the surface. I was held in the presence of pure love and abundance. I let it enfold me as an angel's wings might.

For a moment the air seemed to gather around him whilst the mist evaporated. The sun was high in the sky and shining, but the rays were muted and turned to mauve, bathing us and the little boat and extending across the water to the trees.

I too became still and experienced a calm and peace I didn't know was possible, as if I were being taken back to the source. The feeling stayed with me, although the idea of there being a "source" was both new and yet, as a visceral memory, a given. It was as if Cameron had created a wellspring of light and joy and unconditional love that swathed me and wrapped me.

'Are you ready to talk about Paul?'

His words merged into me. I was not totally aware that he'd spoken, but I felt once again the loss I felt when Paul first died. It was a pain too deep-rooted for floods of tears. I'd shed those already and found no release in them. I tried to speak aloud, but my voice was elastic stretched beyond its limits to the point where it was soon to break. My throat could not overcome the suffocating asphyxiation that overwhelmed me and made my lips too tight to pronounce the words. I instinctively turned my head away and looked towards the trees so that Cameron would not witness my pain. This was private, even from him, but I was grateful he was there.

'He would have loved it here,' I tried to say. 'He loved trees and water.' I made an effort to smile.

Cameron said nothing.

It was a struggle for the words to be spoken. They'd waited for so long for the opportunity, all but given up hope of ever being expressed. They'd been repressed, denied life, imprisoned in my subconscious. Now they were offered freedom they were hesitant and uncertain of their destination. They were safer locked away and hidden. Liberation and freedom was daunting. They weren't yet sure they were ready to greet the outside world.

A single tear found its way down my cheek. 'I was so angry with him for dying, for leaving me. I never got to the hospital in time. He died just minutes before I arrived. Why couldn't he have hung on just for those few more minutes until I got there, so I could at least have been with him, held his hand? It was cruel.' I swallowed and the tension in my throat eased a little. 'We had everything to look forward to. Our whole lives. He should be here. He should be here now. I need him. Ben needs him.' I turned to face Cameron and my words come rushing. 'Why? Why? All the plans we made. All the promises about the future. I'd waited such a long time to meet him. I thought I'd never marry or have a family.'

I gave myself a moment to compose myself.

'He was a firefighter, did you know that? But we talked about him leaving the Fire Service and helping me to set up an international language school. We had such plans, such great plans.' My voice trailed off. I turned away again. 'Sometimes I can hardly remember what he looked like.'

'How did you meet him?'

I cleared my throat. 'We weren't all that young. He was thirty-one and I was twenty-six. We'd both had relationships before, of course, but nothing special for either of us. I was working in Brussels as an interpreter. I came back to spend a few weeks with Mother; she was on her summer break from school.'

Suddenly the longing was on hold and I relived that first meeting again. 'I was driving down the narrow winding lane to her village and I swerved to avoid a rabbit. Next thing I knew I was in a ditch at the side of the road. I wasn't hurt, not even so much as a scratch, but I couldn't open the door to get out. Paul was driving towards me.'

Tears began to well. 'He saw what had happened and he stopped to help.' My chin was trembling, making it difficult to form my words, my breath shallow and punctuated with involuntary sighs, but the memories were treasured and not even the sadness of recalling them could diminish the joy they held.

'He opened the boot, it was a hatchback, and helped me climb out. He had the most wonderful smile. Ben has his smile. You can tell what someone's like instantly from their smile, don't you think?' I said, making eye contact again.

Cameron nodded.

'He insisted on running me to A&E to have me checked over. He said afterwards, when I got to know him, that he could see I was perfectly alright, a bit shaken that's all, but he wanted an excuse to get to know me.' I laughed. 'I felt as if we'd been friends for years. You hear people say that and when it happens to you... it's odd, isn't it? I think we both knew, even then. I don't think I'm embellishing how it really was just to... you know. We actually talked about it, we both said...' I wavered, dipping back into grief.

'What happened then?' he probed softly.

'He drove me back to Mother's and he fixed up with his friend who had a four by four to tow my car, Mother's car, out of the ditch and take it to a garage. I said...' I laughed freely this time. 'I said how can I thank you and he said come out for a meal with me. It sounds so corny, but it was perfect.'

I expected Cameron to say something else. He didn't. His silence encouraged me to keep talking. It grew less difficult to speak; not so choked with emotion.

'It wasn't all straightforward of course, because I lived in Brussels. He came over to spend the weekend now and again, but both of us had to work at weekends sometimes and it wasn't always possible to be free at the same time. We spent a fortune on phone calls. In the end I gave a month's notice, but I had no job to come back to. It wasn't easy for Mother or me when I moved back in with her. Then Paul told me he'd been secretly looking at houses and he'd found three for us to look at together. I fell in love with the one I still live in as soon as I saw it. He said he knew I'd choose that one. Then he said he wanted us to be married when we moved in so I'd better get myself organised quickly because I had three months to arrange a wedding. I said is that a proposal then and he said it does seem to sound like one. You can see why I loved him.'

Silent tears started to flow again. 'That's how it always was with us. Easy and uncomplicated. Even when we argued we used to end up laughing. He just wasn't the kind of person you could stay angry with for long.'

I paused to reflect. 'I miss him. I miss having someone there for me. He would have been a great dad, Cameron. Ben was born with no other relatives except for me and Mother. Paul was an only child and his parents had already died when I met him.'

'You have to be Ben's mother and his father.' Cameron was not asking a question, he was making a statement. A statement acknowledging how tough that was for me.

'Just like Mother.' I hesitated before continuing, 'All the men in my life leave me; my father, then Paul and now even my grandfather doesn't recognise me.'

'And?' he asked gently, but firmly, so I couldn't escape it. I didn't want the "And?" I didn't want to acknowledge or visit "And?". "And?" left me with nowhere to take shelter. The "And?" was too terrifying even to contemplate.

'And... and I'm convinced that something will happen to Ben, too.' The horror of giving voice to my greatest fear, which haunts my dreams and infiltrates all I think and say and do, ripped open its protective binding and became a physical presence in the boat with us.

'Is that why you're here, Cameron? To prepare me? Something's going to happen to Ben, isn't it?' Every fibre of my body was screaming into the silence and the stillness.

'My dearest Ruby, I don't need to prepare you. You live in a constant state of readiness already.'

'So something is going to happen then?'

'I didn't say that, but neither can I give you any guarantees about the future. The future isn't already decided one way or the other. Everyone dies eventually. Few know how or when that will be. It's been said many, many times, because it's true: death is a fact of life.'

I didn't understand. In my mind Cameron was leading up to breaking it to me that I was going to lose my son.

'Then why have you been with him since he was little? Why has he been able to see you all this time if it's not to protect him?'

'The answer to that is simple. He doesn't realise it yet, but Ben is one of us.'

I thought for a moment I was going to be gripped by the fug again, the sensation was similar, but it didn't develop into fug. Instead it manifested as a white space in my mind and body. I felt myself merging into the space so that I and it were not separate. Then it cleared, leaving me feeling as if I'd freshly showered after a long healing sleep.

'Sorry, what did you say? I didn't catch what you said.'

'Your soul knows things that your mind doesn't.'

'I don't understand.'

'Excellent, that's as it should be.'

I stared at him blankly.

'How does it help you to expect that Ben is not safe, to expect that his life will be cut short? How would your lives be different if you were to celebrate every moment and focus on creating happy memories and joyful aspirations for the future? Think of your own experience of growing up. What would you say to your ten year-old self if you had the chance?'

'I'd say… be happy, make the most of every day, don't waste your life worrying, I suppose. Worrying doesn't stop horrible things from happening, but it does spoil the good times. Mother tried her best, but she dealt with my father leaving by pushing herself and pushing herself and pushing me too. She wanted to show the world we were better off without him. She was wrong to do that, believe me, she was thoroughly mistaken. Her bitterness ate up the whole of my childhood. I grew up believing I had to prove myself, had to be a shining example, had to be the best or no one would want me or love me. And of course, I was never good enough, there was always room for improvement.' I was quietly weeping again, my shoulders shuddering, this time for the loss of my childhood and for the relationship I wished I could have had with my mother. 'Bless her, she didn't mean it to be like that, but my whole childhood became a punishment for my dad walking out on her... We never talked about it you know, never.'

Another painful memory exposed, torn from its prison, where it had festered and degenerated into resinous goo.

'So you understand why you're so frightened of living? Do you see how you contrive to prevent the possibility of what you most yearn for because of fear of losing it again?'

'I'm doing what Mother did; filling every minute with activity and work so I won't have time to face how I'm really feeling. That's what the speedboat nightmare is about, isn't it? It isn't about Paul dying, it's about avoiding dealing with it.'

'I can't reassure you that nothing will happen to you or to Ben. You have to live with that uncertainty as everyone has to. Nothing is pre-ordained. There's just "is" and it's the responsibility of everyone to be mindful of themselves and others. Ben has the same chances as every other healthy person of living to old age.'

'So it wasn't fate or destiny that Paul was killed?'

'No. It was an accident.'

'An accident. Yes.'

'You've been very hard on yourself. It's time to learn to be accepting now. No more need for your nightly ritual of pouring over your day and punishing yourself for your shortcomings. You've turned the corner.'

'Thank you. I have, haven't I?'

'There's just one more homework task for you to do. It's the most difficult of all of them. You've been holding on to Paul. He can't move on until you set him free. Do you think you're ready to let him go now?'

It would take time to settle, this new-found freedom, this opening up, this letting go, this trusting and allowing, but I was ready for it. More than just ready, I was hungry, voracious. I felt intoxicated with joy. I couldn't wait to get home to Ben and begin embracing being his mother, offering him the childhood he deserves, the childhood every child deserves. Cameron used the word 'celebrate.' Time to party, I think and I smile.

Cameron passed the oars to me and I rowed back to the landing strip. We left the boat where we'd found it.

'It's time to say goodbye, Ruby. Choose the life you want to live and live it to the full. Everything you need you already have, no matter what adventures life presents you.'

'You really do mean "goodbye", don't you? I'm not going to see you again.'

'Oh, you'll see us many times, though you may not recognise us. We come in many forms, some living perfectly ordinary human lives never knowing at a conscious level of the gifts they bring. We are everywhere, in shopping malls, in the street, on trains, in schools, offices and factories, across nations and cultures around the world. We could be the person delivering your post or serving you coffee or giving you a parking ticket. Yes, really. Wherever you go, you'll meet us. Remember the first few times you noticed me?'

I remembered. 'I thought you were following me.'

'We were. We're closer than you think. You'll recognise us by our smiles.'

'Thank you, Cameron. Thank you so much.'

He simply smiled courteously and with a brief nod, he turned, clasped his hands loosely behind his back and sauntered towards the trees.

I pull on to my drive and switch off the engine. This yoga thing is definitely working, I think. I feel fantastic. I don't remember feeling this free for a long time.

Finally I understand why Jess and Alice have been so concerned about me. It all makes sense. Years and years of suppressing how I really felt. It's been such a struggle. I made my life unbearably stressful, but now I promise myself that I'll no longer agonise over my day before I go to sleep anymore. It's needless and time to stop. Furthermore, I'll keep up the yoga practice every day. Clearly the yoga has helped me make this enormous shift, just as Jess and Alice said it would.

I'll not say anything to them about it yet, I decide as I get out of the car, I'll let them see for themselves. Every day a new beginning, no matter what's around the corner. I breathe in the warmth of the afternoon sunshine. What a glorious evening it's going to be again. I smile.

The boys are in the garden entertaining Mildred and Delilah. Toby is puffing on his empty briarwood and taking a moment's rest after filling his wheelbarrow with grass cuttings from my newly mown lawn.

'How do?'

'I'm good thank you, Toby. You've made a really excellent job of the lawn again, thank you. The garden's looking wonderful. I'd love you to come and have supper with us tonight? You've worked so hard, it's the least I can do.'

'I'd like that a lot. Why don't I go and pick some fruit to have for pud?'

'Lovely. About six thirty be okay?'

'Six thirty it is then.' And he wheels the barrow towards the gate.

I turn to the boys. 'Perhaps you and your daddy would like to stay for supper too, Harry? What do you think?'

'Great, Mummy,' Ben interrupts. 'Thanks. Can we play on the Xbox after?'

'Let's see what Harry's daddy says first.' I laugh.

Matthew is delighted to accept the supper invitation. 'We'd have probably had yet another takeaway tonight. Home cooking sounds much more tempting.'

The boys don't get to go on the Xbox. Instead Matthew is introduced to the chicks and the hens and given a grand tour of Toby's empire. He is as entranced with Toby's expertise and enthusiasm as I had been just a fortnight ago. Ben, meanwhile, is more than happy to show off his knowledge of the fish to Harry and present him to Marmaduke the Magnificent. Marmaduke seems a little less happy about the presentation (he has urgent scratching to do), but he suffers it because it is his beloved Ben that is making it.

It's starting to get dark now so Matthew and Harry make a move to leave.

'About those Italian lessons?' Matthew whispers, lingering at the front door while Harry's collecting his bag.

I smile. 'Si. Sarà un piacere per me. Non vedo l'ora.'

I send Ben to get ready for bed while I busy myself filling the dishwasher.

'I'll be up in ten.'

Ben's looking out of his window, showered and in his pj bottoms as I go into his room to tuck him in.

'It's been a lovely evening, hasn't it?' I say.

He nods. 'I was just watching Ungrampa and Cameron. I waved, but they're too busy talking to notice me.'

'Cameron? Who's that?' I say, puzzled, and look to see for myself. All I see is Toby puffing on his empty pipe in the solar light and chuntering to himself. No one else there. How odd.

Cameron? Must be another of Ben's crackpot names for one of the fish. Whatever will he come up with next? I think as I draw the curtains whilst my son climbs into bed. And yet something makes me pause. I have the oddest sensation that Cameron is someone I've known and loved. The sort of love I feel for my grandfather.

'Are you okay, Mummy?' Ben says. 'You look a bit weird!'

'Do I? Sorry,' I say dismissing the passing ponderings. I grin and kiss him goodnight,

'Sleep tight. See you in the morning, better have a lie in, eh?' I suggest as I head towards the door. 'Love you dots and spots,' I add and blow him another kiss.

'Love you oodles and spoodles, Mum Plum,' says Ben, yawning as he snuggles down.

Before I go to bed, on a sudden impulse, I take off my wedding ring. It's left a mark where it's been on my finger, but the mark will fade in time. I kiss the ring and then put it in the dressing table drawer with the rest of my jewellery.

I fall asleep almost as soon as my head touches the pillow and drift into another dream. I am on a speedboat heading out to the open sea. I can feel the surge of the waves and the spray on my face. I'm at the helm in control of the boat; my hair is billowing behind me. The rising and falling and the buffeting against the tide is invigorating and exhilarating and a tiny bit frightening. I steer the boat around to make a wide U-turn back to the land. As the harbour grows closer, I reduce the speed and cruise to a halt alongside one of the pontoons.

Paul is standing waiting for me. He's just as I remember. I recognise his shorts and polo top. No words are spoken. I throw him the line and he tethers the boat to one of the moorings, then heads away from me in the dazzling sunlight towards the concrete slipway. After a few steps he turns and waves a final goodbye.

He's smiling.

Lesley A

Something Decidedly Oddd

Lightning Source UK Ltd.
Milton Keynes UK
UKHW011130150722
405908UK00004B/815